PRAISE FOR JONAS

"It's an intense thrill-ride from the opening scene to the very last. And, yes, there will be moments when you'll forget to breathe or your shocked gasps will scare those around you. I don't know how Susan May Warren does it, but every one of her novels is spell-binding and *Jonas* is a prime example of the author's incredible creativity and writing prowess."

MJSH, Goodreads

"Warren can always be counted on to show her readers a powerful spiritual insight along with a great story."

Susan, Goodreads

"The author has a talent for bringing spiritual messages through her stories and has again done it masterfully. I closed the book with one thought: WHEN IS NED COMING?"

Sarita, Goodreads

Stock-full of adventure, drama, thrills and romance, Susan May Warren also packs a wallop of a faith message that is sure to reach into your heart and grab hold. God is in the midst of the storm. *Jonas* is a must read and highly recommended.

Laura, Goodreads

JONAS

The Minnesota Marshalls

Book Two

Susan May Warren

Soli Deo Gloria

JONAS

THE MINNESOTA MARSHALLS

ONE

He had to get off this mountain.

Because, if Jonas read the skies correctly, a doozy of a storm was headed his direction.

And Jonas Marshall, with his PhD in atmospheric science, always read the skies correctly. Or at least, with a 99.8 percent probability.

The other point-two percent were simply those God moments that no one saw coming. But then again, that's when people died.

So yes, barring a divine intervention, the altocumulus clouds that had chased him most of the morning, now morphing into dark gray, ragged nimbostratus clutter, would turn this day hike into a soggy, freezing fight for survival.

"C'mon, we need to go."

He said this to his buddy Nixon, who held his cell phone up, taking a panoramic view of the Julian Alps. "Just another minute."

The wind cut through Jonas's Gore-Tex jacket, and he shoved his hands into his pockets against the chill. But he got it.

He could take just another moment to soak in the glorious

view from atop the 2,864 meter high Triglav Mountain. Craggy granite spires, high pockets tufted with white, rumpled the horizon from here in Slovenia to Italy to the west, and across the Austrian border to the north and east.

Gray cliffs fell down to green valleys pooled with moraine-blue lakes and countless spectacular waterfalls. Feeding them were roiling rivers that twined through a thick northland forest, ripe with cedar and pine and the sense of a world untouched.

Probably it was, because Slovenia was largely hidden from the popular tourist hotspots. Jonas had only found it because of Tarek—and, of course, the footage from Walter 01, one of his weather dirigibles, a solar powered, directed balloon soaring over the northern border.

Walt hadn't quite captured the scale of the mountain, the crisp, thin air, the heady feeling of flying as he stood at the top.

Sort of felt like he could just take a step off and soar.

Sometimes, lately—especially since the accident—he wished it.

Shouting in Slovenian turned him, and he spotted a kid, maybe age twelve, sticking his head into the giant white canister at the apex of the mountain.

"Can't believe that kid made it up here." He said it to himself, mostly, but Nixon made a noise, even as he kept filming.

"Next time you invite me to visit, maybe let's not do it on summer holidays," Nixon said.

"Right." He expected the holiday crowds down in the Alpine town of Kranjska Gora, on the banks of the river Sava, where Slovenes escaped with their families for the August holiday. But families and day adventurers clogged the trail through the Krma Valley, despite the technical challenges near the top, with him having to use carabiners attached to cables.

A tiny red flag on the apex of the canister whipped wildly in the wind.

Get off the mountain. He wanted to wave his hands and yell, but probably they had hours left, and maybe he shouldn't be the crazy American on top of the mountain scaring everyone.

But still.

"Nixon—"

"Got it." He pocketed his camera, grinning at Jonas. "Wait until Geena sees this."

Jonas tried to keep his smile, nod, but he just...aw. "How is she?"

"She's good. They have her hooked to a machine that moves her legs, and she sent me a video just a couple days ago of her upright and 'walking.'" He finger quoted the last word with one hand.

Everything inside Jonas burned. "That's great."

"You'll see. She'll be walking again this time next year."

He searched Nixon's face for guile, but only found honesty in his friend's brown eyes. Or maybe faith.

"Here, let's take a selfie." Nixon held out the camera and stepped up to Jonas, lifting it high to catch the breathtaking terrain behind them.

Jonas managed a smile, the camera and sunlight glinting off his mirrored sunglasses.

"She'll love that," Nixon said. "I'll send it when we get to the mountain hut." He pulled on his backpack.

"No internet there, Nix. You'll have to wait until we get off the mountain."

Jonas also shouldered his pack, glad to see the family with the kid had already left the top. Still remaining were a young couple and two women who'd just arrived at the peak.

He walked by them wanting to offer a "Don't stay too long," but opted to keep his mouth shut.

Mostly because he couldn't speak the language, but also because it wasn't his...nope, he couldn't stay silent.

He stopped and turned to one of the women, her brown hair pulled back in a long tawny braid down her back, her eyes shielded by aviator sunglasses. "It's going to rain. Don't stay long."

He wasn't surprised when she just ignored him. But her friend, shorter with a pixie cut to her dark hair, looked past her. "Thanks."

Hmm.

The couple was leaving, so he followed Nixon off the mountaintop, clipping into the line that led down the ridgeline.

An hour later, he'd descended nearly a thousand feet and found himself sitting inside the small gathering room of the Kredarica mountain hut, rain pelleting the windows, shivering as a man stoked a fire blazing in the black stove in the middle of the room. Around him, the family he'd seen shared sandwiches, and the couple had heated up some soup, all of them eating their dinners at the rough-hewn picnic tables. Many were still shivering.

"You were right," Nixon said, handing him a cup of tea, then scooting in beside him. "That mountain is socked in. Hope those women got off it."

He did too.

"Good call to book a night here."

"Sorry about the shared room."

"Hey. It's a hostel. I expect bunk beds. As long as I don't wake up to some kid drooling on me."

Jonas laughed, picked up his tea. "Could be worse. We could be sleeping in a car under an overpass."

Nixon's smile tightened into a thin line. "Yep."

And oh, the air between them stilled, tightened. Nixon looked away. Jonas stared at his cup. Why had he said that? Because of course, yes, they'd been there, done that, but in the case he hadn't been referring to, their car had been thrown by a twister, landed upside down in the ditch, and they'd been trapped in the freezing rain for hours, waiting for help.

While Geena nearly died. So yeah, maybe Jonas should keep his stupid mouth shut.

"Water's boiling," Nixon said and got up, heading for the makeshift kitchen where their freeze-dried soup sat on the counter. He filled the soup as Jonas retrieved the buns they'd purchased in town, now slightly crushed. Some cheese, hot soup, and crusty bread. Yes, it could be worse.

"Tell me again what this grant is about?" Nixon blew on his hot chicken soup.

"Lightning. Storm patterns."

"You finally got to use your balloons." Nixon was back, grinning at him, the Geena specter at least diminished.

"Dirigibles, and yes. I've upgraded them since the last design. Now they're controlled by drones, powered by air and sun, and can stay aloft for weeks. They're programed to fly in a selected area, so we get real data points for specific areas. The black boxes send data down to my app, but it's sketchy here in the mountains, so I have to constantly check on them."

"Have any accidents?"

"One. Came down in a field north of our office in Ljubljana. No one was hurt, but it was a mess."

"How?"

"Wind sheer." He dunked his bread into his soup.

"How much longer on your contract?"

"Another month or so in country, then a few months in Oklahoma sorting out the data. Then maybe...I don't know."

"No more storm chasing?" Nixon had finished his soup and picked up his phone, scrolling through the pictures, occasionally showing Jonas.

Jonas said nothing, watching the family now taking out a deck of playing cards. Outside, the rain roared, and in the distant, low rolls of thunder.

He expected that there might be snow up at the higher elevation.

Yeah, he hoped the women had made it off the peak.

Eventually Nixon let the question die, showing Jonas pictures of the trek up and yesterday's walk around Kranjska Gora, and then Nixon's trip to Venice, Italy just over the border, and then Rome, where he'd finished a gig shooting a commercial for a clothing brand.

Probably a good thing Jonas had gotten out of the storm chasing biz. Gave Nixon a chance to spread his wings.

And that way, nobody else got hurt because of him.

The door blew open, and a man came in, soaking wet, breathing hard. "We've got an accident on the mountain."

Everyone stilled. Apparently, he wasn't the only English speaker in the room.

Jonas found his feet. The man shivered, came up to the heater, still breathing hard. "Big winds. Blew a couple women over."

"Who's hurt?"

"I don't know. I heard them shouting, but it's raining too hard to get to them."

Jonas looked at Nixon, who blew out a breath. Nodded.

"How far up the trail are they?"

"About two hundred meters from here."

"Anyone got climbing gear?" Jonas asked the room.

Silence again. He shook his head and headed toward the door.

The man stopped him. "You go out there, you'll fall off the mountain too."

Jonas brushed his hand away, feeling Nixon step up behind him. "I know how to live through a storm."

The man held up his hands in surrender and stepped back. "Suit yourself."

Jonas zipped up his jacket, pulled up the hood, and stepped out into the gale. The black sky obscured any hope of reading the clouds, the wind moaning.

For a second, his stomach hollowed, and a tremor went through him.

Jonas! Don't let me die!

"You sure about this?" Nixon, grabbing his gear up behind him, steady as usual, as Jonas led him into danger.

"Never pin a weatherman down on his forecast."

Nixon grinned, white teeth against a dark night. "You got this."

Oh boy. But Jonas put his head down, the wind fighting him as he headed up the path.

Yeah, he really needed to get off this mountain.

THE AIR UP HERE WAS COLD, BRITTLE, AND unforgiving.

Probably the perfect end to her life.

"Oh, you're so morbid."

"What?" Sibba Kovac looked at her friend Ina through the pelleting rain as they sat pocketed against the steep grade of the mountainside, trapped on a cliff.

"This is not how we're going to die." Ina sat with one leg pulled against herself, water running down her face and her red Gore-Tex raincoat, the other leg out.

"Maybe. Hopefully." Sibba's nimble fingers ran over Ina's ankle. It didn't feel broken, but she couldn't know. By the swelling, however, Ina was in no shape to walk. "One cold gust of wind could knock us right off this mountain face."

The wind around them moaned.

"Like I said, morbid." Ina's voice was tight with the pain darkness hid on her face.

"I'm trained to think of all the contingencies. And this is not how I want to end. Randomly, in a freak accident—although, given my alternatives, maybe this isn't terrible—"

"Stop. We're going to be fine. Besides, I think I can walk on it." Ina started to rise, then cried out and dropped back down.

"Your ankle is the size of a German panzer."

"Oy. Where did that comparison come from?"

"You know where. I have Nazis in my head after this summer. And clearly you *can't* walk. And it's dark and I don't know how to get us out of here, so we're staying put."

And probably dying on this mountain.

So much for picking up the pieces of her life. Or even escaping them.

Shoot, she was smarter than this. *Think, Sibba!*

As far as she could tell, they'd only fallen about seven meters from the trail. It had happened so fast—the storm whipping up as they'd headed down from the peak, and even though they'd been latched to the cable, they'd slipped a few times on the slick rock.

Then the cable area ended, and a trail led down the slope spotted with snow and shale and death. Probably it hadn't been a great idea to rope up together, but she wasn't going to let her friend tumble down the mountain.

Alone.

Although, maybe, if she'd let Ina go, Sibba would have been able to get help. As it was, she and Ina had worked together to slow themselves in the slick shale and snow and had ended up winded on a sharp plane of rock jutting out into a black abyss.

Frodo and Samwise watching the world shatter around them.

Occasionally, thunder rumbled, and a splatter of lightning would crack open the sky, illuminating the thousand-foot drop below.

So yes, this was exactly what Sibba needed after the summer she'd endured.

"I'm sorry," Ina said now, her teeth chattering.

Sibba still wore her backpack and now pulled it off, holding it between her knees, and grabbed her torch. The light shone on Ina's torn leggings and the swelling ankle. "It wasn't your fault."

"I will walk before I let us perish out here."

Attagirl. But what did she expect? Ina was a fellow soldier—had done a decade in the Slovenian military, and had endured the same brutal summer that Sibba had.

"We should have listened to that guy."

Sibba knew exactly to whom Ina was referring, thank you, because he'd sorta gotten under her skin with his know-it-all American tone. She'd been around enough Yanks to spot them, all arrogant and bossy and—

"How long do you think we've been off-trail?"

They'd slid quite a bit before they'd worked themselves to this place, and then there was the matter of getting Ina settled as well as straightening out her leg and—"Maybe a half hour?"

"How far are we from the mountain hut?"

"I don't know. Two hundred meters, probably? Not far."

"Get me up. I can do this."

Now Sibba shone the light at her friend. Ina winced and held up her hand. Sibba flicked the torch away from her face so her expression hovered just in the glow. "The shale is slippery. And yes, I think I could carry you up, or at least help you...in the daylight. But without knowing where I'm going...we could take a header off this mountain."

"Then you should go, without me."

Sibba focused the light up, just to give their terrain another look-see. "I don't love the idea of staying here all night, but I don't want to leave you, either."

"Give me a sleeping bag."

"I didn't bring one."

Ina looked at her. "What's in your pack?"

"Listen, you said you booked us at the hut. I brought water and some food and—"

"Your glider."

Sibba lifted a shoulder. "I thought, if it was nice out—"

"Fine. Okay. I have a space blanket. And water. Leave me and go get help."

Sibba shook her head. "I don't...I'm not..." She looked up. "It's too dangerous."

Ina grabbed her hand. "Think this out like you would a

minefield. You can see the dangers, but you can also see the way through, right?"

"I'm not superman. I can't see in the dark. And I *can't* fly."

"Most of the time."

"Ha. But especially not in the rain. This could go very wrong."

"Fine. I'll share my blanket with you. But it's going to get cold."

It *was* going to get cold. Sibba had been on top of Triglav plenty of times when the air turned her fingers into blocks of ice even when the sun was shining.

She leaned back and snuggled in with Ina as she unfolded her thin blanket. "Next time you want me to get my mind off...um, *things*, maybe just suggest a nice outing for gelato."

"Don't talk about gelato when I'm freezing."

"Hello? Hello down there?"

The voice made her lean up, and there, some seven meters up on the trail, was a man waving a torch.

"Down here!" she said in Slovenian, but then realized the man had spoken English.

Oh, wait—

"I'm coming down to you!"

Perfect. Now some impulsive bloke would careen down the hill and land on them, or worse, knock them off their perch into the abyss below. "Stay there! It's too slippery!"

Of course the man ignored her. She barely made him out in the dim light of her headlamp as he moved down the slope, working his way from one craggy outcropping to another, like Spiderman.

Or like he might be going through a minefield.

So, maybe she'd been a little hasty in her judgment. Still... *please don't kill us...*

Another man moved behind him, his headlamp catching the orange jacket of the first.

Yep. Mr. America.

But a couple of trapped, injured people on a ledge couldn't exactly complain who their rescuers might be, right?

"Over here!"

Spidey worked his way down to them, taking his time, and finally slid down to the ledge. Truth was, the grade wasn't as steep as it was fast, and the ledge was large enough to pitch a tent, maybe host dinner for a futbol team, so now she felt a little silly when he looked at her, breathing hard, and said, "You okay?"

"We're fine. My friend tripped, and—"

"Oh, wow. That's bad." He'd crouched and now gently touched Ina's ankle. "Do you have anything to splint it with?"

Ina moved his hands from her ankle. "I think I can walk on it."

He gave her the same look that Sibba probably had.

The other man landed behind him. Tall and dark, she also remembered him from the summit. "Good thing you had your light on. It's so dark up here we might have missed you."

"I can't believe you came out in this storm," Ina said, a little bit of emotion in her voice.

"Glad to help," said the first man. "My name is Jonas."

"Ina. And this is Sibba."

He glanced at her, nodded. "I'm glad we found you. It's going to get cold tonight."

She didn't know why, but the concern in his voice caught her, held her. He had dark eyes, maybe blue, and stayed on her for a moment.

He turned back to Ina. "Can you get on my back?"

"I can try."

He pivoted around, still crouched. "Nixon, can you grab her pack?"

"Sure, boss," Nixon said and picked it up. "What's the plan?"

"I'll go up with her. You stay behind me in case I slip. Then we can come back for—" He looked at Sibba, one eyebrow up.

"I can walk."

"You sure?"

"Yes."

"Because you don't need to be a hero. I don't mind coming back for you."

Maybe *she* minded. The fewer people who risked their lives up here, the better, thank you. "Listen, Spiderman. The last thing I need is for you to fly off this mountain trying to save me. I'm. Fine."

He held up a hand. "Okay. But if you change your mind—"

"I hear what you say."

He raised an eyebrow.

Oh blimey. "I'm fine. Really. It's you who we should be worried about. You sure you can climb up this with someone on your back? It's slippery—maybe we wait for rescue?"

"I'm all the rescue you got. Right here, right now."

"But—"

And then he took her hand. Warm, solid, and so painfully... kind? She simply didn't know what to do. Especially since it sort of grounded her. She hadn't realized she'd lost herself a little, let the storm loosen her bones. But yeah, being out here, in the rain, in the wind and even the lightning...

Maybe she needed his grip more than she wanted to admit. Still. "Just...don't fall."

"I got this," he said, his gaze in hers. He smiled, and it in was something she couldn't place. Tease? Trouble? Warmth? "What was it you called me? Spidey?"

"Don't let it go to your head."

"It's already in my ears, like a chant. Spi-dey, Spi-dey."

Of all the rescuers...couldn't she have gotten a nice Swede?

His smile turned solemn. "Okay. You stay behind me. Nixon—"

"I'll make sure we all stay on the mountain."

Then Jonas stood up and took off his jacket. "Ready, Ina?"

Ina leaned up, grunting, and Sibba helped her onto Jonas's back. She wrapped her arms around his neck. "I can help walk."

"Nope. Here's what we're going to do." He handed his coat to

Nixon. "Strap her onto my back—tie the coat around her backside and under her legs. Then I don't have to hold them."

Okay, she had to give him points for ingenuity.

Nixon tied on the jacket, then grabbed Ina's pack. Sibba picked up her own pack. "I'm right behind you," she said to Ina, in Slovenian.

Sibba hadn't put Jonas as a big man the first time she saw him. But then again, she'd barely looked at him.

But he was big. Six foot three, maybe, and strong.

And, apparently, capable, just like he said, because he worked his way up from the cliff, nearly on his hands and knees, grabbing onto boulders and outcroppings. Sibba trekked behind him, also bent over, her hand on Ina's back.

They went slowly, and Nixon moved up beside her to also help steady him.

Jonas's feet dug into the shale, finding purchase, and he grunted now and again, more toward the top as he found the trail. He finally crawled onto the wider path, illuminated by Nixon's headlamp.

Sibba pulled out her torch again.

Rain rivered down the trail, and she cast her light on the path they'd just climbed.

"Don't do that," Jonas said, adjusting Ina, still strapped to him. She'd managed to hold in her moans, probably so as not to rattle him. But her eyes were closed, her jaw tight.

"Don't do what?" Sibba said.

"Don't look down. You'll just scare yourself."

She lived in a state of scared, really, so this...

Okay, this might have taken off a year of her life. Which put her life expectancy at...well, at least today.

She didn't look ahead any farther than that.

But she wasn't going to tell him that, so, "I'm not afraid."

He raised an eyebrow. "I promise. Keep your eyes on me, and you'll be fine. I won't let you get hurt."

Usually that was her line, which felt a little weird.

"Want me to take her, boss?" This from his friend, Nixon.

"No, you light the path. She's not heavy."

Ina seemed in no rush to get off Jonas's back, the way she grinned at Sibba. Oh brother. Fine, he was...capable. And maybe a little heroic. But it didn't matter—she didn't have room for anyone extra in her life, no matter how capable and heroic he might be.

"Let's go," Jonas said, hiking Ina up higher on his back and now looping his arms under her knees.

Nixon moved to the front and shed light on the path as they walked. Jonas braced himself against his friend's shoulder as they reached the rougher parts. But after a hundred meters, the ground started to level out, turned muddy instead of rocky, and despite the chill, the moan of the wind, the pelleting of rain, she didn't hate the walk.

Mostly because it drowned out all other thought. One step. One step more. Next step. Another. She didn't have to think about how close they'd come to disaster.

"You okay back there?" Jonas turned as they came to a rocky patch. "Watch your step."

"I'm not the one carrying a ten-stone backpack, freezing to death without a jacket," Sibba said.

Ina lifted her head off Jonas's shoulder. "What? Eight stone, max!"

"I have no idea what that means," Jonas said, but he was grinning, even as he took a moment to breathe. The rain ran down into an array of light-brown whiskers, dripped off his jaw.

"It means you're doing great," Sibba said, and offered a return smile.

So, maybe not quite as arrogant as she'd first thought.

They finally reached the hut, the place dark, just the glow of the stove illuminating the main room, with tiny lights flickering on the tabletops as they came in. A few people stood in the room in front of the fire, most of them silent, eyes wide, morose.

Some of them got up when Jonas came in and set Ina on a

tabletop. When he untied her, his hands shook. Maybe from cold. Poor man was soaked through. "Anyone here a doctor? She needs her ankle looked at."

When no one moved, Sibba translated.

One of the women moved away from the stove and came over, identified herself as a doctor and asked for details as she then worked off Ina's shoe, her sock.

Sibba noticed how Jonas walked over to the fire, held his hands out, then began to peel off his thermal shirt.

She spotted a hint of a washboard stomach as his thermal shirt rose before he tugged down the inner T-shirt over it. He draped the shirt by the fire.

He was shivering, his arms wrapped around himself, staring into the fire with a tight jaw. As if reliving something.

Or just, suddenly, overwhelmed.

She glanced at Ina, but the doctor was busy examining Ina's injury, so she joined Jonas by the fire. "You okay?"

He exhaled, swallowed, nodded.

"Not a fan of storms?"

"Not a fan of nearly *dying* in storms." He glanced at her. "But no, the storm doesn't scare me."

Interesting clarification. Then Nixon brought over a cup of hot cocoa, and Jonas slid onto the top of a table to blow on the cocoa and sip it. He was handsome in the light, with his light-brown hair twining out of his stocking cap, a hint of whiskers. She liked his hands, the way he gripped the cup, and for a moment, her mind went to his hand in hers.

So maybe she didn't dislike *all* Americans. "Thanks for coming for us. I know I should have gone for help, but I just couldn't leave her—"

"Hey. I get it." He met her eyes. Yes, blue, although when she let herself look, they had shades of green in the center. His gaze fixed on her. No smile, just a grim set to his mouth. "I wouldn't have left my friend behind either." Then he glanced at Nixon, who made a face, then looked away.

Jonas took another sip of cocoa.

Ina made a sound behind her, and Sibba turned to see the doctor probing her injury. She should get back to her— .

"It's okay to be scared, you know."

Sibba turned back to Jonas. "What?"

"Back on the mountain, you said you weren't afraid. But...it's okay to be afraid."

No, it wasn't. Not for her. Not ever for her. Fear made mistakes. Fear got people killed.

"I wasn't afraid." She gave him a smile. "Thanks again."

Then she walked over to the doctor examining Ina's injury.

Jonas and his friend were gone to bed by the time Ina's ankle had been wrapped. Sibba checked the roster of rooms in the hostel, then helped Ina down the hall to their bunk room.

She opened the door. No electricity for lights, but in the darkness, she found a cot and set Ina down on it.

A grunt made her still. Oh. *No.*

She turned on her torch. Faced it toward the ceiling.

In the dim light, Spidey and his buddy Nixon were mostly dead to the world, wrapped in blankets, sleeping on the two lower bunks. She'd nearly set Ina down on top of Nixon.

Perfect.

But for a second, her gaze landed again on Jonas. He had long lashes that gentled his face, turned him peaceful and sweet in sleep.

"Where are we going to sleep?" Ina said quietly. "I'm not sure I can climb to the top bunk."

Sibba walked over to the bunk and pulled the mattress off the top. Put it on the floor, then added the other one. She gathered up the blankets and pillows and tossed them on the mattresses. Helping Ina onto the floor, she tucked her in. Then she lay beside her and closed her eyes, listening to the breathing of the men in the room.

And realized, suddenly, that for the first time in months, her own breath spilled out, full, even, unhindered, the ever-present grip of fear in her gut gone.

Keep your eyes on me, and you'll be fine. I won't let you get hurt.

This, she hadn't seen coming. But maybe, just maybe, it was all right.

"Good night, Ina," she said.

And then she was dead asleep.

Two

Another day to live.

Please.

If she didn't sweat to death first.

"This is unnecessary." Sibba adjusted the chest plate in the Kevlar suit from where it landed on her hip bones and tried to see through the steamed-up visor.

Not a hope.

She took off the hood. Set it on the table in the house where her kit, along with a handful of uniformed police and one particularly nervous rookie bomb disposal expert, watched her.

Or maybe their gaze was on the tractor in the middle of the yard that still sat, as if frozen in fear, after plowing up history.

Dangerous history in the form of a fifty-kilogram German iron bomb with a transverse fuze. It still stuck halfway out of the dirt, having been churned up with the other debris while cleaning the yard after the storm that whipped down from the mountains and through the small town of Železniki. Nestled in the craggy foothills, the town was a relatively recent development, with newer houses sprouting up in the washes and valleys.

"Is this your first callout since the storm?" The question came from the director general of the Hazardous Device Unit out of Ljubljana, a bear of a man named Vlasic.

"No. Had two in as many days. This is the third. But it's the biggest."

Aka, the one that could get more than her killed. She pulled off her gloves and set them on the table.

"It's best you wear the Kevlar, ma'am." The bomb expert, standing behind her—*unnecessarily* far behind her—seemed to be sweating also, his voice shaking a little. Frankly, he almost whispered.

His name was Milovik, according to the nameplate on his BDUs. Young, maybe early twenties. No doubt saw his life flashing before his eyes. And hers.

"Ma'am, please—"

She held up her hand to stop him. "Listen. This suit is designed to protect me from shrapnel propelled at close range—say a grenade or even a land mine. But it's hot and hard to move in and has a higher center of gravity, and I can barely see with my breath fogging up the visor, and frankly, gentlemen"—she turned to the group—"that mother goes off and this entire area is dust and vapor. So the best this suit will do is slow down the quick death that I deserve if I can't disarm this thing."

The air in the room evaporated as all the men simply stopped breathing.

They watched in silence as she climbed out of the suit and left it standing there, as if under its own power. She'd used the Kevlar mostly as a precaution in her first survey of the bomb, scanning for the faded numbers stamped on the fuze head and examining the remaining damaged tail fin. She'd taken dozens of pictures and now took a closer look through her phone.

More silence as they watched. But she was used to this sort of shock and awe and abject terror when working around civilians.

Finally, she put the phone down and opened the BDO box with all the kit inside to immunize the fuze. She quickly catalogued her tools, as if she hadn't already checked the kit a dozen times, before and after every callout, then pulled out her BDO book of fuses. She flipped open to confirm that the directions on which fuze head to drill contained the type 15 early impact fuze specifications.

Then she slipped it into a satchel and hung it over her shoulder. Met the eyes of Vlasic and nodded. "Please get your men back and stay put. I'll be in touch." She lifted the radio.

He nodded. "Good luck, Sibba."

She shook her head. "Nope. Just skill. Counting on luck will get me killed." Then she walked out the front door.

The storm—a local weatherman called it a derecho—had taken off roofs as far south as her town of Cerkno, and frankly, she'd expected a call like this.

Over much of northern Slovenia, like other parts of Europe, unexploded ordnances littered the terrain, buried now after so many years. And not just German ordnance, like here, near the Austrian border, the hotbed of partisan resistance, but American and British ordnance in deeper Slovenia—once Yugoslavia, who had allied with the Third Reich.

So, despite their independence, Slovenia bore the scars of both sides of the war. Scars hidden deep beneath the rugged beauty of a flyover country until events like a derecho, or the wildfires of this summer, unearthed the hidden terrors.

Then the battles of the past revisited them, raking to life the old demons.

She blew out a breath and waited until Director Vlasic and his men got in their cars and drove down the road, parking some fifty meters away.

Might not be far enough, but really, she simply hadn't wanted anyone watching her. She needed her entire focus on the device.

The bomb lay half exposed, a corpse, still lethal in its dormancy, the dirt around it fresh and raw. The smell of old iron mixed with the scent of yesterday's rain, and for a moment, she was following a stranger to safety on a mountain during a rainstorm.

And not sure why, but still wishing he'd taken her up on her offer to fly off it together the next morning.

Maybe because, you know, you only have one life.

Focus.

The wind lifted the collar of her jacket, and she wasn't sweating yet.

But her body had begun its familiar, focused buzz. She reached up then and pressed her finger against the cool gold cross at her neck. Closed her eyes.

If I should die...

Then she opened her eyes and knelt in front of the bomb.

She took out the book and again opened it to the right diagram. Checked it twice against the fuze and markings, then took a felt pen and drew on the fuze.

Then she picked up the hand drill.

She was a surgeon, her own life in her hands.

Keeping perfectly vertical, with just the right pressure to cut through the alloy head, she drilled slowly with continued pressure to the correct depth.

Then she blew out the metal shards to keep any litter from falling into the hole and withdrew the bit.

The screw-threaded hollow needle with a valve went next, creating an airtight seal in the gap. She pulled out the plastic tubing from her kit, along with a bottle of saline solution. This was the tricky bit—connecting the tubing to the needle, then using a bicycle pump to create a vacuum with one hand and with the other, flipping open the valve to release the saline into the fuze.

Then she had to pressurize it with the pump to neutralize the fuze.

The wind tumbled a few broken leaves down the road, lifted her braided hair from her neck, her breath steady, her work practiced.

In her exams, she'd completed this test with three minutes to spare.

But it wasn't a race. Just a pass/fail.

And this time, she passed.

She let out a breath, finally, as she stepped back, packing her tools into her kit. Then she raised her hand.

Triumph. With the fuze immunized, the ordnance could be moved, the payload extracted, and the bomb destroyed.

No lives lost.

Now sweat trickled down her spine, but she unzipped her jacket and turned, lifting her radio. "All clear, Director."

He was already on the move down the road, but he confirmed anyway.

She didn't wait for them to arrive but headed back inside the house.

Nice place. Homey, with a compact dining table set into a banquette against the wall, and a massive, tiled stove in the corner, not unlike her grandfather's place.

So, an older home, and probably it had a couple attic bedrooms and a living room, although children lived here—evident from the drawings taped to the refrigerator in the small kitchen.

Through the west-facing window, the snow-capped Mount Triglav rose in the distance.

"Keep your eyes on me, and you'll be fine. I won't let you get hurt."

And there he was, Spidey, back in her head, still, after a month.

It would help if he hadn't landed in her world like some kind of superhero. Made her feel, at least for a space of time, safe. As if she had a few more tomorrows ahead of her.

She could still see him running out as if to save her life—not in the storm but the next morning as she stood on the hillside, the air a glorious, unhindered blue, her sail on the hillside above her—

"What are you doing?"

He'd stood above her, and if she thought he was handsome in the dead of night, soaking wet, it had nothing on his brown hair tousled in the wind, a thicker layer of golden-brown whiskers, his blue eyes lighting with concern.

Maybe that's why she'd sort of lost her brains. Again. "Would you like to go flying?"

For a second—a long, glorious second—she'd thought he might say yes. Because he took a step toward her.

Then, "What?" His gaze went to the cliff, the drop just thirty feet ahead of her, where she'd launch and...

Right. So maybe she'd misjudged the guy. Not the kind to dive off a cliff. Still, her mouth seemed not to have caught up— "Ina's in good hands, and they're arranging transport for her down the mountain. I'm going to the base to get help. But—I have an extra harness if you want to fly with me."

"I..."

And she couldn't help it. "C'mon. I promise, I won't let you get hurt."

Please. And for a second, she thought—

"Sorry. I—I think I prefer my feet on the ground."

Of course he did. She was the crazy one here, clearly. "Thanks for getting my friend off the mountain! I'll see you at the bottom."

She *hadn't* seen him at the bottom. Which was for the best, probably. She wasn't a fool. She'd trained herself to live in a one-meter view of the world. She didn't have the luxury of anything more.

"Ma'am?"

Sibba turned. Young Milovik came into the kitchen. "Yes, soldier?"

"Should I call the military for removal?"

"Yes. It's safe to move."

On the table beside him, where she'd set her kit, her phone buzzed. She picked it up and opened a text. Ina.

She'd called him two days ago but hadn't gotten through, and then had been picked up by Milovik to attend to ordnances near Lake Bled.

So... She pocketed the phone and turned to Milovik. "I need to go. I need transport back to Cerkno."

"I need to stay until the disposal team arrives."

"Yes."

"I'll take you, Sibba." Director Vlasic.

She gathered her kit—left the Kevlar suit for the military to disinfect—put the gear into the boot of his car, then left them to dig up the past.

The drive back to Cerkno wasn't far, but another unanswered call to her grandfather had her heart pumping.

"Everything okay?"

She liked Vlasic. Mid-sixties, he had a couple grandchildren and was liked, voted in for years in her town of two thousand.

"My grandfather lives in Poče."

A beat. "They got hit. Electricity went down. Might still be down."

Right. Could be why her call didn't go through.

"I know your grandfather. He's quiet. Keeps to himself."

She said nothing.

"Good man, though. Wasn't he mayor?"

"Four times."

He gave a chuckle. "Did he ever take you back to the States?"

She shook her head, looked out the window. The effects of the storm still littered the ditches along the highway, branches down, water running across low patches in the road.

"Why not?"

"He had his reasons."

Vlasic nodded. "I'm sure he's fine. He's a survivor."

A survivor. Yes. He'd had to be.

But one didn't live through war, especially one like Vietnam, without scars. She hadn't seen his PTSD rise to the surface in years, but after the storm last weekend...

And he never knew when the past might show up, either, and destroy everything.

She drew in a breath as the town of Cerkno came into view. Nestled in a valley surrounded by mountains, it was this storybook view of red-roofed homes, a white spire of a central church, and one quaint main street that drew tourists from nearby Ljubljana. That and, ten kilometers to the north, just out the driver's window to the east, the glorious slopes of the Cerkno Ski Centre.

The last thing the tourist industry needed was the rumor of unexploded bombs littering these pine-soaked mountains.

Hence why, after everything, Sibba had found herself back here, forty kilometers from her hometown.

Safe.

Settled.

Living large, one day at a time.

Vlasic dropped her off at her townhome, near the center.

"Thanks." She headed upstairs, dropped her kit, then grabbed the keys to her Citroen Berlingo, a jacket and her backpack, and headed out.

She called her grandfather again on the way up, but again, voice mail.

Really, she shouldn't worry. He managed just fine alone on his farmland, rented it out to a neighbor mostly and lived on his bee money. But he missed her grandmother. And the storm...

She knew every curve, turned right at the V in the road and noticed the effects of the storm on the hay mounds as she drove past farmland.

Twenty minutes later, she spotted Poče. Just a village, a blink on the map, but she knew every storefront, every cobblestone drive, every face.

Her grandfather lived on a farm just outside the village, on a hill overlooking his kingdom. Or at least that's sort of how she'd felt, being his granddaughter.

She cut right again, into his long drive. Ahead, his wooden barn still stood, and across the drive, the whitewashed stone home that had been built by her great-grandfather.

Before it was absorbed into the nightmare that was Yugoslavia.

Before, even, the first war that ravaged their land.

She pulled up alongside the barn and eyed her grandfather's tractor sitting outside. A cat jumped from a high fender and scampered away.

She got out. "Dedi?" The air was colder here, touched with a breath of winter, although reaping the pine scent from the surrounding foothills.

She walked up alongside the barn and stood in the drive. The house seemed cold. Dark. Empty. "Dedi?"

Then, from behind her, a cry.

She whirled and froze. Zuma, his prized Drežnica goat, stood in the open door of the barn, bleating at her.

"Oh, you."

It ran back into the barn.

"Dedi?" She headed to the barn.

And that's when she grew cold.

Empty. The milking cow, Berta, gone.

His horse, Imbero, also gone, his stall open.

And his dog, the old mutt Lenard, hadn't appeared to announce her.

She turned and headed to the house. As usual, the door was unlocked, and she walked in.

Her childhood rushed back to her in the familiar smell of oiled wooden floors, the old coal furnace in the corner of the main room, the drying dill and oregano from the small kitchen, and the scent of Dedi's pipe. She missed the smell of Babička's sourdough bread.

"Dedi?"

She climbed the open stairs to the two small attic bedrooms, her stomach tight.

Both beds were covered in fraying, comfortable quilts.

She stood there, in his empty bedroom, her gaze on his bureau, and her heart thumped.

His Bible was gone.

She pressed a hand to her stomach. He was fine. Probably.

Outside, a rumble thundered from the road, and she walked to the window.

Military transport trucks, two of them, kicked up dust as they lumbered toward the village of Poče.

And sure, it was crazy, but the old stories, the old whispers suddenly rose, consumed her thoughts, and all she could think as she stood there was *Run, Dedi, run.*

SHE HAD TO BE AROUND HERE SOMEWHERE, JONAS JUST knew it.

"She" being weather balloon number four, aka, Frannie, who'd vanished off the radar four days ago near about the time a windstorm swept through northern Slovenia and took off roofs, upended trees, and generally left a wake of destruction akin to a derecho across the plains of the Midwest in America.

No wonder Frannie, and Trixie and Alice, had dropped from the sky, the latter two practically disintegrating in the air to drop into piles of metal and electronics scattered over farmland and wooded areas like Humpty Dumpty. Thankfully, the GPS locators on the black boxes remained intact, and he'd managed to retrieve the radiosondes inside.

Frannie, however, hid from him, her GPS on the fritz, her last known location some thirty klicks from Cerkno, in a valley under the shadow of Mt. Porezen, near a village called Poče.

Just a smudge on the map—maybe sixty inhabitants, total, but large enough to have experienced damage from the storm, not to mention a six-foot dirigible crashing through their main square.

Hopefully not catching fire, since the helium it contained to keep it aloft wasn't flammable, but he'd seen crazy things happen, and the last thing he wanted was for his experiment to turn tragic.

He'd had enough blame to shoulder.

Now he drove along the rutted, two-wheel dirt road winding through foothills crisp with the October cold, the trees lush with reds and oranges, aflame with autumn, reminding him too much of his home state, Minnesota.

Or maybe that was just a byproduct of his recent conversation with his brother, Fraser.

At least, the conversation he'd had *after* Fraser had jumped him while Jonas had been busy breaking into his sister's place in Lake Como, Italy. Okay, not *exactly* breaking in, because Iris kept the welcome mat out, but he'd forgotten his key. Which had necessitated a B&E trick his dad had taught him with the sliding glass door.

Jonas had never expected to get tackled right there in the living room, although he'd given himself some kudos for reacting fast and getting his brother—a former Navy SEAL, thank you—down on the ground.

And sure, Fraser's fitness level may have been a little underdone, but still, big bro had skills, and Jonas was just a weatherman, so hoo-yah and a fist pump for him.

But the triumph had been short lived when he'd discovered that Fraser was in country because their kid brother, Creed, was on the lam with a princess he'd met in Geneva.

Way to go, Creed. Except Creed was apparently also a named witness to a murder, so...

Yeah, Jonas had rolled *that* around in his brain for the past four days since returning to Slovenia.

That and the conversation he'd found himself in after the throwdown with Fraser, about big brother's injury, his future, and the girl he'd joined forces with to find Creed. Pippa something. Bodyguard.

Fraser liked her—Jonas had spotted that from the first. And yes, he'd pushed a little. Confronted him with a *Maybe, if you were honest, you want more.*

He'd meant the words for Fraser, really.

Really.

Okay, in truth, it could be he'd been speaking out of his own heart.

More than running after, or into, storms.

More than returning home after a high-stakes night to nothing more than his sleeping bag and a couple power bars. And the shortwave giving him yet another weather update.

Most of all, Jonas could live without the guilt of—

He nearly missed the turn for Poče, a chip-painted sign that pointed east.

It led him around a farm, through a cluster of trees, down a hill, through more farmland, and then, in the distance, he spotted the stone spire of an ancient church, surrounded by a handful of red-roofed buildings.

Poče.

He pulled over to the side of the road and picked up his cell phone. Widened the map area.

The last known location put Frannie just outside the village, about one kilometer to the southeast.

He spotted a farm in the distance settled into the rolling hills, more wooded foothills rising to the east. Taking out the binoculars, he scanned the fields.

A couple farm implements, but mostly just harvest debris. Still, pieces of Frannie could be scattered all over the field.

He got out, the air brisk although the sun had come out, the sky a bright blue with just a few cirrostratus clouds, high and flat, scattered across the atmosphere.

No snow, at least for a couple days. And a look behind him at Mt. Triglav, jutting bold and white into the sky, said that any weather would have to jockey around it.

For a moment, the memory of his rescue of Ina Novak on said mountain whispered through him.

And not the long stretch of misery carrying Ina to help, but the next morning. *After* he'd slept like the dead and woke to discover that he'd somehow crashed in the room reserved for Ina and her friend, Sibba.

Oops. Or maybe the reservation had belonged to both of them—Europeans didn't seem to worry about those things.

The ladies had already risen, and he'd found Ina and Nixon in the kitchen, with the staff arranging for her descent down the mountain on a four-wheeler. The swelling had gone down, and the doctor from the previous night had agreed to ride down with her.

Her friend Sibba, however, wasn't in the kitchen. And when he'd asked about her, Ina had sent him outside, saying there wasn't any more room on the four-wheeler.

He'd gone outside and seen an orange-and-blue parachute spread on a grassy hillside, Sibba wearing a harness.

"What are you doing?"

She'd looked up at him then, her tawny-brown hair pulled back into a braid, snaking out of her helmet. She wore a lime-green jacket, leggings, hiking boots, and stood up at his call.

He knew his question was probably stupid—he knew what a parachute looked like. And the quick math said she was a paraglider pilot, but—

"Would you like to go flying?"

The question, borne on the wind, carried to him, and he stood there, his mouth open. "What?" He stepped closer so she didn't have to yell, walking around the massive limp silks, now undulating in the rising wind.

The storm had wrung itself out over the mountain, and overhead, a clear blue sky, free from any cumulus, suggested a gorgeous day to, um, fly.

The drop from this altitude swept the breath from his lungs, and he preferred his feet on the ground, thank you. At least, he thought he did.

She shook out the lines of her chute. "Ina's in good hands, and they're arranging transport for her down the mountain. I'm going to the base to get help. But—I have an extra harness if you want to fly with me."

And then she smiled at him. The sight of it undid him, a complete about-face to the woman he'd met on the summit yesterday. She was pretty, in a sort of no-nonsense, no-makeup, just-sunshine-and-fresh-air sort of way.

"I..."

"C'mon. I promise, I won't let you get hurt."

Something about her smile teased, pulled at him, and crazily, the urge to nod, to walk into her proffered harness and clip on, to soar with her over the mountains, swept over him in a wash of heat and light and—desire.

Yes, that's what it was. The desire for something more.

So he didn't know why he raised a hand. "Sorry. I—I think I prefer my feet on the ground."

She raised her hands, as if in surrender, and shrugged. "Thanks for getting my friend off the mountain! I'll see you at the bottom."

Then she picked up her lines and, like a kite, urged the chute into the air. Started running.

The chute lifted her off the ground as gently as a bird taking flight, and she rose on the thermals of the Julian Alps.

He watched her until she became a speck against the blue, and Nixon emerged from the hut to join him.

"Looks like fun."

"Looks like a good way to die."

"Better than most," Nixon had said, said glancing at him.

Jonas gave him a look. Offered a wry smile.

"C'mon, boss, let's go."

He'd followed Nixon down the mountain, but by the time they reached the bottom, Ina had been delivered over to medical help.

And Sibba had gone with her.

Still, she'd left an imprint in his mind. Her, huddled on a cliff with her friend one moment, jumping off a mountain the next.

Calling him Spidey. He remembered that way too much, really.

Maybe that's why he'd told Fraser that he wanted more, back in Lake Como.

Now Jonas climbed over a squat, wooden fence and into the hayfield, past rolled bundles of drying hay, scanning for Frannie, her shiny silver body, or any sign of her.

There. Half buried in the ground, a curved metal spine. Jonas ran over and, as he got closer, spotted the metal nose cone. The back propeller.

More debris cluttered the field, and maybe two hundred yards away, he found the ribbed carcass that had connected to the black box, now twisted and torn, driven into the dirt.

But no black box.

Instead, mounted on the bottom of the carcass, where the black box might have been, hung the remains of a cylinder, burnt and dusty.

He stared at it a long moment, then pulled out his phone and took a few pictures. The silence in the wind combing the field pooled in his ears, running a cold finger down his spine as he processed what he was seeing.

Sometime in the past four days, someone had altered Frannie, attached a device onto her, and from what he could surmise, had detonated said device.

Maybe the storm hadn't been Frannie's demise.

He wanted to detach the device, haul it away, but dirt

cemented the ribs of the dirigible into the ground, and he'd need a hacksaw, or even a blowtorch, to remove it.

Better to find the black box and analyze the flight data.

He walked around the field, scanning the wreckage, digging up fragments of the frame.

No box.

But according to his GPS data, the box had splashed down here.

He turned and looked at the farmhouse, just beyond a far drive. Maybe the owner had found the box...

A rusty red Allgaier tractor was parked near an old wooden barn. The wind had wrecked a hay bale behind the house, and although it didn't seem the farm had sustained much damage, the barn doors hung open. A goat stood in the opening, stared at him, then spooked. In a yard near the barn, chickens waddled, pecking.

The rest of the barn, a rough-hewn structure with open stalls, stood vacant.

Across the dirt drive, a whitewashed stone house with a thatched roof seemed abandoned, but he went to the door and knocked.

Nothing. Not a squeaky board, not the swish of curtains at the window, not a breath of life.

He made to move the door handle when, behind him, rumbling thundered from the road, a stir of dust in its wake. Cupping his hand over his face, he spotted two green canvas-covered troop transports headed down the road.

The trucks rumbled past his little rental Panda and down the hill to Poče.

Maybe it was the Slovenian government, tracking the damage.

He watched them disappear down the hill and was turning to leave when, suddenly, behind him, the door opened.

He turned. Stared at the person standing in the door.

Then, on a wisp of breath... "Sibba?"

THREE

"What are you doing here?"

She asked it in English, and no, it wasn't the welcome her grandmother would have given to a stranger on her doorstep, but Sibba simply had nothing else at the sight of... "Jonas, right?"

Like she'd forget his name. Or how good he looked. Just as good as when she'd left him behind on a mountain a month ago. He wore a pair of brown cargo pants, boots, a puffy lightweight black jacket open over a denim shirt. A thousand percent American with his short brown hair and scruff of dark whiskers, like he'd walked out of an L.L.Bean clothing catalog.

Now he also wore a frown, as if trying to unknot her question. "Yes. Jonas Marshall. Hello Sibba."

He remembered her name. She folded her arms over herself and nodded, her glance going toward Poče. How was it that he'd shown up just as the Slovenian military drove into Poče?

"What are *you* doing here?" Jonas asked.

"I asked you first."

He shook his head, stuck his hands into his pockets. "You own this farm?"

"My grandfather does."

"Sorry about your field. The wreckage belongs to one of my weather dirigibles."

She just blinked at him. "What wreckage?"

He pointed to a piece of metal—looked like a carcass of some ancient animal—protruding from the field. "It went down in the derecho."

Oh. That still didn't explain the military's arrival. Except— "Are you working with the Slovenian military?"

"No. I'm here on a grant, working out of Ljubljana with the University, studying storms and, primarily, lightning."

She had nothing for that.

"So, this is your grandfather's place? Is he here? Can I talk to him?"

Probably he was telling the truth, but it felt terribly coincidental that he'd landed in her life, twice, by happenstance, and the second time was on her grandfather's doorstep.

Her *American* grandfather's doorstep. And all his warnings, his secrets, his fears simply rose inside her, took hold.

Who was this guy? "No. He's not here." She stepped back, making to shut the door, but he stuck his foot into the space. "What?"

He frowned at her. "Are you okay?"

She raised an eyebrow. "You're trespassing."

He held up his hands. "Sorry. Wow. Okay. I just...nice to see you too."

Oh, and now she was a jerk. After all, she'd been the one to... obviously she hadn't been thinking clearly back on the mountain.

But all she knew now was that her grandfather was missing. And the warnings of the past had suddenly risen with painful acridity. "Why do you want to talk to my grandfather?"

He blinked at her. Frowned. "I wanted to apologize and ask him if he saw the dirigible go down. There's this strange..." He then shut his mouth and shook his head. "Never mind." He raised his hand and stepped back. "Glad you made it back to terra firma."

And then he smiled. The sense of it rocked her back, the warmth in his eyes, the genuineness of his expression, the way that he just sort of reached out without guile. And once again, the knot in her chest unraveled and left her weirdly undone.

He turned and walked off the porch and back across the field.

Maybe she should call after him, but...

Her grandfather had vanished for a reason. And until she found out why, she wasn't trusting anyone with an American passport.

Sibba shut the door and watched out the window as he tromped across her field. He stopped at the carcass in the dirt, crouching. Interesting.

She headed to the back room, where her grandfather kept his pack, his boots.

Gone, as she'd suspected.

She pulled off her shoes and grabbed her own hiking boots from under the bench. Grabbed her canvas jacket, the flannel-lined one she used for chores, and a hat.

First, she'd go to town, just to make sure that Dedi wasn't in some crazy showdown with the Slovenian government.

And yes, her imagination had taken over, spun out scenarios that had her grandfather cornered, guns pointed at him, or worse, standing in front of a firing squad.

Blimey. She could thank her grandfather for those deep-seated nightmares, the fodder for a promise to never give away his identity during her travels abroad, especially if she landed in the US. Because, according to Hank Kovac, aka Henry Benson, Corpsman Second Class, US Navy, there was no statute of limitations on desertion.

Apparently, it wasn't unheard of for US agents to appear at the doors of aging soldiers secreted away in places like Sweden or South America and haul them back to the States for court martial.

So no, Jonas wasn't getting anywhere near Dedi.

She slipped out the back of the house and followed the trail through the forest, now partially overgrown, around their farmland and through the foothills into town. Less than a kilometer, but the sun had begun to slide beyond the Julian Alps, a simmer of fire along the jagged white peaks. Shadows filled the tangle of streets, haphazard and turning in on each other. Poče was little more than a village with cozy lanes and pristine avenues. But she loved the cluster of homes, fitted together like puzzle pieces all around a main square. She passed two-story, whitewashed homes, their second-story windows and inset balconies filled with flower boxes spilling late-season geraniums. A few cars were parked in carports, and a tabby ran across her path, but the town felt eerily empty as she made her way to the square.

Ina's childhood home over the Poče bakery was dark and the shop shuttered. And next to that, the café, with the chairs set outside on the cobblestones, had its awning drawn in, the chairs stacked inside.

Probably to protect from the storm. Still, even the wind seemed voiceless here.

No sign of the military trucks parked in front of the ancient, orange-washed administrative building. And the water for the fountain in the middle of the square had been turned off, although with the oncoming cold weather, that wasn't a surprise.

No bicycles were propped up along the fence in front of the Hotel Poče, a two-story B&B and restaurant. She half expected the clock tower to be silent too, but the giant minute hand clicked while she stood there in silence.

She headed for the Poče pub, located in the basement of the hotel via a side entrance.

If her grandfather was anywhere in Poče, it would be at one of the worn wooden tables, nursing a homebrewed lager and bowl of *bograč* soup, a crusty slice of *pogača*. Maybe laughing to a story told by Ciril Golab, Ina's grandfather. Or maybe the barkeep, the burly son of the hotel owner.

But the door at the bottom of the steps was closed. She descended anyway and found it unlocked.

Pushed it open.

Inside, the space smelled of ale and onions, the chairs up on the tables, the long wooden bar empty.

A hollowness swept over her, turning her fragile, shaken.

The town had been abandoned.

A rumble sounded outside on the square, and she turned and headed up the stairs as the military truck now growled to a stop in front of the administrative building. Two men climbed out of the cab, and she expected more from the back, but no one emerged.

They weren't wearing the green-gray BDUs of the Slovenian military. Just work jackets, jeans, and most importantly, they held handguns, loosely, as they looked around the square.

She sank back down into the stairwell.

Voices lifted, the language foreign but—shoot, she could recognize a variation of Slavic. Ukrainian, or maybe Hungarian. Even...Russian?

One of the men pointed to the administrative building, and the other ran inside, breaking the glass door to get in.

The first rounded the vehicle and stood in the square, looking at the vacated houses.

She sank back against the wall, her heart hammering. Closed her eyes.

What was going on?

A moment later, a shout from the administrative building made her look. The man had emerged and now descended the steps.

The first man turned and walked back to the truck.

She held her breath.

Just as he made to mount the truck's footstep, a bark sounded from behind her.

She stilled.

Another bark, high and sharp. No—she groaned as she turned.

Behind her, on the street overlooking the stairs, stood Lenard, his squatty, bulldog body taut as he barked down at her.

As if trying to get her attention.

"Shh. Lenard. Stop—"

She glanced back and, oh no, the man had turned, started heading her direction. Maybe he hadn't seen her yet, maybe she could just hide—

Scampering down the stairs, she closed the door to the bar behind her and fled behind the bar. Sank down into the darkness.

Shouting, probably at Lenard—oh, she hoped—and then, oh! Whining as maybe the man shooed Len away. Please, let him not have hurt him—

The door creaked open.

She closed her eyes, held her breath.

Footsteps scuffed across the cement floor of the pub. They stopped, maybe five feet away, just the pub bar between her and— she didn't exactly know, and maybe they weren't even villains. Maybe her own imagination, and even her grandfather's fears, had stirred up a sinister hue to the entire situation.

Except, hello, *guns*. And then a shout, again in, um, Russian?

She knew enough about the current political landscape to know that Slovenia and Russia weren't in cahoots, despite their former affiliations.

So, nope. Not moving.

Except, his shout had brought more footsteps and another voice.

She made herself very small.

Please, *please*.

"Vot!"

She opened her eyes. A man stood at the end of the bar, pushing open the swinging door—

She took off. Running toward the other end of the bar, headed for the door, and daylight and away from whoever—

A hand grabbed her arm, whipped her around. "Stop!"

Not. On her. *Life!*

She hadn't been in the Slovenian military for nothing. She stomped on the man's instep and shot her fist into his throat, breaking his hold on her jacket.

Then she rounded and pushed through the door.

She made it halfway up the steps before someone grabbed her feet. She landed hard, banged her chin, and screamed.

But she turned as she landed and sent her foot into her attacker's face.

She scrambled up the stairs backward, turned, and ran.

Her assailants were untangling themselves at the bottom of the stairs, and shoot, Len had rounded and was now barking, running after her. She sprinted down the street, cut into another one, and then scrambled down a set of stairs, through a neighbor's yard. Emerged out onto another street.

Shouting lifted behind her—aw, she'd always thought herself faster than this.

She took off down the road, out of town, sprinting with everything inside her.

Behind her, a car engine revved, and she glanced behind her, quick.

Oh—*what?*

A Fiat Panda screamed down the road beside her. It slowed and beeped, and she glanced at the driver.

Nearly tripped.

Jonas.

"Get in! Get in!" He'd reached over and pushed open the passenger door, still motoring down the street, although slower.

She glanced behind her and spotted the truck, now lumbering out of the village.

"I promise—I'm on your side!"

She didn't know she had a side. But maybe, yes. She lunged toward the door, grabbed it and flung herself inside.

Shut the door and turned in her seat, glancing behind her.

"What's going on?"

"I have no idea. But until I do, I'm not interested in being abducted by a couple Russian thugs."

"Me either. Belt in."

She pulled off her backpack and threw it into the back seat.

Then she grabbed her belt. Clicked it, even as he pushed the Panda into fifth gear.

Her laughter sounded almost hysterical as she stared at him, shook her head. "They're going to mow us down in this thing."

"Not the way I drive."

Then he shot her a smile. And again, the sense of something whooshing out of her—fear, maybe—swept through her.

All she could do was hold on as he floored it.

JONAS HADN'T A CLUE WHY SIBBA HAD BEEN RUNNING down the road as if she might be on fire, but he guessed it had something to do with the truck bearing down on them.

And from the way she kept looking back, maybe Jonas should get out and push.

Naw, this little rental Panda might be lightweight and might only have 900 ccs under its skinny hood, but it was zippy and, frankly, the behemoth behind them had to crank down to low gear every time they hit a hill, so—yeah.

Buh-bye.

It helped that before he'd hired Geena to drive for Vortex.com and chase storms around the upper Midwest, he'd done the driving himself. He knew how to think fast, take turns on two wheels, and lose himself into no-man's-land.

"Where are we going?"

"Anywhere. I don't know." It helped that he'd spent the better part of the past three days driving these back roads, searching for his downed weather dirigibles.

They cut sharply and wound around dirt roads that rose and fell over foothills, channeled through thick forests, and spidered off into dirt driveways and rutted two-wheel roads.

"They're determined, that's for sure. You must have really made them mad."

He glanced in the rearview mirror. The truck had turned on its headlights with the fading light, but they were so far behind him—

He turned onto another road, then shut his lights off.

"What are you doing?"

"Hiding."

There. A farmhouse, its lights off. And next to it, a massive white barn.

He pulled into a long driveway, then back behind the bar. Turned off the car completely, then jumped out and pulled hay over the car from a nearby mound.

Sibba had joined him, also cascading hay down from the mound until the car was its own mound of hay.

The sound of the truck rumbled closer, so he grabbed her and pulled her against him, alongside the barn.

Ridiculously, he held his breath.

The truck motored past, up the hill.

She stayed motionless a moment, then shucked his arms off her and rounded on him. He could barely see her in the fading darkness, but he had no problem remembering her face.

Those golden-brown eyes. "Just...what—how—" Her mouth closed, then opened again. "Who are you?"

"Just your local—or maybe international—meteorologist."

She just blinked at him.

"I'm a weatherman."

"A *weatherman.*"

"You know. I predict storms and—"

"Nearly run people off the road?"

His smile vanished. "I beeped. And slowed down, and you had about a half mile of space."

"I could have jumped in front of the car—"

"Why would you do that? Are you a deer?'

She looked at him, and maybe he shouldn't have said that, but he'd thought he was being a little bit of a hero. "I *didn't* run you off the road. I *saved* you." Sheesh. *Twice*, he wanted to add, but maybe that wouldn't go over so well.

"Saved me? I can run faster than your little windup car."

He stared at her. Wow, just—wow. Where was the woman who'd invited him to go paragliding with her?

She folded her arms. Looked away, her mouth tight. "Okay. Maybe."

"Maybe? Listen, Miss Reality Check. You were in their headlights. If I hadn't come along—"

"Fine. Yes. Thank you." Only she said it with a Z at the beginning, like *zank you*.

And shoot, it sent a little zing right through him. Oh brother. Clearly he'd been dreaming a bit too hard about this girl, his brain looping their encounter into a fairy-tale ending.

Hel-*lo*. "You're welcome."

She narrowed her eyes at him, as if dissecting his reply.

"Listen, I'm not sure what's happening here. A month ago, you were asking me to jump into the blue sky with you. And now, what? I'm the bad guy?"

She looked away. Closed her eyes. "Fine. Yes. No."

"Yes? Or no?"

"Both!"

Ho-kay. He held up his hands. "Can I drop you somewhere?"

She stepped up to him. "Who were those guys?"

"I haven't the faintest idea—"

"Then how did you know they were chasing me?" She folded her arms.

"You were *running*."

"I could have been...what do you call it?—*jogging*."

"At top speed? In your hiking boots? And a backpack? Only if you're training to climb Everest."

Her mouth tightened. Then she sighed and released her arms. "I think they were Russians. They tracked me down in a bar after my grandfather's dog—" Her eyes widened, and her voice fell. Maybe he wasn't meant to hear the next part, because she looked away from him as she said it. "Lenard. What was he doing there? Without my grandfather?"

So much there to unpack. "Um, I'm going to need more than that. Because after I left your house, I drove into town and passed these guys going to your place."

She looked at him. "What?"

"They went to the field, where my dirigible crashed. One truck went to your farmhouse."

She stilled, then swallowed, her eyes wide.

"Um. You okay? Something you want to tell me?"

"I don't know!" She rounded back to him. "I don't know, okay? I just know that my grandfather wouldn't leave without Lenard. Not if he didn't have to…"

And then, despite the darkness—*wait*. "Are you crying?"

"No!" But she had put her hands over her face. "Yes. Maybe." She turned away from him. "It's just been a really bad day."

No duh. But maybe his day hadn't quite matched hers, because she walked over to the Panda, past it, and sank down on the ground against the wall of the barn.

Oh. Somehow that was the last thing he'd expected from her.

He followed her. Sat down beside her. "Okay. Let's just take a breath here." He looked over at her. "My name is Jonas. We've met, but not in the best of circumstances, so I'm going to start over. I'm here, researching storms because this area seems to have a lot of them."

She had stopped crying, it seemed, although she'd hardly made a peep before, so who knew if she'd *actually* been crying. Maybe simply hiding.

Which he got. Could be that Slovenia was one giant forested hiding place.

"I invented weather dirigibles. Like giant balloons, only they go where we want—they're programed and driven by drones. Powered by batteries, renewable by the sun. And last week, while I was in Italy, four of them crashed. I've been trying to locate them and retrieve their black boxes, which contain all the data."

She was looking at him now, her eyes shiny in the rising moonlight, her face resting on her folded hands.

And for a second, it hit him that, wow, she was pretty. In a regal, European way—high cheekbones, piercing eyes. And despite the crying, she seemed pretty put together. Brave, even, given the way she'd jumped off that mountain.

But boy, she held the patent on confusing.

"That's what I was doing in your field—looking for Frannie. That's what I call dirigible number four."

"Good, because I don't think Frannie would appreciate being referred to as a number."

A beat, and then she smiled.

Oh, now she was being *funny?*

Okay… "She is a little crabby. Disappeared off our radar for a full twenty-four hours before blipping back up. We thought she'd made it through the storm, but maybe she was damaged, because she went down three days ago. It took me this long to find her."

"Poor girl."

Still being funny?

"Maybe, yes, because when I found her, she had this weird casing on her. Like someone had grabbed her out of the sky and attached a bomb to her."

Now Sibba sat up. "A bomb?"

"Or something. The casing was destroyed, and I'm wondering if that's why Frannie came down. And I searched the field. The black box is nowhere to be found."

"You think maybe these guys who chased me and went to my farm have something to do with the crash?"

"Maybe. If the black box was attached to her, then they could be looking for it. It would have all the data on it about when she was taken and where."

"You don't have that on a computer somewhere?"

"The connection is spotty in the mountains, so no. She goes off the grid for a day and then pops back up a hundred miles from where she went down, and we have no idea what happened while she was dark."

She sat there, considering his words, quiet.

Then she sighed. "I'm sorry, I have no idea what happened to your black box." She got up. "But I do need to find my grandfather."

Right. But, and...wait—"Maybe he saw it crash. Maybe *he* has the black box."

She gave a non-laugh chuckle. "Sorry. I just...he's..." She made a face. "My grandfather is a simple man. Our land was owned by my grandmother's family. They rented it out, and he kept honeybees. Sold the honey locally. He likes to stay under the radar and, since Babička died, he keeps a quiet life. I hardly think he'd take your black box."

Right. "But still, he *could* have it."

She blinked. "Not a hope."

"Could have been watching as it went down and thought, hey, what's that? And picked up the box attached to the device. It's no bigger than a shoe box—"

"He has shoes."

"Not my point."

"He doesn't have your box."

"I've got no other leads."

"I'm telling you—"

"Where do you think he is?"

She stared at him as if debating an answer. "Where did you say you were from?"

"Minnesota."

Another beat. "Where is that?"

"Middle of America. We're a state filled with very nice people who don't like spicy food."

She cocked a head at him. "Nice? Try bossy. Arrogant. Stubborn."

Wow, *really*? But maybe. "No, that's just me. Which you

didn't hate so much when I was carrying your friend off a mountain, so..." He didn't smile and added a shrug.

"This feels like extortion."

"And a little like the pot—"

"The what?"

"Never mind. C'mon. I'm just looking for the black box. If he doesn't have it, I'm gone."

She stepped back, her hands on her hips, looking up the road where the truck had gone. She turned back to him. "Okay, Minnesota. My grandfather has a little cabin in the woods, about a half kilometer from the farmhouse, where he keeps his bees. My grandmother was always a little afraid of having them near the house."

He got up. "We can't go back to your place—not if they're still there. Or watching it."

"I know another way." She pulled the hay off the Panda. "But you might have to get out and push."

He sort of liked it when she tried to be funny.

Sorta.

They cleared the Panda, then he pulled out, kept the lights off, his eyes used to the dark and adjusting under the moonlight, and headed down the road, slower now.

Better to drive in the darkness at twenty miles per hour than to light up the night like a firefly.

The landscape was eerily dark, despite the moonlight—a few lights here and there, but mostly, as they drove by farmhouses, windows unlit, he felt like he'd dropped into the Dark Ages.

"Take a right up here."

He peered down the road. "Where?"

"Here—here—*here!*"

He slammed on the brakes and tried to make out the turn. "That's a footpath."

"The Panda isn't that wide. It'll make it."

"It's a rental."

She looked at him. "It's a couple kilometers from here. We go through this field, then past that farmhouse, and behind it is a pasture. You go through the pasture and then—"

"I'm turning! Sheesh."

He bumped onto the path, praying he didn't kick out the drip pan, and then rumbled across the darkened field. Please, let him not hit a cow. But the moonlight silvered the grasses, and the sky had turned an inky blue, the stars strewn like so many gilded jewels across the sky.

And she seemed to be relaxing, even as she hung on to her seatbelt.

"So, you don't live at the farmhouse with your grandfather?"

"No. I have a place in Cerkno."

"I've been there. Stayed at a tourist farm—Želinc. Great *žlikrofi.*"

"You know Želinc? Go around the house."

They'd reached the other side of the field, jostling onto the drive. He drove up the driveway and around the house.

"See the trail?"

"The goat trail? Yes."

She laughed. And this time it took the tension out of his shoulders.

Okay, he might be having fun. "Nixon and I went to Želinc on our way back from Mount Triglav. Stayed two nights. I was surveying the area for weather events."

She'd turned quiet.

"How's your friend?"

"Ina? Good. Her ankle wasn't broken, just sprained."

"It looked bad. I'm shocked it wasn't broken."

"Me too. It was...not a good night. Stop up here. We'll walk up the mountain."

He pulled into a wooded area and got out. She pulled her backpack from the back seat where she'd tossed it after she'd gotten in.

She produced a flashlight and clicked it on. The beam shone

on a path through the tangled, dark woods. It also lit up the night around them.

"Not afraid they'll see you?"

"It's them or the bears." She worked on the backpack.

She was kidding, right?

Right?

FOUR

Right now, she wasn't alone. And Sibba hated how much she appreciated that.

She might have been overstating her comment about the bears, and maybe she should have kept her mouth shut, because every crack and snap in the forest as they walked the trail raised the hairs on the back of her neck.

If not for Jonas, walking behind her, she might have taken the trail at a faster clip. She didn't know why, but again, just having him around seemed to slow the ever present rattle inside her. Again.

Maybe that's why she'd invited him to fly with her that day. She'd labeled it simply a lapse in judgment then.

Now...

"How much farther?"

"Not much. From my grandparents' place, it takes about ten minutes to walk. But we came from the Gorlic farm, so it's a little farther."

"Bees, huh?"

"His apiary is in a large field near the house. It was started by my great-grandfather. We have one of the largest Carniolan honeybee farms in the region." She stepped over a downed log. "Watch your step."

"I didn't know there was a difference between bees."

"Absolutely. A lot of people raise Italian bees—they're gentler and tend to breed faster. Which means more workers when the nectar comes in."

Their feet crunched on the half-dried leaves, the pine needles crinkling under each step. Overhead, the moonlight bled through the tree cover. She probably didn't need the flashlight, but here and there, the tree cover blotted out the sky completely.

"Carniolan bees, however, are stronger bees. They'll survive better in winter. But they aren't as gentle."

"I thought bees died in winter."

"Wasps and hornets do, but honeybees will often hibernate in the combs they produce, living off the honey. Which is why when you harvest the honeycombs, you don't want to deplete their means of survival. You need to give them someplace to hide."

"So, he raises the feisty, tougher bees." He seemed to be laughing or smiling when he said it. She didn't know what was so funny.

"Native Slovenian bees," she said. "But they make the best honey."

"Of course they do. So, bees means bears."

"Sometimes. My grandfather has been known to have to scare away a hungry brown bear. But he's probably already harvested most of the honey for the season, so probably the bears won't come around."

Silence. "You were playing me."

She smiled. "Just making sure you kept up."

He made a low sound, deep in his throat, and it sounded a little like a bear, so maybe she wasn't that far off.

"The field is just up ahead."

"You know your way around these woods pretty well."

"I helped my grandfather with the bees. He didn't even suit up when he harvested the honey. He taught me to harvest too."

"Weren't you afraid of getting stung?"

"Terribly. And when I first started, I used a bee suit. My grandfather always smoked the bees with pine needles and lavender. I still love the smell. It makes the bees sort of groggy and disguises your smell. Most of the bees inside the hive are drone bees, and they don't have stingers. You just have to watch out for the worker bees. My grandfather taught me how to read the bees, to move slowly, and to remain calm. He'd even let them swarm on his arm and they wouldn't sting him."

"Wow. I have to say...I don't like bees."

"The biggest thing is to use slow, deliberate, nonthreatening movements, and most of all, don't panic."

"Good advice for life."

And in bomb removal, but she didn't add that. Usually her profession sort of sent an awkward silence through any conversation. But yes, her history with bees probably informed her current career, a thought she'd never entertained before.

"So, your dad didn't raise bees?"

"He worked with Dedi when he was young, but he and my mother died when I was a year old. My grandparents raised me."

"Oh, I'm sorry."

"I have an uncle, in America, but it was easier to stay here, so..."

"How'd they die?"

"During the Ten-Day War in 1991 after Slovenia declared their independence from Yugoslavia. The airport in Ljubljana was bombed by the JNA—the Yugoslavian People's Army—and our community was destroyed by a stray bomb. I was found in the rubble."

Silence behind her. She hadn't really told many people the story—after a few years, the details of their deaths had become less important.

"My grandparents loved me. I never really missed my parents, because I never knew them. But it still made me hate war."

They came out to a field, and she stopped. He drew up beside her. "Are those the beehives?"

About fifty boxes sat in the field on long wooden planks, their homes quiet as the moonlight bathed them in an ethereal glow. The cold air had driven the bees inside for the night.

The wind shivered in the trees, and the smell of autumn hung in the air.

"So, Weatherman, is there a storm coming?"

He looked at her, then the sky. "Clouds are high and thin, mostly clear night, so...I think we're safe for now."

Safe for now. She glanced at him. He'd shoved his hands into his coat pockets, turned up his collar, but standing next to her, maybe yes. Safe for now.

She shouldn't have jumped to the conclusion that he was some sort of villain.

"The cabin is this way." She headed out across the clearing toward another trail.

"Why does he have a cabin if the field is close to the farmhouse?"

She laughed. "Because Babička sometimes had a sharp tongue."

He made another sound, like before.

She'd hoped to see a light flickering in the window of the cabin as they approached, but the place was dark, silent. And unchanged since the last time she saw it, with the rough-hewn pine logs, the front porch with a couple old hive boxes still needing repair, a netting hat hanging near the door, the worn bee brush, and a honeycomb extruder on a bench.

She opened the door and shone her light inside. "Dedi?"

The place did seem recently used, the smell of coals in the potbellied stove, the lantern, although snuffed out, in the middle of the table. And his red woolen jacket hanging from a knot in the pine logs.

The two thin beds that ran along the back wall seemed untouched, however. And the kitchen, a simple counter with cupboards over it to hold his ceramic plates and pots, had been tidied. The cast iron pot sat clean on the stove.

Jonas had stepped in behind her. "Not here."

"No." She walked over to the lantern, opened it, cranked the wick up and then took a box of wooden matches from the shelf near the door and lit it. It crackled to life, sputtering, then bathing the room in a soft, warm glow.

Jonas shut the door. "You okay?"

She turned and leaned against the table. "I guess I'm worried. He took his Bible from his bedside stand, which means he was definitely going somewhere. And Lenard...he would have taken him with him for a day trip. The dog can fend for himself, but... Dedi is in his late seventies, and lately I've been worried about his mind. He seems to slip into old stories, stay there for a while."

"Where would he go?"

"I don't know." She slid onto a chair at the table, then set her elbows on it.

He pulled out a chair and sat down across from her. "When was the last time you talked to him?"

"I drove up a couple weeks ago. Made dinner. Picked up a load of honey to sell in Cerkno, at the ski resort. He was fine."

She pressed her hands to her face.

"Hey," Jonas said quietly. "We'll find him."

She looked up. He sat across from her, the firelight flickering across his face. He had kind eyes. That was the first thing she'd noticed about him back on the mountain.

Keep your eyes on me, and you'll be fine. I won't let you get hurt.

Oh no. What was wrong with her that a few hours spent with this man made her say and do crazy things. "Why didn't you go with me that day on the mountain?"

"You mean when you asked me to jump off it with you?" His mouth quirked up.

"Paragliding is not jumping off."

"Technically, you run and jump—"

"I run and let the wing grab the air."

"And if it doesn't?"

"It always does."

"People die running into danger."

"Not if they're careful."

His mouth tightened. Then he sighed. "For a long time, I lived my life by chasing storms. Running toward the potential of danger, hoping to get an up close and personal view of a tornado." He put his hand on the table, running over the wood there. "More times than I can count, I got close—really close. And always seemed to escape anything terrible happening to me, so I got a little cocky and...it finally happened. My team and I were in a terrible accident. Our car was thrown, and we flipped, and my driver broke her neck, suffered a TBI and nearly died. I was fine, however, and...ever since, I've had a hard time living with that."

He looked away, his jaw tight. "I just can't risk letting someone get hurt on my watch again."

Oh.

She got that, better than he could ever imagine.

The words were suddenly right there, on her lips. *I got my partner killed too.*

But then she'd have to tell him about this summer. And the fires. And how she'd failed, so terribly, to keep the worst from happening.

So instead, she just nodded. "And running off a mountain felt a lot like—"

"Running into a storm. Yes." He'd turned back to her, his blue eyes now on fire, emotion thick in them. "So I'm sorry, but paragliding is way outside my wheelhouse right now. I just can't run toward danger...not now."

She sighed. "You missed a great view."

He smiled then. "I'm sure of it," he said quietly.

Oh, this had been a terrible idea. Because sitting here with him in the soft glow of the lamplight...

She was just tired and raw and still a little wounded by this summer. "Maybe we should get back to the car."

"And go where?"

Point.

"It'll be easier to sneak back to the farm and get my car at night, probably." And that felt weird to say. Like they might be on some clandestine spy mission. She ran her hands over her face. "I still can't figure out why they were after me. I mean—"

Scratching at the door made her freeze.

More scratching, then moaning.

"Bear?" Jonas said.

"I don't think bears knock," she said, and got up. Hopefully Russian thugs didn't either, because she opened the door.

Lenard stood at the door looking up at her, his ears perked, his tail busy.

"Len!" She knelt and gathered him in her arms. He jumped up on her shoulders, licking her chin, her ear. "Did you bring Dedi with you?"

A crunch outside, and she stilled.

Looked up just as Jonas flashed his light out into the yard.

Not Dedi, but apparently the Russian thugs had picked up Len's trail, because the two men she'd spotted in the street emerged from the ring of darkness.

Or maybe they'd been followed.

Jonas yanked her inside, the dog scampering in, and shut the door. Rounded on her.

"Please tell me this place has a back door."

No back door. No escape.

No lock on the door.

Jonas put his hand on the door and then his back to it,

hearing his own voice in ominous prophecy: *I just can't risk letting someone get hurt on my watch again.*

Why he'd told her the story of Geena and the crash, he didn't know—it'd just felt right, as if in the quietness, Sibba might understand that him not going paragliding with her wasn't about, well, *her.*

Although, hanging around her wasn't without its drama— "How'd they find us?"

She had backed away from the door, staring at him. "I...I don't know."

Okay, he'd seen that look a few times. The panicked shutdown of an oncoming tornado. "Sibba, breathe."

"I am breathing. I'm thinking."

And then the men were on the porch, pushing at the door.

Len was barking, clearly caught up in the emotions.

Sibba grabbed her backpack and slung it on. Then she walked over to the potbellied stove and pulled a cast iron pan off it. "Let them in."

He stared at her. Len rounded, stood next to her, still barking.

"I don't think I can do that."

Another thump at the door.

"Okay, how about this?" She positioned herself beside the door. "They come in, we go out."

"Hand over the pan, and we have a deal."

A beat.

"C'mon, Supergirl."

Her eyes widened. Then she shoved the pan into his grip.

He nodded, and this time the door shuddered with what he presumed was a body thrown at it.

"Ready?"

He waited until he heard the thunder of feet, then rounded and opened the door.

One of the men came barreling through. He tripped and landed on the floor, Len on top of him, growling.

The second man came in, and Jonas spotted the handgun a second before he batted it away with the pan.

Then he clocked the intruder with a backhand, sent him spinning, dropped the pan, and followed Sibba out the door.

Len shot out ahead of them, on the path toward the field.

Sibba was fast—*really* fast—and ran with a grip on her flashlight, so he got a sort of strobe effect as he followed her.

He caught up as they broke into the field, Len still barking, racing forward, then cutting back to them.

A few of the bees had woken, and a hum filled the air.

"Run!" he said, grabbing her elbow and heading hard for the far side—

A shot speared the air.

He grabbed her, brought her down, rolling with her as another bullet zipped past them. "Turn off the light!"

She fumbled with the flashlight, and in a second, the light winked out.

But they were silvery targets in the moonlit field. And Len—he was going to get them killed, still barking.

Their attackers had laser lights attached to their weapons and now fanned them over the field.

Jonas got up, grabbed Sibba's hand, and pulled her behind a row of hives. "Give me ten seconds, then get up and run."

"Jonas—"

He ignored her protest, kept low and ran down the line of beehives, his gaze on the source of the lights.

Len had stopped barking—maybe she'd grabbed the dog.

The bees had woken, now agitated. They flew around his head, but he didn't swat at them, just stayed still as he crouched behind a wooden box.

The first guy—Jonas dubbed him Igor—had entered the field, now scanning for prey, his friend behind him. They huffed at each other in Russian.

Closer.

The man stood just five feet away, still scanning with his laser.

Close enough.

Jonas stood up, grabbed the beehive, and with everything inside him, flung it at the man.

He dodged, but the box broke, and the bees spilled out in a swarm.

Jonas turned and fled.

Sibba sped out ahead of him—good girl—Len long gone. She vanished into the forest at the far edge of the field to the shouts of the men behind them.

He edged in after her, slowing at the ground turned dark, dangerous.

"Over here!"

He slowed, and a hand caught him, pulled him off the path. He slammed into her. She pulled him into the forest, away from the path. They circled deep into the woods, the field still behind them, away from the trail before hiding behind a massive oak.

"What do you...bet...they have people...at your...car?" She was breathing hard.

Yeah. Maybe. He leaned down and grabbed his knees. "You okay?"

"Yeah. But those bees won't slow them down for long."

"Agreed." Len had stopped barking, now jumping upon them.

"It's okay, buddy," Jonas said and knelt in front of the dog, pulling him to himself to calm him. "Shh." He looked up at her. "We need to keep moving."

"Let's go back to the farm. We can sneak to my car, grab it."

Behind them, in the field, the men were still shouting. A few shots fired and Leo whined. Jonas held him tight. "Shh, buddy." He looked at her. "Do you know the way?"

"Blindfolded."

"Okay." He got up, and for good measure, held the dog. "I'm going to need you to be quiet, pal."

"Follow me. Exactly."

He frowned.

"Trust me."

"Let's punch it."

She looked at him.

"It's storm talk. Lead on, Captain my Captain."

"Americans," she said and grabbed his coat, pulling him behind her.

He followed in silence as they rounded the field, coming back to the cabin yard. Len was scrabbling to get free, but Jonas tightened his hold even as they crouched around the backside of the building.

"They're gone," he said.

"We hope. They could have gone back to the car."

"Or the farm." She drew in a breath. "But even so, I have a plan."

"And your car keys, I hope."

"I left them in my car."

He wished he could see her face, but all he had was the soft sound of her voice, her hand on his arm, the sense of her close to him.

"Again, stay with me. Right behind me."

"Aye, aye, but why?"

She got up. "Because my grandfather was a...careful man. Private. And he might have booby-trapped this forest."

His brain simply blanked out as she got up. *Booby-trapped*? He didn't mind at all when she grabbed his jacket again.

He walked quietly behind her, his heartbeat thundering, trying to unpack her words.

What on earth?

They came out to another thin trail, and she let go of his jacket as they followed it in silence. Len kept trying to wiggle out of his arms, but the last thing they needed was the dog running ahead to alert the troops, if there were any, of their return.

But frankly, he'd dearly like to know what they wanted with Sibba. Maybe, "Do you think these guys are after your grandfather?"

She drew in a breath, glanced at him. "I had thought about that, but...I don't think so."

"Why would they be after him?"

She stayed silent and then put her arm out. "There's the farm."

The moonlight glistened on the farmhouse roof, the farm quiet. A few round hay bales had survived the storm and now dotted the cow pasture, and a massive mound of hay shone like gold at the far end of the field, not far from the trail into the woods.

"I don't see the truck," he said.

"Me either. We'll go down along the edge of the field. Hide behind that hay mound. See my car?" She pointed to her SUV parked by the barn. "I'll go first, get it started, and then pull out and head for the hay bale. You let Len go and he'll jump in. You follow him, and Bob's your uncle."

"Bob?"

"Got it from the RAF. Ready?"

For the first time, he thought maybe not. But, "Yep. I'll get there. With Len."

She looked at him. Took a breath, and in the edge of the forest, the moonlight just made out her face. "Thank you for saving me."

He stilled, then smiled. "It was either that or run you down."

She smiled then too. "Meet you at the car. Don't be late."

Then she got up and dashed out of the forest for the nearest hay bale.

Len fought him, starting to bark. "Hang on, buddy."

She made it to the mound, disappeared, and Jonas flicked a glance at the house. No movement.

She sprinted out into the night, a blur that he could barely make out until, by the barn, her dome light shot on, just a blink, and then the door closed.

Her motor revved.

"Okay, she's all yours."

Len took off toward the car, which headed off road, into the field, straight for the massive hay mound.

He got up, running hard on the dog's trail.

She spun through the field, her lights off, Len racing toward her. Then she stopped a few yards from the hay mound and got out.

Opened her back door.

Len flew inside, and in a moment, so did Jonas, pulling the door shut behind him.

She was already back in the driver's seat, peeling out.

The porch light flickered on outside the house.

Oops.

She broke out of the field, onto the road, and he belted in and grabbed the dog.

"Calm down, Weatherman. You're not the only one who knows how to drive."

He was calm. He was—"All four wheels down, please!"

She laughed, and it sort of speared through him, released something.

Maybe the tightly wound tangle of guilt inside him, that somehow *he'd* been the one to bring danger to her door.

But even if he had, maybe she knew how to face it.

His conversation with Fraser circled back and sat in his brain. *Maybe, if you were honest, you want more.*

His gaze fell on Sibba.

She seemed the kind of girl who took enough risks to keep things interesting, but not enough to live recklessly. Even now she wore her seatbelt, and as they motored out into the dark road, she cut down her speed, turning on her running lights.

So as not to kill them.

Yes, he wanted more. A life with purpose—of course. And he'd had that, really. His data had helped create early warning systems, predict how storms might move or turn.

But he also wanted this...not the running part, but the dog in his lap, a beautiful, intriguing woman in his life.

Running away from danger, not toward it.

He turned, looked out the window. Didn't see any lights following them.

About five kilometers south, she turned on her headlights. "You okay?"

Len sat with his head on Jonas's lap and now flicked a look up as only dogs can. Big brown eyes, a little guilty.

Jonas put a hand on his head. "It's okay, pal. I know you were just trying to help."

"We'll go back to my place, unless you want me to drop you somewhere."

"My office is Ljubljana, so…"

"Okay. We'll figure it out in the morning."

The lights of Cerkno dotted the valley as they descended the hills, and silence fell between them.

"We'll find your grandfather," he said quietly.

She nodded. "And your black box."

Right. He'd almost forgotten about that.

Almost.

They pulled up to a two-story townhouse, and she parked in the drive.

"Okay, buddy, you need to get off me." He went to move the dog just as she turned in her seat.

"What's that…blue stuff on you?"

He looked down at where Leo had pressed against his jacket. Blue dust, and it…glowed.

"What—" He looked at the dog. The blue flecked his coat. He went to brush it—

"Don't touch it!"

He stilled, looked at her. "Why? Is it some sort of plant dander?"

She shook her head, then lifted her hands and checked her jacket in the darkness. "I have it on me too."

"What is it?"

She looked at him. "I'm not sure. But when we get inside, take off your clothes and get in the shower."

He just blinked at her. "What?"

She'd gotten out, now pulled open his door. Len jumped out.

"What are you talking about?" He got out. Looked at himself in the darkness. He wasn't covered—more like scant blue glitter on his body. But it definitely glowed.

And a chill went through him. He looked up.

Her mouth had tightened. "I've only seen this a few times, but...I think this could be radioactive dust."

He just stared at her, her words settling inside, hollowing him out.

"Did you hear me?"

"I...radioactive *dust*? Like waste product?"

"It's sometimes used in creating a dirty bomb."

And now, "How do you know that?"

"I was in the military. We...we had training in this. Let's go."

But he just sat there in the shrapnel of her words.

He should be in Geneva on a romantic holiday.

Instead, Ned Marshall, Petty Officer Second Class, Navy SEAL, sat in the body of a modified Black Hawk helicopter, staring out the open cargo door, watching the sea roll by, green whitecaps and undulating waves that zipped past at 150 miles per hour.

Wishing he'd told his fiancée to go home.

Not that Shae did much of what he told her to do, so maybe he'd modify that to *asked*, politely, fervently. But still, agreeing to her suggestion to wait around in Switzerland while he finished this op—bad idea.

Especially since she'd suggested she do some day hiking in the French Alps. And sure, she'd done plenty of world travelling for her job as a freelance graphic artist, taking photos for advertising spots or marketing campaigns. She'd been in Great Britain, or maybe Lauchtenland, or even Brighton Kingdom before meeting him in Geneva—

Oh, what. Was he. *Thinking?*

He'd been lured by the fact that she'd said yes the night before, when he'd popped the question after four long years, and...

Sheesh, she could tangle up his brain with just a flash of her smile.

So yeah, she'd left for the fun they should have enjoyed together while he, with a text from his team leader, Trini, had left the woman he loved and deployed to a nearby TOC where his team assembled to track down some missing uranium.

Not the holiday he'd wanted. Even though he'd give his life for these guys—Trini, Marsh, Sonny, Cruz, and Mac.

But none of them was a five-foot-five sometimes-blonde with beautiful blue eyes and a laugh that could fuel him for weeks on end during spin-ups.

So no, he'd rather be enjoying a Jambon-beurre sandwich with her at a patisserie on the streets of Lausanne, Switzerland.

Instead, he and his team were getting ready to fast rope down to a 215-foot container ship named *Neptune*, sailing under the Liberian flag on its way to Turkey, carrying what the intel at JSOC said was eighty-eight kilograms of plutonium stolen from the Swiss Institute of Technology in Lausanne, Switzerland, some seven days ago.

Seven long days of surveillance and tapping informants, then a quick mission to track down and grab the cell phone of a now-dead Hungarian middleman named Geza Fezekas, who'd worked as a courier for the Russian Bratva, namely the fringe but lethal Petrov group.

A cell phone that led to the GPS coordinates of one ex-CIA agent, now rogue operator, running around Europe causing all sorts of trouble—a man named Alan Martin. The man had given them the slip in the port of Venice, Italy, but left behind a trail that led them to Transworld Shipping Company and a focused chat with the director. With a little pressure from local operatives, they got the bill of lading and, bingo, they'd discovered something listed as "medical devices."

Right.

Loaded and already at sea, the first stop for the *Neptune* was the Port of Durrës, Albania, where the cargo was scheduled to be off-loaded in a week's time.

So, of course, SEAL Team 3 was deployed to confirm and secure the stolen uranium.

Which landed Ned sitting next to the bulkhead of the passenger compartment, the night so black—thanks to the cloud cover—that he could barely see his own body without his NVGs. He'd already run his mental routine, his hand running over his gear—his loadout and weapons—but now, admittedly, his brain was not on the mission but on the woman he'd left behind—

And couldn't get ahold of.

That's probably what bothered him the most—the fact that after seven days, and just as many phone calls, he was cluttering up her voice mail. And not once had she called him back, even to leave her own voice mail.

He felt a tap on his shoulder and pushed up the NGVs to see Mac—Riley McCord—sitting beside him. Mac had just come back from paternity leave after his wife had given birth to a baby girl in Alaska. "Bull, you got this?"

Ned nodded, regretting, sort of, letting Mac see the way he'd nearly thrown his phone across the room after the last no-go call. "All good."

Then, to prove it, he flipped his NVGs back down and slid the bolt on his M4A1 back to check the round in the chamber. Then he thumbed on the power to his infrared laser target designator and IR illuminator.

"Stay frosty," Mac shouted.

Ahead of them, from the open door, Marsh, XO and Delta Two, flipped a three-finger signal—three minutes out.

Ned ran his hand over his ammo pouches a last time, then played out a mental execution of the mission—

Fast rope to the deck behind the bridge, cross the near football-field-length boat to the cargo deck at the front, then track down the cargo box holding the nuclear material, break in, confirm and contain, and then use that information to put the *Neptune* under international confinement, bringing it to the nearest port to off-load the cargo.

From there, they'd let JCOS track down the intentions of the Petrov group, and he'd return to Lausanne to finish his holiday.

Please.

The Black Hawk pulled up hard and then settled into a hover over the tailfin of the ship. As Ned pulled on his gloves, Trini and Marsh sent the rope bag down, and then Marsh—one of their most seasoned operators, and Ned's first cousin, something that command seemed not to care about—followed it over the side.

Then Sonny, Cruz, and finally Ned stepped up. He wrapped his gloved hands around the rope, hooked his boot around, and down he went, into the cold darkness.

He hit the deck hard and cleared off in a second, leaving room for Mac and finally Trini.

They fanned out, three on each side of the vessel, now attached to each other via the comms circuit. His Peltor earpiece whistled in his ear as the chopper peeled away.

It would wait for their exfil, most likely a water snatch.

And he'd be back in Switzerland by breakfast—

Focus.

They certainly hadn't arrived undetected, although anything at sea, and especially with the engines running, created enough noise clutter that the bridge lookouts might not have heard them. Especially this hour of the night. But they couldn't count on that.

Or the fact that most of the deckhands should be unarmed.

He pushed up starboard behind Marsh and Sonny. Chief

Trini, Cruz, and Mac took portside, and almost in unison, the two teams took the stairs down to the deck.

Marsh stayed back while the others took positions thirty feet ahead. Then Ned held while Marsh and Sonny moved up.

They leapfrogged their way to the front, to the massive stack of containers, and Sonny pulled out a computerized map of the ship on his wrist pad.

Trini's voice came over the comms. "All clear. Move into position."

That meant Trini's team—the portside team—would stay back on overwatch while Ned and Sonny climbed the containers.

They'd run a couple high-level drones over the ship during the past two days and reviewed satellite history, and according to their best data, as well as the manifest and ship profile report, which listed the bay, row, and tier of the container, the one holding the "medical devices," was four stories up in a stack of six.

So, that would be a fun climb.

It always unnerved Ned a little to climb containers set upon each other like Legos. Only, they didn't snap together, and in his mind, one rogue wave and they'd all end up in the sea, him on the bottom of ten tons of metal.

All quiet on the deck, no resistance, and that edged a buzz under his skin. Then again, he hardly expected a bunch of rogue Russians to show up with AK-47s.

Okay, he did a little. If the plutonium meant that much to them.

Which clearly it did, because they'd left a couple people dead, starting with a man named Gerwig Buchen, who'd run the research at the Lausanne facility, his throat slit in a park in Geneva. The night operations manager also, who'd been tortured enough to let in the bad guys before they'd mercifully shot him in the head.

So, yeah, they cared.

But so did the US government, thank you—about not letting plutonium out of international control to somehow end up in a nuclear bomb in New York City, or maybe his home state of Minnesota.

Right. Like a terrorist even knew where Minnesota was on a map.

"Delta Six ascending," Ned said as he came up to the container. Looked up, the green light illuminating the four locking bars, the indentations in the corrugated structure. The CSC plate on the left hand door listed the owner's name, the ACEP data, and the technical data of the container.

Nothing on it that said *Beware, hazardous material,* and maybe it was too much to hope that it had been transported in a special UF_6 Type 30B container.

Which meant he might end this op with his skin peeling off. He glanced at the Geiger counter attached to his vest. So far, nothing.

Sonny, with his bolt cutters, was right behind him.

Ned grabbed the locking bar and scrambled up, his feet in the indentations. Then the next container, same method, then the third.

"You're misnamed, Bull. We should call you Spiderman," said Sonny, behind him.

"No. That's my brother Jonas. He can climb anything." Although, it might be a better moniker than Bull, a playoff of Ned Ryerson's phrase "Ned the Bull" from the movie *Groundhog Day.*

Ned scaled the fourth container—two more above him—and checked the registration. Bingo.

He then used a carabiner to attach a line of webbing to the locking bar cam and the top of the container.

Sonny attached on the other side.

Then they both dropped down, bracing their feet on the sill, their weight held by the webbing. Sonny used the bolt cutters to break open the lock. Then they moved the door handles over, releasing the massive bar.

Sonny swung over next to Ned and opened the first door.

Then he moved inside, Ned following after he'd opened the other door.

Their green lights flashed over the contents.

No massive metal containers of enriched plutonium.

Instead, a crate sat in the middle of the room.

Sonny unclipped his webbing and walked over to it.

"Sonny, hold up," Ned said, glancing at his Geiger counter, which had suddenly started beeping, tiny whining that rose every hair on Ned's body.

"What's the reading?"

"It's over a hundred," Ned said.

"You have three minutes," Trini said in comms, clearly listening.

"Copy." Ned unclipped his webbing also.

Sonny was already prying open the box. Ned helped him tear off the top.

His light scraped the inside.

A nest of six empty containers.

"It's empty, boss," Sonny said. "Nothing here. We've been spoofed."

"Wait—" Ned said, and lifted one of the boxes. The Geiger started to scream. "All Geiger counters are calibrated to Cs-137—caesium." He closed his eyes and tipped his NVGs up.

The bottom of the box glowed blue.

His gut dropped. "Boss, I don't think we're after plutonium." He set the box back inside the container and closed it. "I think we're after caesium-137. This entire box is radioactive. And whoever had it is now in the wind with radioactive waste."

"One minute left," Trini said.

Ned resecured his NVGs, then headed back out and clipped onto his webbing.

Sonny did the same, and in moments, they'd closed the door.

The Geiger counter kept singing. Which meant he probably had dust on his hands, maybe his clothing.

Nothing a dunk in the ocean wouldn't fix, since caesium-137

was water soluble. Hopefully, a dose this small wouldn't take out local fish, but the R-word was never a souvenir he wanted to bring home.

Or to Geneva.

Aw...

And shoot, he already knew what Chief Trini was going to say after they'd rappelled down to the sea and finned out into the black for their exfil, after they'd choppered back to their temporary TOC in Koper, Slovenia, and after he'd stripped down and taken a scalding ten-minute shower.

Expected the expression on Trini's face, on his way to deliver grim news as he walked into the locker room where Ned and Sonny sat in fresh cotton jumpsuits like kindergartners in onesies.

"Sorry, Bull. You're not going anywhere."

FIVE

From Sibba's research, the likelihood of her nose decaying off her body seemed slim.

Still, the amount of glowing blue dust on her clothing had unnerved Sibba as she took a shower, then washed Len.

Before she washed him, however, she combed dust off his fur and slipped the comb into a bag. She'd track down Director General Vlasic and see if his team could analyze it.

Now she sat at her kitchen table, a bag of crisps open, an orange Fanta on the table, Len at her feet, her laptop open, wearing leggings and an oversized University of Ljubljana sweatshirt, wool socks. She'd pulled her wet hair back into a ponytail.

In the bathroom, the shower ran. She'd told Jonas to stand under the water for five minutes at least. Wash his hair twice.

He'd given her another look, the question again on his lips—*How do you know that?*

The answer she'd given him in the car clearly wasn't enough. But she also remembered their conversation on the way to the cabin. *"I just can't run toward danger...not now."*

She couldn't help but wonder if that included being around her. So no, she could just keep her profession quiet for right now.

Besides, he was going back to Ljubljana in the morning.

For now, she'd given him her old bathrobe while she washed his clothes.

But first, she'd gotten out her Geiger counter, the one in her EOD kit, and run it over his attire. CPM rate landed just above fifty, but he'd only been exposed for an hour. Unless he'd picked up the dust in the fields.

Still, acceptable rates were up to 150 CPMs.

She checked her clothing too. She had less dust, mostly on her shoes, but she'd found it in the pores of her hands, too, so maybe when she'd fallen on the stairs coming out of the bar in Poče.

Or even at her grandfather's house.

Not enough effective radiation to contaminate the water, so she washed his clothes and hers. Sprayed off her shoes.

She heard the shower turn off. It felt a little strange to have someone else in her shower.

No, a *man* in her shower.

A man in her apartment, even.

And then said man started to hum. Sure, it was in the bathroom, but at this time of night, with the silences around them, the sound of it just filtered through the door and out into her main room.

She couldn't place it, but she knew the tune. Something from her childhood.

Something that knew its place in her heart, even if she couldn't name it.

She clicked on a site about radiation poisoning and was reading the wiki about it when, "Oh no, is it that bad?"

The voice jerked her, and she gasped. Turned.

"Sorry," Jonas said. "I thought you heard me come out." He wore her white bathrobe—thankfully it fitted around his waist and hips, but it pulled at the shoulders and revealed a bit of his chest, and why had she thought this was a good idea? Because it only made her suddenly, keenly aware of his presence here. Solid build, muscular, and he hadn't shaved, so it only made him ridiculously attractive in a fish-out-of-water sort of way.

She turned back to the computer. "No. My Geiger counter got a hit, but it isn't enough to do serious damage. We'll have to bring a sample of the dust into a lab to find out what it is."

"But it *is* radioactive." He put one hand on her chair and bent over her, and wow, that was an issue, because he smelled soapy clean and husky, and suddenly her mind was on the way he'd tackled her in the field.

Strong arms, bracing them both for the fall, the sense of his body covering her.

Protecting.

She drew in a breath and got up. "Fanta?"

He'd stepped back from the chair. "No sugar before bed." He turned back to her computer. "This chart is terrifying." He sat down in her chair. "Help me understand this."

She leaned over his shoulder and pointed to the chart. "Radiation is measured in both ionizing events detected per second or minute and displayed as count rate or CPM, and a radiation dose rate, which is called a sievert, or SI. It measures the health risk. The dose rate and the CPMs are combined to create the reading. Anything below 100 CPMs is considered acceptable."

"Meaning my skin won't slough off in a week, but I'll get cancer in ten years? Maybe I'll take that Fanta."

She slid onto a nearby chair. "No. We have radiation all around us. It's in the soil, the water, the air. And there are natural substances that can be radioactive—the most common is a substance called caesium. But it's only radioactive as a by-product of nuclear fission. Cs-137 is the most common, and the most lethal, and this is what a Geiger counter is calibrated at. One microsievert per hour would equal about 120 CPM."

"And how bad is a one microsievert dose?"

"Nausea and vomiting within six hours. Maybe a headache."

"That doesn't sound so bad."

"Leukemia within a month."

"Oh."

"And, if not treated, death within six to eight weeks."

He stared at her.

She smiled. "But only a five percent death rate."

"That makes me feel oh so much better."

"Still have time to go paragliding with me." Oh, she didn't know why she said that. She got up. "I can make you some toast." She pulled out a loaf of bread.

"I'm suddenly not hungry."

"Nauseous?"

Silence. She turned. He appeared white.

"Oh, too soon?"

"How can you joke about this? We could be—radioactive!"

"We're not radioactive." She turned, bread knife in her hand. "We don't even know what kind of dust that is. Could be...anything."

"How is Cs-137 made?"

"It's the nuclear waste of uranium-235."

He sat back. "Okay, now I'm feeling nauseated."

"Should I get you a garbage can?"

He pressed his hands to his face.

Oops. "Sorry." She sat down at the table. "Listen. I took a sample from Len. We'll get the substance checked in the morning."

Jonas stood up. Walked over to the light. Turned it off.

He stood, a white marshmallow in darkness.

"What are you doing?"

"Looking to see if I glow."

"Oh, for—stop." She got up, flicked on the light. "You're freaking out."

"And you're not." He cinched his bathrobe. "Which sort of unnerves me. Are you in the least worried that your eyeballs might turn to liquid?"

He was funny. Or maybe he wasn't kidding, but she liked him more than she should probably.

"No. And if they are, there's nothing I can do about it now."

"We should go to the hospital and get radiation meds."

She walked over to the sofa and picked up a blanket. "Or you could try and get some sleep."

"Where are my pants?"

"Still wet."

He considered her. "You're *not* concerned, are you?"

"Nope." She had pulled a pillowcase from her ottoman storage and now slipped it over the pillow. Tossed it on the sofa.

Silence, and he had crossed his arms over his chest, leaning one shoulder against the wall.

"What?"

"What aren't you telling me?"

"I promise, nothing."

"You aren't afraid to jump off a mountain, or stick your hand in a beehive, or even drive with the lights off. And now your cells might be turning to liquid and you're like, hey, drink a little warm milk and up the wooden hills you go."

"Up the wooden hills?"

"Something my mother used to say. Stairs. To bed. But, really. Does nothing phase you?"

She sighed and sank down on the sofa. "I'm a little unnerved that my grandfather is missing."

"Right." He ran his hand behind his neck. "I forgot that."

A beat. Silence. Then, "But, no, I'm not easily rattled, I guess." She got up and grabbed a duvet from the ottoman space. "Your time is your time—you can't do anything about it. So why worry?"

He just stared at her. "You're not worried about dying?"

"Every day could be your last." Ask her parents.

Ask Erazem, or Hedwig, or any of the brave firefighters she'd seen vaporized this summer.

Ask Rok.

In a blink, there he was, dressed in turnout gear, standing with the fire backdropped behind him.

The next, the world exploded around them.

She dropped the sheet, her hands suddenly, weirdly shaking at the rush of emotion. No, not here, not now.

"Sibba, are you okay?"

She swallowed and forced a smile. "Yep. I'm fine." And now, shoot, her eyes had started to burn. She blinked hard and looked away.

He stepped up to her. "Wait. What is going on?" He touched her arm. "Every day could be your last? Where did that come from?"

And it was hard not to give in to the softness of his voice, especially with him standing there in her puffy bathrobe. Like he might be a friend.

Again, just like in the mountain hut, everything simply unwound, and she found her breathing hiccupping, her eyes filling.

Aw. "Sorry." She tore away.

"Why are you apologizing?"

"Because the last thing I want is to..." She closed her eyes.

Silence.

She took a breath. "Listen. Fine. Okay." She took a step away from him. "I...I recently lost someone close to me."

"A boyfriend?"

She shook her head, looked away. "No. We worked together, but I made a mistake. It was my fault he died."

Jonas just stood there, his eyes narrowing. "I have a hard time believing that."

"There it is. And so, you know, you just have to...just, hold things loosely."

"No, you don't." He walked over to her. "You don't have to hold anything loosely, especially people you love."

No, no... She pressed her hand to her mouth. "Jonas...I... really. Please, I..."

Although his body didn't move, his mouth did, tightening down to a firm line.

"I'm just tired."

"Go to bed, Sibba." He gave her a small smile.

She fled to her room and shut the door.

Sheesh, she'd nearly broken down right in front of him. She hadn't even cried at Rok's funeral.

Pulling off her sweatshirt, she climbed into bed, pulled the duvet over her. Stared out the window.

Oh, she didn't want to think about Rok. Or the rest of the firefighters.

But there they were, inside her brain, and even as fatigue consumed her, the fire pulled her in.

The choking smoke, the heat, the roar of the flames. A too-hot turnout suit—

"Over here! This way!"

Rok, motioning to the firefighters, trapped in the town of Temnica, now in flames.

Her, standing in the middle of the field, the smoke billowing up to turn the sky to charcoal. "Run where I tell you! Exactly!"

Rok nodding, running the path she'd shown him.

Already, fire breaking through forest around them, burning the grass.

Four firefighters, their helmets blackened, their jackets singed. And Rok, running hard for the chopper.

The fire, so fast now it could catch them, climbing up a tree, shooting off the top, like fingers beseeching the sky.

"Run!"

It chewed the grasses, reaching out to grab Hedwig. He went down and she screamed as Erazem rounded back—

"Run!"

Rok, now, helping Isak, who also tripped.

Then they were down, and the fire swelled around them.

Rok popped up, pushed Isak in front of him. Matik ran past them, hard for the chopper.

Rok tripped and she left the chopper, running hard—

Somehow, he stood then, the fire behind him, a backdrop of writhing flame.

Rok—

The explosion slammed her to the ground, and Rok simply disintegrated.

She couldn't breathe. Couldn't—

Wetness across her face. She threw up her arms, fighting—

"Sibba, wake up. I got you. I got you. Breathe!"

She opened her eyes to Jonas grabbing her, holding her arms. "Breathe."

Oh. Her breaths came fast, over each other, then suddenly she was twisting off the bed, holding herself, hyperventilating.

Len was on the bed, barking.

She couldn't catch her breath.

"Okay, okay, come on, don't do this." Jonas bent down, put his face close to hers. "Breathe out of your nose. Close your mouth. In and out now, through your nose."

She tried, and he breathed with her. Out through her nose, in through her nose, out—

"That's right. Good job."

She kept the rhythm until her chest stopped seizing, until her breaths became full.

Until the panic loosened its grip.

She stood up, trembling. "I'm okay."

"Right." He took her arm and led her back to the bed, sitting down next to her. "That was...loud."

She looked over at him. Len pushed himself onto her lap.

Jonas picked up the dog. "You kept yelling *run*, and for a second I thought maybe I should run. And then I realized that you were also whimpering, so...sorry, I didn't mean to break in, but actually Len came in first—"

"It's okay." She closed her eyes. "It's just a..."

"Memory. Probably one I dragged up, right?"

She made a face. "I try not to think about..." She looked away.

"What was his name?" Jonas said quietly.

"Rokko. He was twenty-eight."

"That's young."

Not in her business.

"Yeah."

"How'd he die?"

"He was trying to rescue a group of firefighters."

"Was he a firefighter?"

"Actually, no. He was EOD."

She glanced at him, and he just kept looking at her. "Explosive Ordnance Disposal."

"I know," he said slowly, his gaze hard on her. Probably piecing together her words. Her job.

"This summer, along southwestern Kras, there were massive fires. It also happened to be the location where a dozen World War One battles were fought. And nearly five hundred unexploded bombs lay in wait."

She pushed off the bed and went to the window, her back to him. "EOD had marked the roadways where the ordnances were, and we were systematically disposing of them, but a handful of firefighters were trapped in a city that had been evacuated, and Rok tried to get them out."

Outside, the night was still deep, thick. "He was killed during the evacuation."

More silence, and she knew, just knew he was going to ask.

"I'm so sorry, Sibba. That sounds awful."

Oh. Or maybe he'd already figured it out. But in case he hadn't: "Mostly because I was the one who marked their route."

The bed creaked and he stood. She turned and didn't care that her face was wet. "Twenty pound Coopers, all World War One era. We landed a chopper to get the team out, and I thought I'd found them all—I used a state-of-the-art Foerster locator, and..."

She shook her head, didn't even bother to wipe her cheek. Stupid tears. "I missed one."

"Just one."

"That's all it takes." She met his gaze. "And that's why I can't fall apart, Jonas. Because the next second, I had to get off the ground and load into the chopper the people who lived."

"Including you." He made a face.

She lifted a shoulder. "I don't count."

He stepped closer, and she wasn't sure why she let him wrap his arm around her and pull her tight against him. "Sibba."

Maybe she was just tired. And worried about her grandfather, which had spilled out into this emotional wreckage.

"You absolutely do count."

Oh, no, no, he wasn't going to get under her skin, make her care. Start feeling again.

Not when she'd developed a nice, deep scab over her heart.

ADMITTEDLY, JONAS HADN'T EXPECTED TO END UP here. Not in a puffy bathrobe, feeling half-naked and sensing that he'd stepped into something bigger than he wanted to understand.

Because if he did the math right...

Sibba disposed of bombs for a living.

And that felt, well, like a *bomb* in the middle of his chest, given the thoughts he'd been having about her.

The kind that entertained asking her out for dinner after they found her grandfather, and after the right people determined that their organs weren't going to dissolve inside their bodies.

But really, he was blind not to have seen the truth—this woman wasn't afraid of danger. And if she could stick her hand in a beehive, yes, she could dismantle a bomb.

So much for staying away from danger.

But still, he couldn't help but want to reach out to her.

Tough, stoic Sibba.

No wonder she hadn't gotten worked up about the, um, radiation poisoning. Although, if a guy were to go, getting blown up might be quick and painless, or at least so quickly over that—

No. He'd still give that a one-star, would not recommend.

This moment, however, when he held Sibba in his arms—yes, all five stars.

Because, if he were to admit it, he'd been a little lonely since...

Maybe longer than he had realized.

Sibba put her hands to his chest and pushed. He let her go, stepped back. "You okay?"

"Yeah. I just...sorry. I didn't mean to drag you into my dark places."

"Hey. Remember me? Storm chaser? I'm exactly the person you want around when the lights go down and the wind kicks up." He winked, and then felt like a fool.

Seriously, Jonas?

"Maybe I should make breakfast."

"At three in the morning?"

"Or...get some shut-eye?"

"And dream about Rokko and the guys again?" She made a face.

"Right. All I'm going to think about is my fingernails falling off."

"So, dinner?"

"Pizza rolls?"

"What?"

"What do you do when you come home late and need something to munch on as you watch hours of *Friends*?"

He got a smile.

"Posmodula," she said, and pushed past him.

He followed her out into the kitchen, where she flicked on a light. Pulled out a bowl and flour.

He sat down in the kitchen chair. He'd emptied his pockets and now picked up his phone.

"My grandmother used to make this for me while we waited for bread to bake." She'd put some yeast in a bowl, added hot water, salt. Now she stirred it. "What are you looking at?"

"The wreckage of the dirigible." He scrolled past the pictures he'd taken in the field, landing on the ribbed carcass that had held the black box.

"How did you get into storm chasing?"

He set down the phone. "Storms always held a mystery to me. I have this memory of being a child, maybe five or six, and coming downstairs during a terrible thunderstorm. I was scared, I think, but I found my grandfather—he was living with us at the time— sitting on our big stone porch, watching. I came out to him and sat on his lap, and he wrapped this big blanket around me, and we just sat and watched the storm. The lightning spidering across the sky, the deep roll of the thunder. The wind, moaning as if it were alive. Sitting there with him, those strong arms around me—I wasn't afraid anymore."

She had added flour and lard and now stirred it with a wooden spoon. "Dedi is like that. Calm. Solid. He..." She glanced at him now. "He saw his own trauma. Learned how to face it. Mostly."

"Oh?"

"No, it's nothing. It's just, sometimes as he gets older, he's back there, you know? In war."

He knew little of Slovenian history, just that they'd fought for their independence from Yugoslavia. So probably, her grandfather had been a part of that.

"So, you weren't afraid of storms...but when did you start chasing them?"

"I was in high school, sitting in my classroom—about eighteen—and one day, a storm headed our direction. Our teacher told us to go to the gym, and I headed to the parking lot, and ever since then..."

She had dumped out the dough onto a stone board, was stretching it out.

"That looks a lot like pizza to me."

"It's better than pizza. It'll knock your shoes off."

"Socks?"

She frowned even as she opened the fridge.

"It'll knock your *socks* off. But that's close. Where'd you learn English?"

"It's taught here in the schools, but mostly, when I was seconded to the British Army to learn EOD."

"You trained in Great Britain?"

"With the RAF, and then with the Royal Engineers."

"For how long?"

"Four years. Then I came back and spent the next two disarming bombs for the Slovenian military." She'd opened a jar of cream and was now slathering it on the dough. "I've spent the past two years as a freelancer."

"Why'd you get out?"

She added salt, and leaves from some fresh herb she had growing in her windowsill. "I lost a friend."

He stilled. "Oh no."

She opened her oven and stuck in the bread, set a timer, then turned and wiped her hands with a towel.

"Did you know that, if a bomb goes off, you'll have a much better chance at survival if you're standing next to something solid?"

"I don't want to ask how you know that."

"During World War Two, the RAF, Russia, and the US Army dropped 2.7 million tons of bombs over Europe. Ten percent of those bombs never exploded."

She dropped the towel on the counter. "They call it the Iron Harvest, and over the past fifty years, over six hundred EOD personnel have been killed trying to clean it up. Slovenia had divided loyalties—we had both Allied and Axis fighters, so we got the best of both bombings."

He leaned back. "I had no idea."

"Always watch where you stand." She winked.

He didn't. "That's a little terrifying."

"Someone has to walk up to the bomb and ask to be its friend, at least enough to figure out its tricks and disarm it. That's me. But now, I work alone."

And maybe he was imagining it, but it sort of felt like she might be drawing a little line between them, as if he'd moved too far into her space.

No worries. Because the last thing he wanted was to worry about the woman he loved—and no, he didn't love Sibba, so hypothetically—walking out the front door, knowing that she might not be coming back.

"Now I get why you jump off mountains."

She smiled, and for all the darkness that seemed to be cluttered up inside her, she could light up a room—not so much with a dazzling light, but with a sort of softness, the kind that offered a shelter in a storm.

And he liked storms.

The timer on the stove went off, and she pulled out the bread. Crispy and brown around the edges, it had curled up a little on itself. She slid it off the stone and onto a plate, then cut it into pie wedges.

Set it on the table. "It's hot."

Grabbing a couple napkins, she set one in front of him.

He wasn't surprised in the least when she picked it up, tossing it between her fingers, then bit into it. Then she dropped the piece on a napkin and fanned her mouth. "Ot, Ot." Then she closed her mouth. "Mmm."

He went to pick up a piece, then dropped it. "That's hot."

"Chicken."

"I prefer *wuss*, thank you."

She laughed, her hand in front of her mouth.

Now, there was the sunshine.

He picked up the piece, blew on it, and took a bite. Yes, hot, but the cream—sour cream, with a hint of marjoram and maybe garlic—filled his mouth, along with the bread. He swallowed. "Wow, that's good."

"Better than pizza rolls?"

"Not even in the same galaxy."

She nodded, took another bite. Then she reached for his phone. "What's this?" she asked after she swallowed.

"That's a picture of the device on the bottom of my dirigible. It was tampered with."

She set down her piece of posmodula. "That's a bomb casing. It looks like an old iron bomb, the kind that was dropped from airplanes." She widened the picture. "Except, this here—" She showed him a gauge. "That's an altimeter. This bomb was set to explode at a certain altitude."

Behind them, Len got to his feet. Barked.

She stilled, then got up and disappeared into her bedroom.

He turned off the lights. Grabbed his phone. Backed into the room and knelt next to Len. "Shh, buddy." The dog's body had stiffened.

Then Sibba came out of the bedroom, and even in the darkness, he could make out a handgun.

Right. Military.

The doorknob wiggled on the front door.

Sibba stepped back, and he stood beside her. Sheesh, why hadn't he become a SEAL like Fraser? Because, hello, what good was identifying nimbostratus clouds when—

The door swung open.

Beside him, Sibba stiffened. And Len barked, then took off for the intruder, who stood in the frame, dressed in army-green fatigues, a backpack, a woolen cap.

The man bent and caught the dog, pulling him into his arms. Said something in Slovenian.

Jonas had already done the math by the time Sibba dropped her gun.

"Dedi!" She ran toward him, landed on her knees, and pulled him into a hug.

He wrapped his arms around her with more words that Jonas didn't understand.

Finally, he got up and pulled her with him. She flicked on the light.

Time could have pulled him out of the pages of a war epic, complete with steely, battle-weary eyes, a wiry gray mustache, thick beard, and most of all, the army-green attire of a bygone era.

Vietnam.

And on his breast pocket, a name.

Benson.

The man looked at Sibba, then at Jonas, and his smile fell. Then he stepped forward, and though the man had to be in his late seventies, he looked at Jonas with an expression that could fell a man and said, in perfect Midwestern English, "Who are you? And what are you doing with my granddaughter?"

And for a second, Sibba was back in his head.

Run.

Nope. Instead, he stuck out a hand. "Jonas Marshall. We've been looking for you."

Which were exactly the wrong words, apparently, because just like that, the man pushed Sibba behind him. And lifted an ancient double-barreled hunting rifle.

"I'm not going anywhere."

Jonas stilled. Looked at Sibba. "Um."

"Dedi," she said, and launched into Slovenian. Which Jonas dearly hoped translated roughly into, "Grandpa, this is a great guy who helped save me from some Russian thugs (twice!) and who is most definitely on our side. And see, even Len likes him."

Which maybe was true, because Len came over to Jonas, wiggling like, *Look who's here!*

He crouched and rubbed the dog's ears as Dedi-slash-Benson turned to Sibba and answered her in the same tone. Which Jonas hoped wasn't, "And what is he doing here, dressed in your bathrobe?"

Jonas stood up. Good question. "This, I can explain," he said, and they both turned and looked at him like he might be interrupting, so he headed to the bathroom. Where his clean radioactive clothes were drying.

Still soggy, but he pulled them out and worked on the pants, pulled on the shirt.

At least he no longer looked like a cream puff.

He returned, barefoot, his socks soggy, to find her grandfather at least disarmed, the gun by the door, again crouched by his dog, listening to Sibba.

Glancing now and again at Jonas.

So he hoped that was going well. He offered a smile. Folded his arms over his chest.

Dedi lifted a hand. Stood up. "Fine. But let's ask him."

Jonas drew in a breath.

"Are you working for the government?"

Again, perfect English. Oh. Um. "Not...really."

A bushy gray-white eyebrow went up.

"I told you, Dedi. He's a *weatherman.*"

Storm chaser.

But Jonas offered an innocuous weatherman smile. "I don't know what's going on here, but...I'm just a guy who ended up sort of...actually, I'm not sure what I'm doing here."

Sibba gave him a look. "Thank you for that."

"It looks like Grandpa is good, so...maybe I should..." Leave?

In what?

She waited for him. Smiled.

"Okay, so it's a little early to find an Uber."

"You'll never find an Uber in Cerkno," Sibba said. Crossed her arms, almost smugly.

What—

Her grandfather stood up. "Wait, you're saying that you're the one who crashed a zeppelin in my field?"

"I...yes. Not purposely. The storm—"

"Then this belongs to you." The man went to his backpack, opened it, and tugged out a black box.

The black box. Jonas went to reach for it.

The man pulled it back. "Not so fast. First, I want answers, starting with why my village was bombed."

Six

Jonas needed sleep. Because maybe six hours of shut-eye would untangle the questions in his brain.

Instead, he stood at the window, staring out at the muted darkness, the smallest glimmer of gray just lifting off the faraway mountains.

And really, after the story Henry Benson, aka Sibba's grandfather, had just told, he might never sleep again. He'd have to wait until he got back to his lab in Ljubljana and unpacked the black box's data to confirm his suspicions, but according to Henry...

Someone had dropped a dirty bomb on Poče.

Or tried to. The storm had mitigated much of the radioactive dust, although it embedded the soil, the nooks and crannies of the street, and would have infected the population—all forty-one men, women, and children—if Henry and the current mayor hadn't already taken them all away, hiding them.

Because even Henry knew that Russians invading their city and prowling around couldn't be good.

"We had enough run-ins with them when I served in Vietnam that I knew something wasn't right. They drove into town about a week ago, tested the water, the soil, and then left."

The old man had sat at the table, finishing off the posmodula, drinking a cup of tea, winding out his story in English.

This was, of course, after Jonas had given a full biographical account of how he'd ended up in Slovenia, and most particularly, the Benson field.

Or rather, the Kovac farm, because Henry had taken his wife's maiden name when he moved to Slovenia.

Escaped might be a better word, because although Jonas didn't have all the details, clearly, he'd taken an unauthorized trip straight from Vietnam to Eastern Europe.

Are you from the government?

It wasn't hard to figure out the math. Henry Benson was a Vietnam deserter.

Now the old man lay snoring in the recliner in Sibba's small family room.

Leaving Jonas to sort out what to do next.

We started to get nervous about why they were there, and when we saw the dirigible circling the town for a couple days, rumors started—the kind that got people scared. Jaka and I took pictures, and it looked like one of those old-time zeppelins with a bomb attached.

Sibba had joined them at the table, nursing her own cup of tea.

"Or course, I was thinking tear gas, the likes they dropped on Cambodia. And then, about six hours before the storm hit, the Russians parked their trucks on the road out of town. It was then that we decided to evacuate the town."

"How?"

"We took them on foot to a secure location in the woods. We couldn't go farther because of the storm. They stayed there, and I went back for Jaka and his brother, Lan."

"So, the residents are safe?"

"Yes. Hidden. But Jaka and Lan are sick."

Sibba had met Jonas's gaze then. "How sick?"

"Nausea, vomiting. Headaches, diarrhea."

"Were they in the town when the bomb exploded?"

Henry had nodded, and the knot formed inside Jonas. "They stayed to monitor the zeppelin...and then the storm came through and they couldn't leave."

"When did the bomb detonate?" Jonas asked.

"A few hours before the storm. It crashed in my field."

"Dedi. Did you stay in town too?" Sibba had reached out to him, then pulled her hand back.

"I was at the farm. Went out to check on the debris right before the storm. Retrieved the black box. I wore a gas mask." He'd walked over then and pulled out said mask from his pack.

Looked like something issued in the 1960s.

"Then I went to check on Jaka and Lan. Took them to where the others were staying. I didn't plan on returning, not for a while, and finally came here. But Sibba wasn't around, so I headed back to the farm. But when I saw that our Russian friends had returned, I got nervous. So I came back here to see if I could track down Sibba."

He shot her a look of affection that made Jonas miss his own grandfather.

"You think you'll be able to find anything about what happened in this box?" He touched it, and that's when Sibba had gotten up and gotten a bag.

"I hope so."

Sibba had handed Jonas the bag for the box. Then she'd turned to her grandfather and sent him off to shower, with another bag for his clothing.

"I still have some of your clothes here from when you last stayed," she said, and disappeared into the bedroom.

Jonas hadn't wanted to suggest that he might have worn those instead of the silly bathrobe.

Henry emerged from the bathroom in a pair of polyester pants and a blue sweater.

Or maybe not.

It was during Henry's shower, however, that Jonas had decided to pry.

And he'd started with the obvious.

"Is your grandfather a Vietnam vet?" He kept his voice low as he helped Sibba clear the table.

"Yes," she said, and glanced behind them. But her grandfather was in the shower.

"Deserter?"

"Yes. He was injured and was sent to Japan to recover. Instead of being sent home, his orders were to return to combat. So a number of Japanese activists helped him escape to Sweden, where he was granted asylum."

She rinsed off a plate and handed it to him to dry. "He'd been given new papers, so he used those to travel and finally ended up on my great-grandfather's farm, working as a day laborer. Where he met my grandmother. And stayed forever."

"Wasn't Slovenia part of Yugoslavia at the time?" He finished drying the plate.

"Indeed." She handed him another plate. "Which is why he felt safe. America wasn't going to track him down in a communist country."

"But what about the pardon Carter gave all the draft dodgers in 1977?"

"Draft dodgers. Not deserters. There's no statute of limitations on desertion. He could still be brought back to the US and be court-martialed. Thankfully, they've stopped executing deserters—"

"America never executed deserters."

"Not since World War Two, but ask Allen Abney what happens."

"Who?" He put the plate away in her cupboard.

"Deserter. Arrested in 2006 for deserting in 1968. He was fifty-six years old. The sentence for desertion during wartime is now five years." She lowered her voice. "Can you imagine my grandfather going to prison for five years? He'd be eighty-three when he got out. *If* he got out."

"Who is going to find him in Slovenia?"

"Anyone. And America and Slovenia have an extradition treaty, so..."

Jonas had raised his hands. "Your secret is safe with me."

She sighed. "He has a son who lives in America that he hasn't seen for thirty years. And grandchildren. His parents died long ago, but I think he'd like to visit their graves. Especially now that Babička has passed. More than anything, I want Dedi to see his son again, my uncle Marek."

She turned back to the sink as her grandfather came out of the bathroom. He dropped the bag with his clothes by the door. "So, do we burn these?"

"We'll bring them to the hazardous materials unit in Ljubljana," Sibba said.

Jonas had his own ideas. His brother worked with some private security group that might have the right resources, although probably Sibba was right—they should alert the Slovenian military.

Except, that would lead to questions and then to Henry's doorstep.

No wonder Sibba had been so secretive when she'd opened the door to him back at the farm.

"We need to get Lan and Jaka to medical help," Henry said then.

"And you tested," Sibba added.

Yes, this was going to get complicated.

Her grandfather had stood there then, in the light, and something had simply washed over him.

It looked a lot like defeat. "I just can't seem to escape war."

Another beat and Sibba nodded.

Henry grabbed a blanket off the chair. "They're hiding at the old partisan hospital near Dolenji Novaki. We'll get them in the morning."

Then he sank into the recliner.

Sibba turned off the kitchen light, just the light from her room illuminating her face. She, too, looked tired.

And Jonas had the terrible urge to reach out and pull her to himself, like he'd done in her room. To tell her that maybe, if he could, he'd figure out how to make everything all right.

In fact, his entire body pulsed with that hope, and sure, maybe it was the guy inside who ran toward the storm, wanting to understand it, to survive it. But also, maybe it was simply Sibba. And the fact that she stood alone. Strong, but maybe a little weary.

"C'mon. I promise, I won't let you get hurt." His words to her a month ago on the mountain crept back, clung.

Except, she'd drawn that invisible line between them, so he didn't move, didn't reach out.

Tried to mute the strange feelings budding in his heart.

"I'm going to bed."

He nodded. "Good idea. Try and think only happy thoughts..."

"Thank you, Jonas. I..." She wrapped her arms around herself. "I..."

"Next time, I'll say yes."

She frowned.

"When you ask me to go flying."

A smile slid up her face. "You'd better."

You'd better. He let her words settle inside him, along with her smile, a sort of balm to the crazy day.

He'd cleaned up the kitchen, then headed to the sofa. But he woke up early, to Henry's snores.

Got up and fixed himself a cup of coffee. Now, standing at the window, the earliest hint of dawn simmered against the mountains, the firelight of the sun turning the white peaks to gold.

How had the Russians gotten ahold of his dirigible? If they

were even responsible. But given their testing of the soil and the water prior to the attack, then afterward...

But why, and why Poče? Or was Poče simply a random small town. For what—testing the effects of a dirty bomb? Because clearly this was some attempt at that.

Yes, he needed to get the box to the right people, find out what kind of radiation they were dealing with.

But first, probably, he had to help Henry and Sibba rescue the people of Poče.

When he'd asked God for more, he'd maybe meant a little less than this.

"I DID MENTION THAT I'M JUST A WEATHERMAN AND not, say, a Navy SEAL, right?"

The words came from Jonas, who stood with her on a cliff overlooking the gorge where the occupants of Poče now hid at the old Franja Partisan Hospital.

Oh, he was funny, but Sibba didn't smile or laugh, because, well...

They could probably use a special forces operator right about now. Mostly because the Russians who were blocking the road, clearly searching for the hideout, seemed serious. And out here, in the middle of a forested countryside, no one was around to ask questions.

Except, maybe, she, Jonas, and her grandfather.

When Jonas had spotted the trucks this morning, the ones that had tracked them around Poče yesterday, Dedi had directed Sibba to a farmhouse off the main road.

There, they'd taken another two-wheel rutted path into the forest all the way to the end of the road, then gotten out and walked a half mile up a hill.

Her grandfather had handed her a monocular, aged and

battered, and pointed to the trucks kicking up dust on the road, clearly searching for the group.

"How did they find them?" Sibba asked. She handed the monocular back to her grandfather.

"Maybe they followed me. I came yesterday to check on everyone." Her grandfather stood up. "But for now, they're safe. Let's go."

Her grandfather had turned into some kind of guerrilla fighter, despite his age. Suddenly, despite the fact he'd deserted, the stories he'd told her about his missions on Vietnam before his injury clicked in turned vibrant and real.

Tough. Determined. Resolute. For the first time, she saw him as the soldier he'd once been.

Before his country had betrayed him. She'd always grown up with a disdain for America.

And then she'd met Jonas. Who'd sort of blown apart everything she believed about the United States. Sure, she'd met Americans in London and around the UK, but they'd always been arrogant tourists, needing their selfies or souvenir pictures.

But Jonas...

Sure, he'd made to leave last night, but she couldn't blame him after the way Dedi went after him.

Who she couldn't blame either.

So, to find them both asleep, peacefully, in the main room this morning had seemed a hint of a miracle.

Jonas had slept fully clothed, his arm up over his eyes, as if struggling to catch some winks. He'd looked peaceful, despite his pose, and it had occurred to her that since she'd met him, even a month ago, he seemed to be always moving.

Always rescuing.

C'mon. I promise, I won't let you get hurt.

Indeed. She didn't know why those words curled inside, like a whisper, winding around her as she showered, again, and took her own clothes and bagged them.

Maybe it was because she always said them to others.

Never, however, herself.

But with Jonas's words last night, about saying yes the next time she invited him to fly...shoot, he had her thinking about tomorrow, and the days after that. Like she actually might be around.

So maybe he was more trouble than she wanted to admit.

Dedi had been awake by the time she emerged from the shower. He'd made toast and tea, and then Jonas rose and disappeared into the bathroom. He emerged smelling clean.

They ate as Dedi explained the location of the hideout. "It's a partisan hospital used during World War Two. The Nazis never found it, so Jaka and I figured it was a good place for our people to hide."

She vacuumed out her car, then bagged the contents. Then she ran her Geiger counter over the inside. With the reading negligible, she okayed it for travel.

The fact was, whatever radioactive waste the attackers had dropped on Poče had been mitigated by the storm, the water diluting it, the wind scattering it.

So maybe God had intervened, used the storm to save them.

And that thought sat inside her like a burr. Because she didn't know a God who intervened.

Who cared.

"We can take this trail down," Dedi said now, pointing to a mostly hidden path. "They used to blindfold patients when they brought them here so if they got caught, they couldn't reveal the location."

As they hiked down, he turned to them. "Be careful where you walk. They mined this area."

Jonas looked at her, his eyes wide. Mouthed, *mined?*

Yes, she heard that too. The narrow trail led to a gorge where a wooden bridge spanned a dry riverbed, the logs worn, a couple at jutted angles.

"Careful where you walk. Some of these boards are rotted." Dedi headed out over the bridge, the boards creaking as they made their way through the gorge, then up wooden stairs and across a cliff face.

They entered a cave, a wire attached to the granite from which lights hung.

"Is this place mined too?" Jonas asked.

"No. But they used to park snipers on the cliff above it."

Their feet scuffed along the rocky floor. "How do you know about this place?" Sibba asked in English.

"Your great-grandfather showed me. Did you know that he was American too?" Dedi looked at her.

"No, he wasn't. I saw pictures. He was a partisan."

"Shot down during a bombing raid. Injured and rescued and brought here. Stayed, even though his fellow Americans were smuggled out."

The cave tunnel spanned maybe four meters, another three meters high. Light from the other end muted the darkness, but the cool breath fell upon her skin.

"I think it was one reason he took me in," Dedi said. He looked at Jonas. "I was a patriot. I just didn't have any more fight in me. Took me years to shake the demons."

Jonas nodded. "Yeah. Some of us don't even have to go to war to have demons. I can't imagine what it was like."

"It was hell. A place even God feared to go. Or at least I thought so for a long time." He held his arm out as they came to the end of the tunnel. "Wait."

They stood at the mouth of a canyon that opened up into forest. But beyond the tunnel, not even the wind stirred the thicket of oak and pine. A trail wound into the clutter.

"The hospital is deep inside that forest, in a pocket inside the gorge with steep walls and narrow passageways. Once you go in, there is nowhere else to go but through."

"You're saying if the Russians have found it, then we're walking right into an ambush."

Dedi pointed at him.

"Then onward we go."

Her grandfather smiled. "He might be a weatherman, but he has a soldier's heart." He said it in Slovenian and glanced at her.

She frowned. "Dedi. Don't—"

He put his fingers to his lips.

Oh, she hoped he wasn't getting any ideas. Because as soon as Jonas helped them rescue the people of Poče, he was back to his life.

And she was back to hers, one day at a time.

Pine scented the air, and the forest seemed to breathe again as the wind shivered the leaves.

"I feel like I'm in an episode of *Band of Brothers*," Jonas said quietly. "Or maybe that part in *Forrest Gump* where he's in Vietnam."

"Run, Forrest, run," she said.

He looked at her. "Are you being funny?"

"What? Did I say it wrong? Dedi has that movie."

He shook his head. "You are the most confusing—we're walking into a possible ambush, and you're quoting movie lines."

"You never know when your laugh might be the last."

"You need to stop thinking that way."

Her smile fell. "No, I don't. If each day is my last, then I live it to the fullest."

"Maybe. But pleasure isn't just for the moment. Pleasure can be found in hoping for things too. If you never look past right now, if you never have to hope for something, then you miss out on the long-awaited dream."

"What long-awaited dream?"

Dedi walked ahead of them, head down.

"Family. Home. Children. Love."

"Not for me."

Jonas frowned.

"EOD and a happy ending are mutually exclusive."

"Do they have to be?"

His gaze found hers, settled there a moment.

She drew in her breath, slowed. "Yes. I live with a one-meter view of the world. It's the farthest I can look ahead."

"One meter is very small."

"About three seconds. Enough to know that you're in big trouble."

"Sibba—"

"No." She met his eyes, the deep blue of them, something in them he suddenly couldn't—or maybe shouldn't?—say. "I can't lose another partner," she said softly.

Jonas finally nodded, his mouth a grim slash, and walked out ahead of her.

At least that was over. But her chest had started to burn.

Dedi slowed as the gorge narrowed, the trees closing out the light overhead. He held out his hand and they stopped.

She, too, felt like she was in the middle of some epic war movie. Maybe about the French Resistance. All she needed was a bicycle.

"Let's go."

In all her years living in Poče and then Cerkno, she'd never discovered this place, although she'd heard rumors of it.

A river ran through the canyon here, and she guessed that it somehow meandered away from the dry riverbed, not far from the cave. A fine mist rose into the air, as if the breath of angels.

"The buildings were washed away in '07 after a flood. The Slovenian government rebuilt them, but they're replicas of the originals," Dedi said as he led them across a bridge over the river. "This is a retractable bridge, the last line of defense."

He pointed to a dozen simple pine buildings all tucked into the groove of the gorge, nestled against the sheer walls, a thin walkway between them.

"This bigger building is the infirmary, but there are four other buildings that housed the wounded, as well as a surgery, kitchen, laundry, staff quarters, and even an X-ray cabin."

Jonas stopped, shook his head. "It's like the eye of the storm. Calm and peace inside the chaos."

Dedi stopped outside the big infirmary. "Remember what I said about finally seeing God in the middle of war?"

Jonas nodded.

Dedi smiled. "I've learned that God is in places we least expect to see him." Then he opened the door.

Sibba followed him in.

A dozen bunk beds with people seated on them, some huddled in blankets, a couple children sitting on the floor, one of them playing a handheld Nintendo.

"Get ready to go," Dedi said, now in Slovenian, and he walked over to a man lying on the bed. "How's the headache, Jaka?"

The man wore a pair of jeans, a woolen sweater, appeared in his early fifties. On the bunk next to him lay a younger man, late twenties. Right—she remembered Lan now. He'd been just a few years younger than her in school.

"Better. And the nausea is gone." He sat up. "But a few more have gotten sick."

"Where is Lana?" He helped Jaka up.

"She's in the kitchen with some of the other women. But she's not well either."

Sibba didn't want to say it, but...

"The radiation poisoning has spread," Jonas said.

She looked at him, shook her head. Some of these people could speak English.

"Let's get out of here before we're trapped," Dedi said. He turned to Jaka. "The Russians who bombed our town are now looking for us."

Jaka was a thick man—shiny head, white, close-cropped beard. A benevolent man who smiled, jolly and vocal about his love for Slovenian beer. Now, he groaned as he stood, grabbed onto Dedi's shoulder. "We can't go back to Poče."

"Sibba has a plan."

Jaka looked at her. "Sibba. We were worried for you this summer. Henrik said you were fighting the fires."

"Something like that. Let's get you out of here."

The women were already bundling up their supplies, their children. A few wore backpacks, many sturdy shoes.

Her father and Jonas visited the other cabins while she helped assemble the children.

The boy with the Nintendo pocketed it, and she stopped a ball that escaped from the younger boy. Maybe five or six years old.

She handed him the ball. Cute, with curly blond hair that flopped around his head. Blue eyes. "My name is Sibba," she said.

"Petea."

His mother came up and took his hand. She smiled at Sibba, then pushed out of the infirmary and followed the others along the bridge. Forty or so, most of them tromping along in quiet, some of them coughing, a few with their arms over the shoulders of others.

She spotted Jaka's wife, Lana, leaning against him as she walked.

They needed medical help as soon as they exited this gorge. Her plan was to call Director Vlasic and ask him to send trucks.

Maybe scare the Russians away.

At the very least, the radiation in Poče, as well as the remnants of the bomb in her grandfather's field, could be dealt with safely, the people here treated, and their country put on alert for more dirty bombs.

Dedi walked at the front of the crowd, Jonas somewhere in the middle as the group headed along the walkway and back through the forest. The hospital seemed to close up behind them as they headed toward the cave. No wonder no one had found it.

Petea unlatched his hand from his mother's and started to kick his ball. He'd scoot ahead, kick it, then catch it and turn and kick it to her.

His mother played with him, kicking it back. The sound of his laughter lifted, bouncing off the cave walls.

"EOD and a happy ending are mutually exclusive."

Sibba glanced ahead and spotted Jonas walking with the kid

who was playing Nintendo. They seemed to be conversing in English, or at least trying to.

"Do they have to be?"

She drew in a breath. Yes, they did.

They were drawing closer to the other end of the tunnel, and as she emerged, she spotted the trail of people walking across the bridge. It swayed over the dry riverbed, a three-meter drop below.

Little Petea had grabbed his mother's hand, his ball under his arm.

She dropped back, waiting for the last to pass, and watched from the ridge as Petea and his mother navigated across the bridge.

It swayed, and Petea grabbed for the rail.

His ball dropped, bouncing on the riverbed below.

He shouted, but his mother pulled him across as Sibba followed down the stairs and out to the bridge.

"Petea! Come back!"

Sibba looked up and froze as Petea scrambled down the bank after his ball, perched in the middle of the gorge.

"Be careful where you walk. They mined this area."

Dedi's voice swept through her brain, and maybe not only hers, because suddenly, Jonas appeared, scrambling after the kid.

"Stop! Stop!" he was yelling.

Petea had run out to his ball, picked it up. Turned to run back—

Jonas reached him, swept him up.

"Don't move!" Sibba shouted.

He stilled, looked up at her.

Nodded.

"Just stay there."

He nodded again and she pushed past people on the bridge to the other side. Dedi had run down the path to meet her.

"Was there water under this bridge during the occupation, when this hospital was built?"

"No. Dry bed."

She blew out a breath, looked at Jonas. "Just stay where you are. I'll get you out of this."

JONAS DIDN'T EXACTLY KNOW HOW HE'D ENDED UP IN this riverbed, just that when the kid had taken off for his ball, something inside him had simply ignited.

Twenty seconds later, he was balanced on a rock in the middle of the semi-sandy dry gulch, holding a kid in his arms.

A kid and his little orange ball.

And him, an island in a sea of mines, because as soon as Sibba screamed, her "Don't move!" had cemented him into place.

Nope.

Because suddenly, every step had turned lethal.

"I'm not going anywhere," Jonas said, his gaze on Sibba.

The little boy squirmed in his arms.

His mother—Jonas guessed at that, but he'd seen the kid playing with her in the cave—leaned over the bridge and yelled at him. In Slovenian, of course.

But the kid stopped struggling. Instead, he started crying.

Yeah, Jonas felt a little like doing the same. Not really, but, well, maybe.

"I'm coming to you," Sibba said then from the opposite shore.

He wanted to shout at her to stay put, that he could figure this out, but, like he'd said, he wasn't a Navy SEAL. And he hadn't a clue how to get out of here without blowing himself, and maybe too many bystanders, into unrecognizable pieces.

So, "Okay!" he shouted back to Sibba.

Because she was the EOD superhero here.

She had armed herself with a long stick that she'd broken off a tree and a number of hats and scarves. Then she took the stick, maybe four feet long, crouched and extended it, slowly pushing it into the dirt at an angle.

After a moment, she pulled it out and stepped into that spot. Then she turned and dropped a hat in her previous footprint.

The crowd had gone completely silent as she turned and repeated the drill.

Hats, scarves, a towel, another hat. She took big steps, but not so large that she lost her balance.

She was halfway across the riverbed when she looked up at him. Offered a wan smile.

And he heard her words, spoken on their way to the camp. *I can't lose another partner.*

He'd never understood them more than now, as she crouched and moved the stick under the earth, maybe two inches. Stopped. "There's a mine here."

His entire body turned cold, painfully aware that he'd probably stepped three inches from that spot.

She took her stick and broke it at the top, shoving it upright near the spot, propping it up with a rock. "See this?"

"Got it," he said.

She probed away from it and found a safe spot for her next step. Then the next.

By the time she reached him, four such sticks rose from the riverbed, a couple that she'd retrieved from the fallen debris.

And through the clutter, a pathway made of hats, scarves, towels, and one red child's mitten.

She stepped up to him then and met his eyes. So much calm in them, it reached into him, through him.

And then she blinked.

No, not calm, because for a second, emotion flooded her gaze. "You okay?"

"So far," he said.

She put her hand on the little boy's back and spoke to him in Slovenian. Then looked back at Jonas. "I'll help you put him on your back."

Taking the ball from the boy, she put it between her knees. Then she lifted him, holding him around the waist as Jonas turned in place. The boy climbed onto his back, his arms around Jonas's neck.

His mother was shouting at him from the bridge, and the boy clamped his legs around Jonas's waist.

Jonas grabbed his legs to steady him, then turned back to Sibba. She held the ball under her arm.

"I'll go behind you," she said. "Walk exactly where I marked the path."

He nodded, but she hadn't moved her gaze from his.

"Exactly, Jonas."

And he didn't know why, but he leaned down and pressed his forehead to hers. "Breathe, Sibba. I got this. I will walk in your footsteps."

A beat, and she finally nodded.

Right. Good. And here went the rest of his life. He stepped out onto the red mitten.

So far, still alive.

He eased off it, then stepped on the next marker, a white towel.

Leaned off that to the next marker.

He didn't look behind him, but he could hear her steps, small crunching sounds in the sand.

It felt a little like playing *the floor is lava*. Only, with real consequences.

Especially when the kid shifted his weight while Jonas was mid-step.

"Hey. Stay put," he growled, and all likeness to the game vanished.

They finally reached the riverbank, and here, it was just six more steps up the bank. But going up, his arms useless for counterweights, turned out to be harder than he thought. Still, he stepped on the black stocking cap, then a lavender patterned scarf, two more berets, and finally let Dedi and another man pull him to safety on the road.

The little boy's mother ran up, grabbed him off Jonas's back, crying.

He turned and spotted Sibba also being pulled to the road. She had shoved most of the debris into her jacket as she crossed, still holding the ball.

She handed it to a man, maybe the boy's father, then shed her jacket and let it fall, with the debris, onto the road.

People moved in to grab their belongings, but Sibba turned to Jonas, put her hands on his chest and backed him away.

Moisture edged her eyes, and she was breathing hard. "Don't...ever—"

Then she wrapped her arms around his neck and embraced him.

Oh. *Oh.* His arms went around her, and he held her, feeling her tremble.

"Hey," he said softly. "I'm okay. You're okay. We're fine."

She just kept holding on.

And yes, he got it. Especially in view of the story she'd told him about Rokko.

So he just held her, put his head down against hers, feeling himself start to breathe again also.

She finally let go.

He released her. Met her eyes. They were reddened, as if she might have been fighting tears. But for the first time, he got a good look at them—golden brown, with variations of green woven in, and gold in the middle. Intriguing. Beautiful.

"Thank you for not dying," she said softly.

"Anytime." Then he winked, and she smiled and pushed away from him. Turned to her grandfather and shouted something.

The group had begun to move along the path, and she waited until most of them had gone before she moved onto the trail.

He stayed with her.

She reached out then and took his hand.

Maybe so he wouldn't walk into danger again, but he held on, just for a while.

She dropped his grip as they came out of the forest, near the farm, and then she ran ahead to her grandfather and pulled out her cell phone.

Her grandfather herded everyone into the farm's barn, and then they waited until some vans and a truck pulled up.

Slovenian police, by their uniforms, and Sibba and Henry stood talking for a long time to what seemed the man in charge, while Jonas helped people into the vehicles. He finally joined them.

"Jonas, this is the director general of the Hazardous Device Unit out of Ljubljana, Director Vlasic," Sibba said.

A big man, solemn demeanor, he reached out his hand, and Jonas shook it, introducing himself. To his surprise, the man spoke English.

"Thank you for your help here. We'll need a statement of what you saw at the Kovac farm when we get to the hospital."

"Of course," Jonas said.

But what he really wanted was to get the black box to his lab.

No, what he wanted was to find out if he might be radioactive, his insides melting. Then, to his lab.

And after that, maybe figure out what that embrace had been about.

Probably relief. Nothing more.

And probably that was for the best. Because he'd never felt quite so undone as when he'd watched Sibba work her way across the minefield. *EOD and a happy ending are mutually exclusive.*

Yes, yes they were.

He needed his car, left back at the farmhouse by Poče, so he mentioned this to Vlasic, who instructed one of his men to fetch it. "We need you at the hospital."

Right. Jonas tossed over the keys, then found himself in the car with Sibba, following the caravan to Ljubljana.

The beautiful capital city was located in a massive valley

under the shadow of foothills and mountains to the north and west, and under the purview of a twelfth century castle perched on a cliff. He'd been utterly charmed by the cobblestone streets, the bridges over the Ljubljana River, the beautiful churches, the Baroque cathedral in the middle of the city, the massive pink Church of the Annunciation, the open kitchen food market.

A treasure, tucked away in a country most people didn't know existed.

"Where are we going?" he asked Sibba as they wove their way into the city, heading for downtown.

"The University Medical Center. They will know what to do."

"Does this happen a lot?"

"Dirty bombs deployed in our country? No. But they're familiar with the fallout of unexploded ordnances, and we share a nuclear power reactor with Croatia, so there are protocols in place for disasters." She glanced at him. "I'm pretty sure you're not melting from the inside."

"There you go again, trying to be funny."

"I'm hilarious." She grinned, and he couldn't help but grin back. Maybe her approach wasn't terrible—moments of stress softened by bad humor.

He could get used to it.

They parked with the others and were met by a team who'd been briefed and set up tents in the parking lot. Garbed in protective gear, the staff met the group, ushered them into privacy to disrobe, sent them to showers, then provided clean attire in the form of cotton scrubs.

Two hours later, Jonas sat in a sterile room, waiting on his blood test, having been administered a dose of Prussian blue with crackers. Sibba sat with him, her hair down and drying, wearing the same green scrubs, translating as one of Director Vlasic's men took his statement.

They'd already verified his identity via a call to the lab—thank you, Tarek—and his passport from his backpack when Vlasic's courier retrieved his rental car.

The call to his lab also confirmed his authority to dispatch the dirigibles, two of which were still in the air, according to his last check-in.

But he was getting worried, because if the Russians—or whoever—had grabbed Frannie from the sky, they could get their hands on Farah and Sally.

Five and six.

Vlasic and his team asked him about the men he'd seen chasing Sibba and then tussled with at her cabin, and the make of the transportation. Trucks weren't common in Europe like they were in America, so that worked in their favor.

Then they quizzed him about the blue substance.

Or rather, the caesium-137, identified in the radiology lab at the university.

"I don't know how I picked it up. Mostly it was on the dog, but also my boots, so probably in the field..."

A fist had formed in his gut the moment they identified the substance. But the doctor confirmed that his dose had been low—at acceptable levels.

Although, to Jonas's mind, when was it ever acceptable to be radioactive?

Sibba had jumped in then, in Slovenian, and a long discussion had ensued, with hand gestures and looks of incredulity, and he would have liked to have added his own voice to the discussions of how, when, and why.

About then, the doctor buzzed in and confirmed that his blood test was clear.

Finally, they finished, and Sibba translated the conversation.

"Mostly, they want to know why Jaka and Lan have higher levels of contamination. They think it's because they were in town when the bomb deployed."

He'd gotten up and now headed toward the door. "Will they be okay?"

"Yes. They are on a schedule of Prussian blue, and no one else was significantly affected. They think the nausea might have been from the soup they made to feed everyone—although, in my mind, it might be fear."

She held open the door and walked out into the hallway with him. "That's the purpose of a dirty bomb—yes, it's harmful, but often the radioactive particles are washed away or caught by the wind and disseminated so that they aren't as potent." She carried her mask, which she'd taken off during the interrogation, after the doctor had reported back her blood test findings. "Although, it's different after a nuclear meltdown. Then the radioactive waste is so potent you can get readings across an entire country."

"So the storm saved the city," Jonas said.

"Maybe. Depends on how much caesium-137 they dropped. But yes, it looks like it."

They were standing near the doorway now, him carrying the backpack they'd already checked and returned to him. He pulled the strap onto one shoulder.

She smiled at him. Her hair had dried, mostly, into tawny waves around her shoulders, and he had the crazy urge to reach out, let the silk fall between his fingers. And then that felt creepy, so he shoved his hand into his pocket.

Silence fell between them.

"I need to get to my lab," he said finally.

"And I need to check in on my grandfather." She met his eyes, her lip caught in her teeth.

"Then...I guess—"

And then she took a step up to him, lifted herself on her toes, and kissed him.

He froze, not sure exactly—then, okay, he was a go. Slipping his hand behind her neck, he held her to him, kissing her back. Nothing crazy, just a sweet kiss, but it held heat and longing and the taste of what-ifs.

Ten seconds longer and he might have dropped his backpack,

added his arm around her waist, pulled her to himself, maybe even backed her against the brick wall for something...more.

In fact, the old words stirred inside him. *Maybe, if you were honest, you want more.*

Yes, yes he did.

He wanted Sibba.

The smell of her—cotton and the lavender scrub of the hospital soap—circled up around him and—

She let him go, stepping away. Met his eyes. Then, slowly, she smiled. "Take care of yourself, Weatherman."

He stood there, numbly nodding as she turned and walked down the hall.

Twenty-four hour pass, and Ned had already spent six of it getting to Geneva.

A train to Ljubljana, a flight to Innsbruck, and then another hopper to Geneva, then a commuter train to Lausanne, and all the time, not an answer from Shae's phone.

And now he stood in the lobby of the Alpine Hotel, trying not to raise his voice. But—

"I rented that room for *two weeks*. I have four days left on my rental." He knew he sounded tired, but after being poked and examined for the past twenty-four hours, and later determined that no, he wasn't going to die of imminent cancer or his bones dissolving, he'd been given the *all-clear and hurry back* by Trini to track down Shae.

To tell her that maybe she shouldn't stick around and wait for him to return from what he'd hoped was a brief spin-up.

With nuclear waste caesium-137 on the loose, their team had been among the spec op groups tagged to track it down and put jack back in the box. Hopefully *before* the Petrov group could unleash another brand of terrorism into the world.

Ned had been read into the event this summer attached to the same group—one where they not only tried to EMP-bomb Air Force One and take out President Isaac White—again—but tried to unleash a biological weapon into the happiest place on earth.

He wondered if his brother Fraser had been on that op, mostly because he'd heard that Jones, Inc. had been a player in that takedown. But Ned hadn't talked to his brother for the better part of six months, and last he'd heard, from his dad just two weeks ago in Geneva, Fraser was back in Minnesota, holding down the family winery.

Been there, done that, and Ned was in no hurry to return to the daily chore of farming, cleaning out barrels and fermenters, bottling wine, and occasionally acting like a tourist guide around the vineyard.

Good luck, Fraser.

Poor guy had left the teams about two years ago—hadn't really explained why. And he didn't exactly have a girl to tug him away either.

"Sorry, sir," the desk manager said now, a thin man with a pressed dress shirt and a fade haircut. Very European, with a touch of French. "We had to release your room to the local police for investigation."

"What?" Ned said.

"Yes. We had a break-in, and the guests were attacked."

Ned stilled. Last he knew, his brother Creed had taken the room. "Was anyone hurt?"

"I don't know."

"I need to talk to someone who does know." Ned gave the man a look that suggested it wasn't a request.

"I'll get my manager." The clerk vanished through the door to the back.

Great. Ned had left his suitcase in Shae's room, however, so hopefully she still had his hiking gear, his other civvies.

He'd like to change out of his cargo pants and T-shirt, get in a shower, and then maybe take Shae to dinner before he had to catch his midnight flight back to Slovenia.

If he could find her.

The manager appeared through the door, an older man in a suit, dark complexion, his hair graying on the sides. Seemed an older version of the desk clerk. "Can I help you, sir?" Same French accent too.

"I wanted to know what happened in the room I rented."

"I'm sorry, sir, but that is a police matter—"

"My brother was in that room."

The man stopped, took a breath. "As far as I know, your brother and Princess Imani escaped without harm."

Ned blinked at him. "Princess—who?"

"Her Royal Highness Princess Imani of Lauchtenland was one of the guests. Unfortunately, we did not find this out until after the incident."

"Please elaborate."

"All we know is that someone broke into the room. They escaped over the balcony."

He took that in, let a beat pass. "Was anyone hurt?"

"Yes. But...we don't believe it was our guests."

Interesting. So the woman Creed had been with was a princess.

That dog.

"We refunded your room to your card, sir."

"How about my other room—the one under Shae Johnson's name?"

"I'm afraid that is private information, sir."

Ned leaned into the desk. "It's being charged to my card. All I want to know is if it is still being rented."

The man considered him a moment, maybe taking in the two-day beard growth—he'd planned on shaving after he'd gotten into his room—and the not-so-hidden fatigue on his face, along with the tightening of Ned's jaw, and maybe decided on compassion.

Or fear.

Whatever worked. But the man pulled up the reservation on his computer. "According to our records, that room is still being rented."

The words released a knot in his gut.

"Perfect." He shouldered his pack and headed up the stairs.

He'd rented the Alpine Hotel because it was quaint. Small, with only three stories, the place had once been an old apartment house, the rooms renovated but still historical. Shae's had a fireplace in it, a small sitting area that overlooked a dining courtyard, and a partial view of Lake Geneva.

The getaway had been a last-minute grab of time away from the teams and a chance to connect with his family. Creed had run in some international track meet. He didn't win, but it gave Ned a chance to catch up with his family. His sister Iris had even been there, and he hadn't seen her in over a year, what with her busy reffing schedule.

He'd finally decided it was time to formally pop the question to Shae. She'd been incredibly patient as he went to BUD/s, then the year of SQTs, another year of first-year training, and then he'd been selected to join Team 3, which had shipped him to San Diego, and he'd spent a year just getting used to the team, cementing his skill set.

The fact that she'd followed him first to San Diego, then to Pensacola, then back to San Diego—yeah, he didn't deserve her, and he knew it.

But now was their time. And for the next eight hours, he was going to make the most of it.

He headed down the hallway and found her room, the corner suite, and knocked on the door.

Stood, listening to the quiet, the thump of his heartbeat.

No footsteps to the door, no turning off of a shower or opening of a balcony door. He knocked again, waited.

Still, no answer.

He headed back downstairs.

"Are you sure she hasn't checked out?" This he addressed to the manager, who still stood at the desk, scanning the computer.

The man looked up. "Like I said, the room is still rented. As to the occupant's whereabouts, I'm afraid we don't monitor our guests' activities."

Right.

He walked over to the lobby sofa, an art-deco affair with rounded arms in royal blue velvet, and sat down. Refused the urge to lean over, put his feet up.

But wow, he was tired. And maybe the kind of tired that meant he needed the sunshine of his fiancée's smile, something to remind himself why he did what he did.

"You're clean." Trini's voice whispered into his head. Maybe, but his life felt cluttered and busy and complicated, and the only thing that wasn't was—

Laughter, and he would have recognized it anywhere. He sat up, looked toward the door...

She came in with the sunshine, her hair pulled back, the gold in it bright against the light browns. She wore a fleece, a pair of jeans and tennis shoes, a backpack over one shoulder, and held the door open for someone behind her.

A man. Tall and lean, with a dark blond ponytail and red whiskers, hiking boots, a vest, and a silly-looking stocking cap. He wore a satchel and laughed in response to something she said. "You can't be serious—"

"Ned?" Shae stopped, standing in the lobby, and Ned rose, his heart a fist in his chest.

He looked at her, then at the man and then—

"Ned!" Shae dropped her pack and ran, slamming into him so hard he almost didn't catch her. She wrapped her arms around him, her face in his neck. "Oh my gosh—what a surprise!"

He embraced her, his gaze on the man by the door. The man smiled, but it seemed forced to Ned.

Or maybe he was just attributing that to his own smile.

Then Shae leaned back, took his face in her hands, and kissed him. Not a chaste kiss, but not too intimate either, something that shook him out of the crazy head-space he'd briefly landed in and made him focus.

Shae. He kissed her back, his arms around her, molding her to himself. He'd missed her.

She tasted of coffee and chocolate and new mornings and everything he'd jumped on a plane for. So maybe he'd overreacted there, because a big part of him—probably fatigue and stress—wanted to walk over and get serious with this yahoo who was so friendly with his, um, *future wife*, that he might be laughing at one of her jokes.

Teasing her.

She leaned away, and moisture glistened in her eyes. "I was worried. I hadn't heard from you."

He blinked. "Honey. I've called you every single day since I left."

Her mouth opened, then closed. "Right. Oh yeah. I was getting charged crazy data fees and not even getting service, so Dana here told me to switch out my sim card on my phone for something local. I'll bet it didn't keep my number."

Dana, huh?

At the mention of his name, said Dana came forward, his hand, out. "Dana Munson. Fellow traveler."

He had an accent. Swedish, maybe.

Ned met his grip. It was a little roughened, so not a complete pansy, despite the satchel and ponytail.

"Ned Marshall."

"She's mentioned you." Then Dana looked at Shae and winked.

And what was that about?

"Did she mention that we're engaged?"

Dana nodded. "As a matter of fact, she did." He was still smiling.

Ned didn't know why he didn't like him. Just...didn't.

Shae slid her hand into Ned's. "I met Dana the first day you were gone. I did a day hike up Mount Blanc, and he and his friends were hiking too, so they adopted me."

Yeah, he'd bet.

"We've been all over Switzerland. Even hiked up the Matterhorn. Dana's been great to show me around."

Mm-hmm.

Dana was grinning at her, and yeah, Ned knew that look.

"He even decided to stay behind to keep me company after his group went on to France."

"How nice of him." He looked at Dana. No smile.

Dana's fell. "Yeah. But now that you're back—"

"I'm back."

"Good. She was worried." Dana now met his eyes, and the games were over.

"Mm-hmm."

"And lonely."

"Really."

"I wasn't lonely." Shae stepped in. "It was just nice to have some people to share the sights. And Dana's been here before, so this morning he took me to his favorite breakfast café."

"Thoughtful."

She tugged on his hand. "Yeah. But now that you're here...we can explore the city. Maybe go into Geneva."

He so wanted to tell her the truth, but not here, not with Dana staring at him.

And him staring back.

"Let's go up to your room," he said, glancing at her. "Mine was given away."

She made a face. "I heard that. Came back that night, pretty late, and all the commotion had already happened. I called your folks a few days ago. They said Creed was okay and back in Minnesota with Fraser."

Interesting. But good. He put his arm around her. "Thanks for checking in with them."

"I'm so sorry about the sim card," she said. "I never even thought..."

"It's okay." He pressed a kiss to the side of her head. "I was just a little worried too."

"She was just fine," Dana said, and now Ned looked at him. Took a breath.

"I'll take it from here. But...thanks."

Maybe he was reading this all wrong—

"Shae, you have my number if you need me. Or if you're left here alone, again."

And that was just it. "Dude—" He loosened his hold on Shae's hand, but she grabbed it and gave it a tug.

"C'mon, sailor."

Right. The last thing he wanted to do was spend one more second doing anything but kissing Shae. Or just talking to her, letting her know that she was the one constant, good thing in his life, and that, shoot, he'd waited way too long to ask her to marry him.

They headed up the stairs, and she opened her room.

Her presence filled the room—from the fragrance of her shampoo to the art pieces she'd painted and left to dry. He walked over to a canvas and picked up a watercolor of the Genevan boardwalk, moonlight casting on the water. "This is gorgeous."

"Thanks. I felt really inspired, I guess."

A few prints of photos were propped on the dresser, most of them landscapes, some of architecture, others were street scenes.

"And this." He'd picked up another painting, this one of a mountain with a river flowing through it.

"Yeah, that one is the Rinderhorn hike."

"You went on that with Dana?" He set the picture down.

"And his friends, yeah."

He walked over to the window and scrubbed his hands over his face. Oh, he didn't know why this was bothering him so much.

Maybe since he was the one who was supposed to hike the

Rinderhorn or whatever with her, or walk down a moonlit boulevard. Or eat at breakfast cafés.

He hated Dana a little. Ridiculous, but still...

"I was really worried about you," he said.

"That makes two of us. I called you too. But you never picked up."

He turned. "That's because my phone is set to spam any number I haven't approved."

She stood there, having dropped her backpack on the bed, her pale blue eyes on him, and he just wanted to cross the room and pull her into his arms.

Forget whatever had happened this week.

But for some reason—aw, it just sat in his chest. "What if Dana and his people weren't...weren't good people? What if they'd found out you were alone and...I don't know, tried to kidnap you? Or rob you or..." And his voice dropped low. "Or rape you?"

Her smile had fallen. "Ned. I was fine."

"I know, but—"

"Don't you trust my judgment?"

His mouth opened. Closed. "It's not that—it's just that the world is a dangerous place."

Her eyebrows rose. "And you're telling me that? The person who saw her boyfriend murdered before her eyes, went into hiding for years, and then stood up to the murderer. Me?"

Right. But, "You're just so..."

"Naïve? Stupid?"

"Independent!"

She blinked at him, and oh, that was probably the wrong word.

"I meant...I just...I just need to know that when I'm not with you, you're safe, is all."

Again, this wasn't quite coming out right. But maybe it was. Maybe— "I can't do my job if I'm worried about you, Shae.

Twenty-four hours ago, I was...anyway, my team depends on the fact that I'm not distracted."

She had stood, listening, and now folded her arms over her chest. "Ned. I know you need to be focused. But you can't be distracted by the what-ifs—"

"I couldn't get ahold of you for a week! *Over* a week!" And oh, this was not going at all how he'd hoped. Or wanted. But he couldn't seem to stop himself. "Shae, do you have any idea how it feels to call and call and not get an answer? My brain conjured up all sorts of nightmares."

She just blinked at him. "You're kidding me, right? Because, hello, that is *exactly* what it feels like to be dating you. And I guess to be married to you. An active duty operator who leaves in the middle of the night and comes back whenever he feels like it—"

"It's *not* when I feel like it—I'd be here all the time if that was the case. But it's my job."

"I get that! But you can't expect me to just sit here and wait for you. Wait. Doing what? Sitting in my hotel room?" She raised her arms. "Like a dog? By the door? Thump, thump, my tail is wagging. My master is home!"

Wow. He held up a hand. "No. I just...yes. The thought of something happening to you while I'm gone—"

"And what about the something that happens to *you*, Ned? We're not even married. If you died, your parents would find out before I did."

"That's not true. Trini would make sure—"

"And if Trini died? And your team—the point is, I'm *nothing* to you."

His mouth opened, and she held up her hand. "At least, officially. And yet I've followed you around the planet for four years. And you have the crazy nerve to tell me that I should have stayed put in this hotel room while you went off...who knows where, and for how long—" She reached for her backpack.

"What are you doing?"

"I'm getting some air."

"With Dana?"

She had flung her backpack over her shoulder, turning for the door. Now she stopped, turned back. "Wow. I never pegged you for the jealous type. Dana is a friend. Nothing more. Because…I am engaged to you."

He stared at her. And she stared back.

"Or maybe I'm not. Because as much I as I love you, Ned, I can't live in a cage, waiting for you to show up in my life. I have one too. And you're going to have to accept the fact that I get to live it, even when you're not around."

Then everything shucked out of him when she took off the ring, the one he'd spent two months' pay on, and set it on the dresser.

"Shae—"

"When you can accept that, when you can start trusting me, then we'll talk about the future." Then she reached for the door.

"Shae, don't—"

She turned, her eyes red. "I love you. Only you. But I've lived in fear, hiding and worried, every step calculated and measured and…it was prison. And I can't live like that, Ned. Not again." Then she turned and opened the door. "I'll be back later. Please don't follow me."

"Shae—c'mon! That's not what I meant!"

But the door closed.

He turned and wanted to put his fist through the fine plaster of the old building. What just happened? His entire body shook, his gut churning.

Okay, right. So he'd been a jerk—he got that part. But certainly, they could figure this out.

He didn't care what she said. He turned and headed to the door. Opened it.

Not in the hallway. He ran down the hallway, took the stairs.

Not in the lobby.

He pushed out into the street, bracing himself for the sight of her walking with Dana.

Nothing. Not even Dana.

He took off down the street, running—maybe he'd simply lost her in the crowd. He sprinted a block.

No sign of Shae.

Turned and sprinted back the other way, two more blocks.

She'd vanished.

He gripped his knees, bending over to catch his breath. *I'll be back later.*

Later just might be too late.

Seven

"I thought I'd find you here."

The voice came from behind Sibba, her grandfather's tone low and gentle against the soft wind, the rasp of autumn leaves brushing across the square. The three soaring chestnut trees turned the sunlight into a clutter of shadows across the cement, the massive wall with the names etched into the face.

"I just had to...I don't know."

"Find yourself again?"

Dedi sat beside her on the wooden bench that faced the creamy white monument.

She said nothing.

"Not all the victims' names are on that wall," he said.

Maybe not. But somehow, since Slovenia had built the monument to the victims of all wars and added her parents' names, she'd started visiting every time she came to the city.

Or most times.

Often, right after a callout. She didn't know why the urge cycled inside her this time, but somehow, walking away from Jonas, then turning at the end of the hall to see that he'd gone, had left a hollowness inside her.

Not that she'd expected anything different.

Still, after she'd checked on her grandfather, she'd walked the four blocks through the city to the monument. Sat on the bench and stared at her parents' names in the marble for a long time.

"I don't know why I like being here. It's quiet." She'd picked up a fallen chestnut and now rolled it between her fingers. "I feel less alone here."

"You're not alone, *mucek*." Her grandfather put his arm around her. "Your parents loved you so."

She let herself sink into his embrace.

"I told you they found you in the rubble—it was a miracle you lived." He pressed a kiss to her forehead. "You keep testing that miracle."

She met his eyes, and they held a sadness. "Sorry."

"Your grandmother and I never understood why you chose such a dangerous life."

"It's because of you, Dedi. You taught me not to be afraid."

"And are you?"

She frowned.

"Not afraid."

She stared at the monument, the thousands and thousands of names. So many lives lost. "I'm always afraid," she said softly.

"This is why you are still single."

She rolled the chestnut between her hands. "It wouldn't be fair to leave someone behind."

"We always leave someone behind, Sib. Be honest. Your fear is this." He gestured to the wall. "For you, the promise of love is not greater than the fear of loss."

"Love? Dedi—"

"I saw you. And that American, Sibba."

She bit her lower lip, the feeling of Jonas's hand behind her neck, the taste of him on her lips. So crazy, but she couldn't help herself from kissing him, as if she'd stepped outside her body and let another person take over.

A person she both feared and longed to know.

However, if she hadn't pushed him away, finally, *that* Sibba might have taken over. Started making declarations and promises that...

Well, hope wasn't an ally.

"I don't need to be married to be happy."

"No. But a partner, in love, walks the road with you. Helps to make sense out of the life we live. Gives it meaning."

She opened her mouth, but he held up his hand. "I'm not saying you don't have meaning alone. But it is one of the ways God helps us survive, even—to use your grandmother's term— bloom. God is love, and that love is often seen best between a husband and wife. And children. Loving someone gives life meaning, no matter how long it lasts."

She offered a smile. "I hate war."

"I hate war too." He sighed. "But as long as evil persists in the world—and it will until Jesus returns—there will be wars." He looked up at the monument. "But we don't stop living just because there is war. There is still love. There is still joy. That's a lesson that took years for me to learn, and I might have lost it again if it weren't for you."

He took her hand. "Your grandmother's love helped me survive after we lost your father." He looked at her. "And you," he said, softly. "You gave me a purpose, a reason. Our miracle. You brought me back to faith, mucek. God gave us you to love, to show me life wasn't bereft of meaning."

Her eyes burned.

"The truth is, when I deserted my country, I was bereft of faith. Believed that God had abandoned me. Even after your grandmother married me, I was a hard man, angry at the world, at God who allowed war. Your grandmother loved me despite all that. And then your father was born. I didn't want to imagine that God might have found me, blessed me. And then after him, Marek. He, too, seemed a miracle, but I didn't want faith. It seemed too...ambiguous." He looked at the monument, swallowed.

"And then you were born. A girl whose name means light.

And you were, Sibba. Light and joy, and I wanted to believe that God cared. That despite my fears—the way I ran away—he still loved me."

"And then the airport was bombed," she said quietly.

He nodded. "We were distraught. I was angry—not just at the JNA but at God. It felt like a trick. He'd found me and brought war back to my life."

He cupped his other hand over hers. "And then...then they found you. Unhurt. Can you believe that? Fires and rubble around you, and you lay in your father's arms, untouched. And it was as if my heart burst open and I saw it."

"Saw what?"

"The hope of salvation. The fact that into the middle of our darkness, God reaches out and saves us. This is the miracle of Jesus. Of redemption."

He smiled at her, closed mouth, but she could see the hope in his eyes, a faith there that seemed to liven his expression, change him.

And oh, she wanted to believe.

But, "I don't feel saved. I feel that if *I* don't go out and defuse the proverbial bombs, then they'll simply explode, and then we'll be left with the fallout. I don't feel safe or loved...most of the time I just feel...angry."

She looked at the monument. "I feel like hope was stolen from me. And now it's mocking me." She stood up. "*God* is mocking me, if there is even a God."

Her grandfather raised an eyebrow.

"Okay, I've done the math, listened to the arguments. And I can't deny that God—or some creator—exists. I just...I don't want to have to reckon with the disappointment of trusting Him only to have Him fail me."

"Have you ever trusted Him?"

She blinked at the soft question. Narrowed her eyes. Opened her mouth, closed it. "I have prayed."

"When Maja was killed. I know."

She turned away. No, she wouldn't cry for old griefs. "Yes."

"The point of prayer isn't the *answer*, Sibba. It's the fact that we turn to God. That He takes us in His arms. That we are His. Blessed are the poor in spirit, for theirs is the kingdom of heaven."

"What does that even mean?"

"It means all the things. Grace and hope and love and...safety. But it starts with a bereftness of faith."

"I would rather have my prayers answered."

"Your prayers are always answered." He stood up and looked at the monument. "Maybe just not the way you want."

He touched her shoulder, squeezed. Then he walked up to the monument.

Frankly, she hadn't prayed for so long, she didn't know what answers God had given her, or hadn't.

Poor in spirit.

At the monument, Dedi pressed his hand to the wall, bowed his head.

It starts with a bereftness of faith.

She walked up to the monument and stood beside him. Her gaze trekked up to their names. Luka and Brita Kovac.

But a partner, in love, walks the road with you.

For a moment, she was standing on the riverbed, Jonas's forehead to hers. *I will walk in your footsteps.*

No. Her footsteps were just going to get him killed. And it didn't matter anyway.

His footsteps had led him out of her life.

But in a different place, different life, different world, she might have run right after him.

"You sure you're not contagious?"

Jonas turned to his research partner, Tarek, and gave him a

look. "I took the blue pill. And I had my blood tested. I'm not bleeding from my eyes, and neither will you."

Tarek raised an eyebrow, then turned back to his screen, where the data from Frannie's black box downloaded into their shared server.

In his late twenties, Tarek was wiry and smart, with round glasses, blond hair that hung behind his ears, and so much energy he could be plugged in and used as a generator, his feet always tapping, his brain always on overdrive.

He'd already done a deep dive into caesium-137 and its possible side effects, none of which Jonas wanted to hear.

What he wanted to know was where and how the Russians got ahold of the nuclear waste.

Or better yet, who exactly had snatched his dirigible from the air and used it to terrorize a small village.

"You showered?"

"Please. Twice. And I went home and changed clothes before coming here. My other clothes are in a bag at the hospital." Which, actually, was only located a few blocks from his office-slash-lab in the College of Geodetic, Environmental, and Civil Engineering.

Too close, really, because his brain was still stuck on that kiss.

That. *Kiss.*

But she'd walked away from him and, really, probably saved both of them heartache.

Because he'd seen the look on her face as she dissected that minefield. She *wasn't* afraid. Or if she was, she hid it under layers of calm. Which made her brilliant at her job.

Not so much as a life partner.

Aw, who was he kidding. The heart wanted what the heart wanted, and right now, it was back at the hospital, or on her doorstep, so he could continue their kiss.

"Hello, Jonas. Come in, Jonas."

He sighed and looked at Tarek. "Sorry."

"The download is done, and I went ahead and opened it to sort the data."

Their office wasn't large—it didn't even have windows. Just two long tables, numerous computer screens, a mini fridge, and a dart board.

And it smelled like an old basement.

Which it was.

Jonas tried not to think about the fact that he'd gone from high speed action chases across the Midwest to staring at a screen in a darkened room. No wonder he wanted more out of life. And kissing Sibba hadn't helped at all. Especially now that he was back in the cellar.

Three flatscreen televisions hung from the wall, all of them tuned to local weather channels. Another screen—connected to the GSP monitoring system—tracked weather balloons five and six: Farah and Sally.

It looked like Farah had stayed on course, her trajectory over northern Slovenia, through the mountains.

Sally, however, had veered off, heading south toward Croatia.

"Have you tried to get Sally back on track?" he'd asked Tarek when he came into the office.

Scared the guy, who'd been eating a bowl of pork dumplings. The smell made Jonas's stomach roar. He hadn't eaten since this morning, some toast and jam.

Tarek passed him over a thermos. "My mom made them this morning."

Jonas handed Tarek the black box and took the thermos. While he ate, Jonas spilled out the story of the past twenty-four hours. Tarek set up the box for download.

He'd given Jonas a look when he got to the radioactive part, but Sibba had put her Geiger counter on the box, and despite the proximity to the bomb, it had bare traces. Probably, the storm had washed the dust away.

Now Jonas picked up the thermos to finish off the dumplings while Tarek gave him the lowdown.

"According to the GPS history, Frannie went offline four days ago, somewhere west of Poče."

"So, how?"

"Maybe someone intercepted our radio signal. If they were closer, and the signal stronger, it's likely they could have overridden our signal."

"What about our RFID? They'd have to have the same radio frequency identification to intercept."

Tarek was nodding. "Right. It's possible we were hacked and the RFID duplicated."

Jonas set his fork down. "Hacked? How? This part of the building is in a Faraday cage."

"I read an article about hackers who siphoned passwords and other data from computers using radio signals generated by the computer."

"Radio signals? How?"

"It's malware. It's downloaded onto the computer, and then it generates radio signals that can transmit data."

"But we have software that protects against malware."

"They can take it from your phone, too, through the FM radio receiver built into mobile phones."

"There are FM receivers in phones?"

"Yes. Part of the emergency backup, when internet and cell networks are down."

Jonas pulled out his phone and opened the app that controlled his drone. "I can't even communicate with Sally."

"They might have changed her RFID remotely."

"Has she gone down yet?"

"Maybe. But her GPS is still working, so maybe not."

He got up and stared at the screen. Sally sat just north of the border to Croatia.

"Let's hope she crashes before they can grab her."

"And who is *they*?" Tarek asked, his gaze on his screen as he typed.

"Not sure. Sibba said they spoke Russian. But why would Russia drop a dirty bomb in Slovenia?"

"Russia is out of control. They have rogue groups operating all over—Ukraine, Chechnya, Georgia—I even read an article on the dark web about an assassination attempt by the Bratva on the American president." He glanced at Jonas. "You know anything about that?"

"I know the VP-elect was accused of being involved in a plot. She just stood trial. I didn't watch the news, but I think she was convicted. But you're saying the Russians worked with her?"

"Just a theory on the internet. Okay, so the GPS clicks back on twenty-four hours later, and she's just northwest of Poče. According to the data, she circled Poče for two days, and then the storm hit." He frowned.

"What?"

Tarek turned to another screen and pulled up a Doppler screen. "According to the Doppler history, the storm front didn't hit Poče for another hour." He ran the history, the storm front moving over the map.

"Let me throw in the time stamp of Frannie's crash."

A blink appeared on the screen, and then Tarek ran the program.

Frannie's light blinked out before the front passed over it.

"So it wasn't the storm that crashed it." He'd considered it when Henry had told him his account, but seeing it on the screen was proof. "It was a dirty bomb, deployed over Poče."

"What's in Poče?"

"I have no idea. It's a village full of innocent people."

"Maybe it was just out of the way enough that they thought they wouldn't get caught," Tarek said.

Evil. Jonas got up. "I'm getting a pop. Want anything?"

"You mean a Fanta, and no. Tea for me." He pointed to his cup.

Jonas headed down the dark hallway, then took the stairs to the main floor and across the lobby to the lunchroom. Vending machines stood against the wall. A few students sat nursing tea or eating sandwiches.

He used his card and bought a Fanta. Opened the twist-off and stood at the window. Outside, leaves had scattered across the lawn, under a beautiful, blue-skied day, although the sun had started to slide beyond the buildings, and long shadows stretched into the yard.

A man and woman walked hand in hand down the sidewalk, talking, smiling.

No fear of the future. Just...walking.

He took a long drink.

If there were international terrorists on the loose, Russian or not, probably Fraser would know what to do.

Jonas pulled out his cell, checked the time, and dialed. Six hours behind, Fraser should just be getting up.

If he was back in the US by now.

The phone rang, then ran over to voicemail.

Jonas didn't leave a message.

Okay, so if Fraser wasn't in the States, maybe his buddy Hamilton Jones would know what to do. Fraser worked for Jones's private security firm, and it felt like Jones had contacts all over the world.

He did an internet search, found the Jones, Inc. website and then the contact information in the footer.

Dialed the number.

It would probably go to a voicemail—

"Jones here."

He stilled.

"Hello?"

"Uh—Hamilton Jones?"

"I don't have a timeshare, and my car warranty isn't expired—"

"My name is Jonas Marshall."

A pause. "Fraser's brother?"

"Yep. I was trying to get ahold of him—"

"He's, uh, sort of on an op right now—"

"No problem. Actually, maybe you're a better person to ask. So...I'm in Slovenia, and I think some rogue Russian group set off a dirty bomb in the area."

"A *what*?"

"Dirty bomb. It's filled with radioactive—"

"I know what it is. But—seriously?"

"Yes. And I know this is crazy, but Fraser seems to be into all sorts of things, and I just thought maybe—"

"Hold please."

The line went quiet. Jonas took another sip of his drink. Watched a couple kids kick around a soccer ball, and his mind went to the boy he'd rescued today.

Yeah, that could have gone all sorts of wrong. Talk about God intervening—

"Jonas. I have a man named Logan Thorne on the line. He runs an under-the-radar group that hunts down terrorist activities around the globe, and that's all I can tell you, but he's the guy you want to talk to. Logan—this is Jonas, Fraser's brother."

Another voice came on the line, resonant and unruffled, not unlike Ham's. "Hey, Jonas. Thanks for calling. Tell me about this dirty bomb."

Jonas pushed his way outside and stood on the back step of the cafeteria entrance, his voice low as he detailed his information. He didn't know why, but just telling someone outside Slovenia, someone who might make sense of the bigger picture, eased the knot in his chest.

"You don't have any idea who these men were?" Logan asked after he finished.

"Nope."

"And where is your device now? The one shot down."

It wasn't—never mind. "It in a field near Poče. Probably the property of the Slovenian police, or maybe the military by now. But I have pictures."

"Okay. Send those."

"I also met the Director General of the Hazardous Materials Unit here. His name is Vlasic."

A pause. "Okay, got it. All right, listen to me, Jonas. You did the right thing calling us."

Only then did he realize Ham was still on the line, because he cleared his throat. "We'll take it from here."

"Actually, that's the problem. Uh, I have another dirigible that has gone off course. We think maybe Sally has been hacked."

"Sally?"

"Weather balloon number six. She's no longer under our control."

"Where is she?"

"The southwestern corner of Slovenia, near the Croatian border. It's possible that we could get her under control again if I can get close enough to hack the radio transmission. I built in a sub-frequency that allows me to control her, but it's line of sight."

"Very good, Jonas. You sit tight. I'm going to send someone to you. She'll track down Sally and stop her from being used for any terrorist activities."

Terrorist. But, "Yes, sir. Let me know how I can help."

"Well done, calling your brother. You're the storm chaser, right?"

He stilled. What, did this no-name organization have some sort of dossier on him?

"Ham told me that Fraser keeps him updated. I'm a storm man myself."

"I'm more of a weatherman now."

"You did the right thing calling this in. Ham, stay on the line. Jonas, I'm going to ping you after this call. Send me your address and those pictures."

"Yes, sir."

"You can hang up now."

"Yes, sir."

He pressed end and stared at his phone, not sure what had just happened.

Except, clearly he knew even less about his brother's life than he thought.

Jonas stuck his phone in his pocket, went back inside, dropped the empty bottle in the trash, and headed down the stairs.

Even as he pushed open the door, he knew something was wrong. Tarek was on his feet but hunched over the computer, typing fast.

"What's going on?"

"She's gone."

"Sally?" He might have guessed Sibba, but he hadn't actually gotten a handle on that yet.

"Yes. Her signal just went dark. I'm trying to pull her up on satellite, but it looks like she went down in the area of Snežnik, just north of the border."

Jonas stepped up to his computer and pulled up the map. "It's really dense in there. Forested. Is it mountainous?"

"Not like northern Slovenia, but there is some rough terrain."

"Can I reach it by car?"

Tarek stood up. Looked at him. "Um. Maybe. Yes. At least part of the way."

His phone pinged. Logan Thorne, requesting the images along with his location. He closed the text. Pocketed his phone. It wouldn't matter. By the time anyone got here, he'd be long gone.

"I'm going to forward you a text. Send the location to that number." He reached for his laptop, closed it, and dropped it into his backpack. Then he grabbed cords—laptop, his phone charger.

"Where are you going?"

Would it be too sappy to say, Where his heart wanted?

And yes, it was a desperate move, and maybe unnecessary, but frankly, he didn't know where else to turn.

No, *correction*—didn't *want* to turn anywhere else.

"I'm going to get help. We've got to stop Sally from deploying another dirty bomb."

EIGHT

She wasn't running. Not really.

She just needed to get some air under her.

And okay, maybe escape the memory of Jonas and the strange impact he'd made in her life. It wasn't like she'd never met an attractive male before.

But she'd never randomly, abruptly kissed a man like she had Jonas, so there was that.

Oy.

"Are you sure you want to do this? Maybe wait until tomorrow?" Ina's voice came through her Airpods as Sibba finished adding another fleece to her accessories pack. She wasn't taking a lot of gear—just enough for one night, one trek up the mountain.

And a gliding trip down.

"There's still plenty of sun left. And I'm not going up Triglav—it's too far up. I'm staying at the hut on Razor Mountain." She pulled the drawstring on her pack, tightened it down.

"I thought the hut was closed for winter."

"I talked to Kat, the caretaker. She said the winter room is open, and I'm the only reservation. It's just an hour from there to the top of the mountain—I'll be there before the sun goes down."

"And tomorrow."

"Tomorrow, I fly." She carried the pack out to her main room, where Dedi sat in the recliner watching the news. "I checked the weather, and it's going to be a gorgeous day."

He glanced at her, took in the pack, and his mouth tightened into a grim line. But he gave a nod and said nothing.

"Are you sure? You got checked out for radiation poisoning?"

"I'm fine, Ina. They gave me meds. And my bloodwork was clean." She opened her refrigerator and took out her chilling thermos of water and a piece of Tolminc cheese. Then she grabbed a pack of instant soup from her cupboard, a packet of dried chicken, and sliced off a hearty chunk of the baguette she'd purchased on the way home.

"I don't like it. I know you—this feels like a reaction jump."

"Reaction to nearly getting my insides dissolved? Yes—"

"No. This is about that guy. What was his name?"

She drew in a breath. "And now I regret telling you—"

"Why? I still can't believe you met up with Spiderman—isn't that what you used to call him? What are the chances?"

"Yeah, apparently he's also a weatherman, and he was doing some research in the area, so hence why he was there. But yes, I could hardly believe it when I opened Dedi's door to see him standing there."

"I remember him being strong."

Sibba had added the food to her pack, now cinched it up, but at Ina's words, the memory of him tackling her in the honeybee field, or even the sight of him carrying little Petea across the riverbed... "Yeah. He's strong."

"And hot. Or maybe I dreamed that part up."

"You didn't. Blue eyes, brown hair—except he hadn't shaved, so typically American."

"Sounds horrible."

Sibba laughed. "A nightmare."

Ina also laughed, and Sibba could imagine her sitting in her office in Ankaran at the Slovenian naval base, overlooking the Adriatic Sea.

"So, what are you running from?"

"Why did I call you again?"

"Because you know, deep inside, I'm right. You like this guy, and as usual, you're running full speed the other direction."

She carried her pack outside to her car, where her glider was already packed from her last trip up, and hooked it to the bottom of the glider pack. "It seems like the only way to get him out of my head."

"Why do you want him out of your head?"

"Because if I can get him out of my head, maybe I can get him out of my heart."

Silence. Oh, she hadn't exactly meant to... "Forget I said that."

"Hardly. Sib—I don't remember the last time you cared this much about someone."

"My point exactly. And I barely know him. Think of the trouble I'd get into if I—"

"Why this guy? What is it about him?"

She checked her cockpit carry bag, checking the battery level on her variometer, then clipped her helmet to her pack and closed the back of her SUV.

"I don't know. It's weird—that day he carried you off the mountain, I guess I just liked the way he showed up and didn't panic."

She turned then and stared at the faraway mountains. The sun had just started to fall, turning the peaks gold, the sky above a deep magenta mottled with high, flat clouds. "And then in the mountain hut, it felt so...safe to just be in the room with him. And the same over the past two days. Even when we were walking through a minefield. He makes me feel like I'm not alone."

"What if—"

"No, Ina. I *am* alone, and that's the way it has to be."

Ina went quiet.

"Besides, he hasn't exactly shown up on my doorstep asking to stick around in my life. I know what the EOD designation does to a relationship. Poor guy—I even kissed him—"

"You did what?"

"It was—impulsive. And right, too. Like, a goodbye, maybe."

She opened the door to the kitchen. Dedi was up and perusing the fridge. Pulled out a container of eggs.

"You're not running from him. You're running from yourself and the fact that you really want him in your life."

Dedi smiled at her, and she heard his words again. *But we don't stop living just because there is war. There is still love. There is still joy.*

"It doesn't matter what I want. Life isn't about want. It's about what is. Duty. Responsibility. You know that better than I do. How's the new job?"

"Considering the Navy only has two ships, and most of what we do is patrol the border, there isn't a high need for a translator. But I'm on the ready."

"A good change from this summer."

"Anything would be a good change after this summer. I've never heard so much cussing in four different languages."

"That's what you get for being so smart. Not everyone can speak eight languages. I'm surprised they let you transfer to the Navy. Who'd they get to fill your shoes as NATO liaison?"

"Oh, I'm still on call. But some young guy out of university. He can even speak Farsi."

"I hope we never have a need to speak Farsi." Sibba had closed the boot of her SUV. "I wish you were here to check in on Dedi. But I'll be back tomorrow."

"Your grandfather can take care of himself and a small nation. Don't worry. Have fun. Don't die."

"No promises."

"I hate you."

"You love me."

She pulled out her phone and hung up, then tucked it back

into her pocket. "You sure you're okay here tonight?" She directed the question at her grandfather.

"Please leave. I know when you have a burr in your britches." He took out a pan. "Just don't get yourself killed."

She walked over and kissed his cheek. "I won't."

"Just in case you do—where are you going?"

"Razor's peak. I'm staying at Kat's hut tonight."

He glanced out the window. "I guess you still have plenty of sun." He reached out and pulled her close. "Come back with your head on straight."

She didn't ask him to clarify, but in her definition, that meant a new perspective—one without Jonas Marshall in it.

Two hours later, she'd driven to the trailhead, unloaded her pack, and hiked up the two kilometer trail to the Razor Mountain bivouac hut. Formerly an Italian military post, it had been converted over the years to a chalet with an expansive view of Triglav Mountain to the east. She reached the hut before the sun set, and watched it disappear behind the slopes of Tolminski Migovec to the west while drinking her soup.

In the main room, a stove pumped out heat to the winter room, or the lofted area above the great room, where she'd stowed her gear. A nip hung in the air, cooler up here, and she guessed tomorrow's ride might be chilly.

But she loved the feeling of freedom.

"I brought you some tea." Kat Rupchik came out onto the porch, dressed in a down jacket, a knit hat. She handed Sibba a warm mug. "Chamomile." She wore age and sunshine on her weathered face, kind eyes. She ran the place year-round, sometimes acting as a rescuer, often just a therapist for travelers who needed an escape.

Or a reminder of all things good. Sibba knew her well. "Thanks," she said, blowing on the tea. "I'll add more wood before I go to bed."

"Very good." Kat stayed for a moment and stared out at the

view, the mountains turning to darkness. "It's late for you to come."

"I needed to sort some things out."

Kat nodded, drew in a breath. "The Lord is my shepherd. He makes me lie down in green pastures. Or mountains—either one."

It wasn't the first time Kat had quoted scripture to her. Now Sibba just nodded. "Good night, Kat."

"Sweet dreams, Sibba." She let herself inside.

Sibba sat on the porch a long while, nursing the tea. Seeing Jonas emerge from the woods in his canvas jacket, his wind-blown hair, those whiskers. *But a partner, in love, walks the road with you. Helps to make sense out of the life we live. Gives it meaning.*

She got up and went inside. Tossed more wood into the massive black stove, then ascended into the loft that housed ten cots. She'd already laid out her sleeping roll, and now pulled off her shoes and jacket, keeping on her leggings and thermal shirt.

Then she lay on the bed, staring at the ceiling, the lean strip of moonlight that cast into the room through the window. *Into the middle of our darkness, God reaches out and saves us.*

Yeah, well, He would not only have to reach into her dark—or at least shadowy—heart, but He'd have to show her a path beyond her own steps.

She closed her eyes, but her mind played games with her, stirring into her slumber images of Jonas, him laughing at her attempts at humor. Or the look in his eyes after she'd kissed him.

Just before she ran away.

She rolled over. The place had cooled. Maybe she should add more wood. Getting up, she headed downstairs in her stocking feet. She had just opened the stove with the hook when outside, footsteps sounded on the porch.

She didn't think that Kat was expecting anyone else.

The door knob rattled, and she stepped back, still holding the stove hook when the door opened.

He stood against the darkness, the moonlit world behind him, his face obscured. But the outline of his form made her still.

She knew. It was her heart first, then recognition set in as he walked into the room, lit only by the firelight.

He still hadn't shaved, and wore a stocking cap over that brown hair, but his eyes—oh, they found hers and latched on, such an intensity in them that she felt the storm inside.

Or maybe it was just inside *her.* "Jonas?"

"You're a hard woman to find."

He looked good in a lightweight parka, his backpack, hiking shoes.

Too good. "What are you doing here?"

He stiffened. Oh, that's not what—but yes, what. Was. He doing. *Here?*

"I mean, oy, it's a long hike up this mountain."

He seemed to breathe then, and pulled off his hat, even while turning to shut the door. "Yes, it is. I had to hike the last half kilometer by flashlight."

Only then did she see the headlamp attached to his hat. He shrugged off his pack, set it on the ground, then put his hat on top of it.

Turned back to her.

Then it was just them standing in the semidarkness, the heat of the stove between them, him slowly undoing her world. "I need you, Sibba."

And surely, no, he didn't mean it like it sounded. "You...need me?"

But yes, *I need you too.* The words were in her chest, her throat, on her lips—

"Yes. I think there's another dirty bomb set to explode. And I need your help to stop it."

Well, then. Okay.

Heart attack over.

Maybe.

"I promise, this is the fastest way down." Sibba stood, harness on, her fluffy orange-and-blue chute spread out across the grassy hill.

A five-hundred-meter drop at the far side of the hill suggested there was no turning back, and Jonas had simply mentioned that. Sort of as a joke.

Not really.

"I won't let you get hurt." She held up a tandem harness.

"I trust you." Really, he did. And the calm skies, the sunshine, the scent of the piney mountains around him—this was a good day to fly.

And they did need to get down the mountain pronto, so...

Besides, what was he supposed to do with that grin she flashed him? She wore a helmet and had pulled out an extra in her pack, along with the additional harness. She also wore gloves and a layer of fleece over her leggings and shirt.

"Are you sure your chute will hold me?"

"We call it a wing or sail, and yes, unless you're over thirty stone. Then we might be in trouble."

"What is that in English, please?"

She cocked her head at him. "Four hundred pounds."

"I might be."

"Doubtful."

"I ate a lot of cheese."

"You do look a little bloated this morning. And you snore, so maybe you're fatter than you look." She grinned at him, the sunshine in her eyes. "Just come over here and snap into the harness, Santa."

He'd do anything for that smile. In fact, he'd had a hard time wiping from his brain her expression when he'd barged into the hut last night.

Sure, she wore surprise, but despite her words—*what are you doing here?*—something had flashed in her eyes that looked a lot like delight. As if, despite the fact she'd walked away from him, she wanted to see him again.

So, fist pump for the weatherman who hiked an extra three kilometers to track her down. And yes, he'd used the non-excuse, but very real danger, of another dirty bomb as a way to see her, but he wasn't sad that she'd smiled and nodded and agreed to help him.

Provided he started with how he'd found her.

She'd closed the stove but lit a lamp, and they'd sat in the great room under the flicker of a wick, and he'd told her first how Sally had gone off the radar.

No, first he'd told her Tarek's theory of how the Russians had hacked poor Frannie, then his phone call with Logan and Ham, and *then* he'd mentioned that Sally had vanished.

"You think she's being rigged with a bomb?"

"I don't know. But we need to find her."

She'd worn a long-sleeved thermal shirt, a pair of black leggings, pink woolen socks, and had let her tawny-brown hair down, pushing it behind her ears now and again as she traced out an imaginary map of Slovenia on the wooden table top. He'd pinpointed where he thought Sally had landed.

"That's just over the Croatian border. And while we're not currently in a border war with Croatia..." She shook her head. "Let's hope she landed in Slovenia."

"And that something simply went haywire in her GPS system, and not that she was hijacked."

Sibba had drawn up one knee, held it to her chest. "Hungry?"

"I ate some eggs with your grandfather when I went to your house."

"That was four hours ago."

"A little hungry."

"I have cheese." She got up then and went upstairs while he unzipped his jacket, pulled it off, and then unlaced his boots too.

The chill had found his bones, and he'd sat in front of the heater, warming his hands, when she came back down carrying bread and cheese and a knife.

About that time, a woman emerged from a side room wearing

a fleece jacket and sweatpants. Sibba said something to her in Slovenian, then introduced her as the caretaker. Whatever Sibba said to her seemed to satisfy her, and she shook his hand, then headed back to her room.

"Thanks," he said as she sat down again.

"Kat's good people. She understands wayward hikers."

"Is that what we are?"

She looked up from where she was unwrapping the cheese. "Maybe not lost. But definitely wayward."

He raised an eyebrow.

She looked away and started to slice the bread. "I guess that Dedi told you where I was."

"Drew me a map and offered to go with me."

She grinned at that, offering a small laugh. "You'll love this cheese. It's called the King of Mountain Heaven."

"That's some cheese." He took a bite. "Sweet. And tangy."

"Yep. I love it with butter and bread." She handed him a piece of bread. "We should probably save the rest for breakfast. We'll need it before we fly."

He'd stilled then, and she'd laughed. Raised an eyebrow.

Okay, then. "I'll go flying with you."

Dire words, but he meant them.

Mostly.

Because now that the sun was up and he'd had a full night's sleep, he found himself standing on a cliff with probably too much cheese in his gullet for what was about to happen.

He stepped into his harness, which felt like a flimsy chair, and snapped together the straps. His backpack had been strapped onto the bottom, a lot like her extra bag.

She stood in front of him, checking his straps, tightening them while he held up his hands.

"How long have you been doing this?"

"I learned in the UK from some RAF pilots. Got instantly hooked. There are clubs, and I belong to one, but I prefer to fly alone." She tightened down his chest strap. Met his eyes. "Except for today."

"Yet you had a tandem harness and an extra helmet in your pack."

She put on her sunglasses, then went around behind him and picked up a carabiner, hooking it onto his harness. "I was going to take Ina flying on the mountain. I hadn't unpacked since that day. I just forgot about it when I drove out here."

She attached the other carabiner and locked it down, then tested it. "Too much on my mind, I guess."

Wow, he'd love to follow up on that. But at the moment, he wanted *nothing* on her mind but getting them off this mountain. Alive.

"Usually, I'd fly with my solo wing. The tandem sail can get a little unwieldy—"

"What?"

"—without a passenger. Although, last time I used it, it was fine."

"How unwieldy?"

"Don't worry, you're great ballast."

"I hope you're not flying for tips."

She laughed as she attached the wing to her harness with the carabiners.

"So, is this going to feel like I'm falling?"

"No. Like you're flying, Spiderman." She was sorting through the lines, making sure they were straight.

"Usually, flying comes with a choice of almonds or biscotti."

"I gave you breakfast."

"I'm not sure if I should regret that yet."

Silence.

He glanced behind him and saw her check a small device. "What's that?"

"A variometer. It'll tell us our speed and alert us to any air pockets. If you weren't with me, I could use it to help me find thermals. And it tracks my flight." She shoved it into a pack at her hip. "Okay, listen. When the wing starts to fill, we're going to run a little down the hill—yes, that one with the cliff at the edge—"

He had lifted his hand to point. She pushed it down.

"—and the wing will lift us off. If something happens, we have plenty of room to abort."

"Abort? Is that a thing?"

"I've done this nearly a thousand times, so don't panic, just listen to me."

"Panic?"

"I can feel your heart beating."

"No, you can't."

"It's like the thunder."

"I'm as calm as a tropical day."

"Here's the reserve chute line. Don't touch it."

He held up his hands.

"In fact, just hold on to your harness, here and here." She banged the straps at his shoulders.

"I am attached to you, right?"

"You're not going anywhere without me."

That was more like it.

"Run when I tell you—not at top speed. We're not in a race. Just enough for the wind to fill the canopy. It'll lift us off gently."

"Gently?"

"You won't even notice."

He'd bet he would.

Behind him, she turned to face the wing. "Ready?"

"Punch it!"

"Whatever that means. Okay, steady..." She tugged on the canopy, and he glanced back to see it rise. "Three, two, one...walk."

She turned back around, and he started to walk. She fell in step behind him as the canopy rose above him. The lines began to tug up.

"Faster. But don't sit down. Let it pull you—"

Already the canopy had risen, yanking him up.

His feet whispered against the ground—and then with a whoosh, he was flying.

The ground dropped out below, the cliff falling away, and just like that, they were soaring. Not weightless, but he sat back in the harness seat, holding on to the straps where she'd instructed.

"So...?"

"I'm a fan."

She laughed, and it fell like sunlight into his heart. He looked back, and she held on to two handles, the brakes, moving them to direct them.

They soared over trees, the granite peaks rising around them. "Watch the birds—you can spot the thermals." Her voice in his ear, and he watched as a hawk rode the wind. The variometer sang, and in a moment, she'd directed them toward it, and suddenly they rose.

"Did you catch that thermal?"

"Yep. I need to circle again to grab it. Lean in."

She tugged down on her right hand, let out with her left, and he felt them rise again.

Below, the greenery rose up the peaks, the horizon stretching so far he could see Triglav peak and beyond.

"As the day heats up, the thermals will rise from the valleys. You could be up here for hours flying the valley breezes."

"How do you not get lost?"

"Read the sun's shadow on the trees."

She rode the thermal around the mountain, then turned them south and directed them toward another slope. "There'll be a beautiful heat pump up this little mountain, the way the sun is on it."

Below them, in the distance, he spotted the parking area, their two vehicles like toy cars. Around it, thick spires of pine trees turned the foothills into a mass of green.

"We're going to follow this ridge, get high, and then curl around into the valley and give ourselves a beautiful landing."

"How fast are we going?"

"I try and keep our ground speed around thirty."

He had no idea what that meant. But the air had chilled his face, his hands. No wonder she wore gloves.

They soared over the backbone of the ridge, with its granite outcropping and chutes of early season snow. Jagged mountains, as far as he could see, and below, gullies and valleys, shadowed by the rising sun, rivers tumbling through.

He took a breath, let it fill him.

"Right?"

He looked back.

"You were humming."

He hadn't realized that. But yeah, this felt like a humming situation. "Maybe a John Denver song. 'Rocky Mountain High.'"

"I don't know that one. My grandfather loves 'Free Bird.'"

Jonas laughed. "That sounds about right." He held out his hands. "'If I leave here tomorrow, would you still remember me...'"

She laughed as she turned them toward the valley.

"The valley wind pulls the thermals along the corridor. You want to stay near the warmer slopes, the ones with the sun on them. We'll get some lift from the valley heat, but I'm going to turn into the wind to slow us down."

The sky was dotted with thick, fluffy clouds, and he pointed to them. "Those are cirrocumulus clouds."

"Does that mean rain?"

"They're made of ice crystals, and they can mean a front is on the way, but no, no rain today."

"How do you tell the different kinds of clouds?"

"Height. Thickness and form. The storm clouds are the cumulonimbus—which look a lot like an anvil. They can mean thunderstorms. And then there are the nimbostratus. Gray, low, hide the sun. Gloomy. You'll get rain. There are a lot more, but mostly, don't fly around the thick, gray clouds."

She pulled on the brakes, and the variometer sang.

"What are you doing?"

"Cutting our forward speed. We're down to five."

They were dropping, the wind thicker down here.

"Keep your feet up until I tell you. I'm going to put us down on the field there, north of the parking lot."

He spotted it, and the ground seemed to almost drift toward him, closer and closer.

The variometer kept singing even as they glided down to the field.

"Feet up," she reminded as the ground rushed to them, and at the last moment, she pulled up, and they fluttered down, gliding in to their harnesses until they sat on the ground.

The wing fluttered down behind them.

He just sat there, the sense of the earth immense around him.

"You can almost feel it all fall back to you, can't you?"

He unhooked his harness, climbed out. "Feel what?"

"Life. The smallness of it all." She sighed as she unhooked his harness.

He held out his hand, and she gripped it as he pulled her up. She unhooked her helmet and pulled it off, her hair, which had been pulled back, whipping around her face.

"Life is not small, Sibba. That's only our perspective from here. But when we get up there, we see that it's massive, so much over each horizon."

She looked at him, her gaze in his, searching.

And oh, he wanted to kiss her. To put his arms around her, tell her that she didn't have to live a one-meter life.

Instead, he took off his helmet. "I'd really love it if, after all this is over, you'd teach me to fly."

She blinked for a second, then drew a breath, and then slowly, with a smile that spread up her face, she nodded.

For today, that would be enough.

NED MIGHT NEVER SLEEP AGAIN WITH THE AMOUNT OF caffeine zinging through him.

"So you just came back?" The question came from Sonny, who sat backward on his chair, leaning on the front, chewing on a toothpick as Master Chief Chester Nez gave them the briefing from JSOC about the missing caesium-137.

Ned would like a briefing on his missing fiancée, thank you.

They sat in the dining room at a safe house not far from the Slovenian naval barracks, a handful of Slovenian spec-ops guys seated across a long dining table, a couple of EOD experts leaning against the window sill.

At the head of the room, a woman in her early thirties, pixie-short brown hair, green eyes, wearing the gray-blue BDUs of the Slovenian Navy, translated what Nez, on a secure video transmission, was saying. Ned leaned over from where he sat next to Sonny as his commander waited for the woman to finish translating.

"I waited until nine p.m., then went to the airport. The last thing I needed was to be AWOL as well as dumped."

"She hardly dumped you," Sonny said, his voice low.

"The ring is in my gear." Ned sat, his arms folded, watching the screen, trying to keep his mind in the game. "I didn't want to take the chance that she meant it, so I took it. But that feels like dumped to me."

Sonny's mouth made a grim line as he nodded.

Maybe what Ned needed was exactly this—a high-stakes, high-action operation that demanded his full attention.

Otherwise, he'd be on a plane back to Geneva...or maybe the US, if Shae had decided to go home. He wouldn't know, of course, because she hadn't given him her new number.

Sweet.

"We found CCTV evidence of a small team of operatives breaking into the container after it was loaded into the secure container storage at the yard. The container was loaded as scheduled, with no indication that they were loading nuclear waste—even though it was empty."

"Any idea as to who stole it?" Trini stood next to the screen, feet out, arms folded over his massive chest.

"Still trying to identify the group. Not sure if they're connected to the Petrov Bratva or not, but we do know where we think it ended up. Or at least part of it. According to the records at the Swiss Institute of Technology. Unfortunately, the caesium is nearly as dangerous as the missing plutonium."

"Which we have no lead on at the moment," CPO Marsh said. "So, two priorities—the plutonium and the caesium-137. Perfect. The world just got a little more dangerous."

"A lot more dangerous, because it looks like whoever stole the caesium-137 isn't afraid to use it. According to intel, from sources in Slovenia and outside normal channels, there are reports of a dirty bomb that detonated here, in northern Slovenia."

Which was why Team 3 was still here, holed up in a house overlooking the Adriatic Sea in a country most people couldn't point out on a map.

Ned took another sip of coffee—cold now—as the translator relayed that information to her people. They were nodding, their expressions grim, and he got that.

A dirty bomb, regardless of its effectiveness, did as much or more damage spreading fear.

"What does the Slovenian government know about this bomb?" Trini asked Nez.

"Their government knows—it was reported by the Director General of the Hazardous Device Unit out of Ljubljana. But other than the location of the deployment, they're still investigating."

"Which means they have nil," Mac said. He glanced at the translator. "Don't translate that."

She raised an eyebrow.

"That's why they called us. Or rather, we called them," Nez said.

"Why—"

Nez held up his hand. "We got the call from an outside source—"

"Reliable?"

"Yes," Nez said. "He works in a lab in Ljubljana and found the caesium-137. American. One of our non-military partners sent a contact to meet him, but when they got there, he wasn't there. They found his assistant, however, murdered."

Non-military partner. Some outside, non-government-affiliated group, maybe, that the US had been utilizing more and more for their war on terror. Like Jones, Inc., the outfit Fraser worked for.

It still bothered Ned that Fraser had left the teams. Although he knew they'd never work together, he'd still hoped for the insider camaraderie of training with him.

"So why call us?" Trini said.

"I need you to meet up with the contact and track down this informant. He seems to believe there is another bomb at play, and we need to confirm and then shut it down before more caesium-137 is released."

"Is this priority over tracking the plutonium, sir?" Trini asked.

"For now. Button up this guy. Let's get this information and secure the caesium. Without anyone getting exposed, please. Bull and Sonny."

Ned gave him a half salute. Sonny raised his toothpick.

"I'm sending you the info package. This is a joint mission, Team Three. The Slovenian operators and EOD need to be read in on it, although we'll take point. Trini, let me know when you have the operation package put together."

"Copy," Trini said, and Nez signed off.

Ned blew out a breath, scrubbed his hands down his face.

"Tired?"

"I'm running on fumes." He picked up his coffee, then got up for a refill at the pot boiling sludge in the kitchen.

Sonny, Mac, and Cruz followed him.

Cruz grabbed what resembled a Bismarck, a puffed pastry with a filling.

"There's lemon in that, so beware," Mac said. He reached for the pot and filled his cup. Ned set his on the counter.

Mac filled that, too. "So, how was your twenty-four?"

"Unfulfilling," Sonny said for him as Ned took a sip of the black.

Mac raised an eyebrow. "Didn't get to see your girl?"

"Oh, he saw her all right—and she gave him the heave-ho—"

Ned held up his hand. "That's enough, Son. Just...leave it."

Sonny made a face, shook his head.

"What happened?" Mac grabbed a piece of what looked like a rolled cinnamon roll. "I love these. *Potica.*"

Whatever. "I overreacted about a friend she'd made, and we got into it." He took another sip of coffee and looked out the window.

Their safe house sat on a hill overlooking the red-roofed homes, towering cedars, and a quaint and glistening Adriatic Sea. The kitchen was small, like most European homes, but the room connected to a large dining room area and a small but comfortable living area.

Most importantly, it housed all six of them, even if they'd had to double up. He'd taken his thin duvet and flopped onto the floor when getting back late last night.

Not that he'd slept much anyway, his argument with Shae like thunder in his head.

"I was a jerk." He looked up at Mac.

Who just nodded, his mouth a tight line of understanding. "Easy to do when you're stressed out. Who is this friend?"

"Nobody. Really, nobody." He reached for a pastry. "And Shae's right. She's not reckless—trust me, she has her reasons to be suspicious of people. So if she trusts this guy, I should too—"

"A guy? She made friends with a *guy*?"

"A Swede." He said it with an emphasis on the *ee*.

Mac laughed.

"I was just tired. And worried about her—she hadn't answered my calls for a week."

"That's a long time."

"No longer than she has to wait to hear from me."

"That's different."

"Is it? It feels like maybe I have a different standard for her."

Mac set down his coffee. "The difference is that we're not in touch for a reason. If she goes off the grid...that *is* different. I think you had a reason to worry."

"She switched out her sim card—and with it, the number."

"Still. She should have texted you." Mac added more coffee to his cup. "But I get it. I want to freak out every time Larke doesn't answer my call. I think maybe something's happened to the baby, or maybe she's in trouble. But that's just because that's the world *we* live in. That's not their world. They don't have terrorists hunting them down. So yes, when they go AWOL, it feels different."

"Yeah. I just wish I could have stuck around until cooler minds prevailed. Now I'll have to wait until we round up this informant. And track down a bunch of radioactive waste. And maybe hunt down missing plutonium—"

"Stop, please. One mission at a time, okay?"

"Right." Ned finished his pastry. Not bad. Refilled his cup as Mac headed back to the dining room.

Maybe he should call home. See if Fraser could just check in on her—he still had friends in San Diego that could swing by her place, right?

He was pulling out his phone when, "Hey, Ned, you'd better get in here."

The voice belonged to his XO, Marsh. Who then stuck his head out of the door, gestured with a nod.

Huh. Ned headed into the room.

Mac had sat back down along with Sonny, and the Slovenian operators grouped around a joint computer, brought in by their team leader.

But on the big screen, the info package had loaded, with the picture and name of their missing informant on the screen.

Ned stilled. Looked over at Marsh, who took a breath. "What is this?"

"That's our informant. The guy who called in the caesium-137 bomb."

No, that couldn't be right. The picture was taken from his Vortex.com website, the one with him sitting on his outfitted caravan with the satellite mounted on the roof and a very smug-looking storm chaser leaning against the hood in jeans, a T-shirt and boots, the wind in his brown hair. He smiled at the camera, the kind of smile that always made Ned feel like maybe, when he was around, everything would work out.

He put his coffee down slowly, drew in a breath. "That's my brother, Jonas."

The room went silent.

"What?" Trini said now. "This is your *brother*?"

"Yeah."

"Does he work for the government?"

Ned probably wore something of an incredulous look, because Trini raised a hand in defense.

"He's a storm chaser. Or was. He got into an accident about six months ago that really derailed him. I saw him just a couple weeks ago, in Geneva."

"Geneva?"

"Yeah, a few days before we got called out."

More silence. And it clicked.

"He doesn't have anything to do with this...I promise. He's a *weatherman*."

"A missing weatherman," said Trini.

"I know him too." The voice came from across the table. The female translator. "He helped me off a mountain about a month ago."

"What mountain?"

"Triglav. It's...here." She turned her computer around and pointed to a place on a digital map of Slovenia."

"And where did the bomb go off?"

She moved her finger over, just a millimeter. "Just here. About fifty kilometers away."

"Hmm," Trini said, folding his arms over his chest.

"I'm telling you, guys, he's not involved," Ned said.

"I'd have to agree," Marsh said. "I don't know my cousin well, but...he's not the kind to get involved in an international terrorist plot."

Ned didn't know what he meant by that, but, "Jonas is...not complicated. He loves storms. He's very smart—probably the smartest Marshall I know—sorry, Ford."

Marsh lifted his hand.

"And he's a patriot. I promise, he might be in trouble, but he's not a terrorist."

Trini nodded. "Okay, then. We need to find him."

"I know where we start," said the interpreter. She'd introduced herself earlier—Ina, he thought. "We start by finding my friend Sibba."

Really?

"How do we do that?"

"Let's ping her cell phone, for starters," Ina said, and turned her computer back around.

"Do you know Jonas's number?" Cruz asked, at their own ops computer.

Ned pulled out his phone and scrolled to the number. Read it out.

Cruz keyed it in and let the program run. The GPS tag pulled up about the same time Ina pulled up her tag of her friend's phone.

"They're west of here," she said, and turned the computer around again.

It matched the ping on Jonas's phone.

That was easy. Too easy, maybe, but he'd take it.

"Let's go get him," Trini said. "Cruz, grab the drone." He turned to the Slovenian team. "This is a fluid op. You stay behind us and do everything we tell you. We're on point."

The Slovenian team was led by a tall, dark-haired man with equally dark eyes. Ned had heard the naval team was fairly young, but this man seemed in his late thirties, so maybe he'd been on the Army side of spec ops. He said something in a low voice to Ina.

She nodded and turned to Trini. "Just remember that you're on Slovenian soil, Commander."

"Of course." He turned to his team. "Let's gear up—don't forget protective masks."

"I happen to know that your brother was already exposed to the caesium-137, but he wasn't infected," Ina said.

Hopefully Jonas knew better than to take that risk again.

The team dispersed to their gear, but Ned, however, walked into the kitchen. Dialed Fraser. Maybe he'd heard from Jonas.

And while he was at it, he could find Shae—

Except suddenly, finding Shae felt a little...overreacting. She was fine. And he had a brother to find. One who was definitely in trouble.

Fraser's phone didn't pick up, so he dialed the family line at the winery.

It went to voice machine. Oh, fine. "Hey, um, Fraser—tried to get ahold of you, but you didn't pick up. Hope you got Creed home okay. I just wanted to let you know that I think I tracked down Jonas, and there's a plan to extract him. And I think we found him in time. As long as he didn't get too close, you know? So, I guess we'll see. I just wanted to give you an update. Don't tell Mom and Dad—they have enough on their plate."

Marsh walked into the room, frowning at him.

He turned to the window.

"Maybe I wasn't supposed to say anything, but I don't have time to record another message...just...stay put. I'll call you if I need you, but for now, don't worry...I promise I'll find Jonas and bring him home."

The machine beeped—he was out of time.

Hopefully by the time Fraser picked this up, they'd already have Jonas in hand.

And then, maybe, he could tick off one box on his list of nightmares.

NINE

"**R**eady to save the world?"

Jonas had asked the question over two hours ago as they'd left her house in Cerkno, after dropping off his low-riding Panda rental and switching to her SUV for the drive.

She'd answered quickly, the words just falling out of her. "Let's—what did you say? Punch it."

"Now you're talking like a storm chaser," he'd said.

She'd laughed, but frankly, the closer they got to southern Croatia, the more her stomach tightened. It had taken them two hours to get back to Cerkno. She'd picked up her kit while Jonas petted Len, and then he received a text from someone in America.

He'd gotten on the phone then, and maybe woken someone up but had a not-quiet, pacing conversation outside where he used words like "can't wait" and "radiation poisoning" and then "hurry up."

Then he'd hung up and headed back inside, a grim look on his face.

She'd made them a couple sandwiches while he prowled around the kitchen, silent.

He'd finally explained the call when they got inside her SUV.

"My contact in America sent an agent to my lab in

Ljubljana—apparently, that's the address that Tarek sent them. Apparently, they are pretty hot that I'm not there. But I sent them the pin, so maybe they'll find us at the dirigible location."

She hoped they showed up armed, because their arsenal included a couple ham sandwiches and her kit, as well as a suit—because who knew but Jonas would want to follow her into danger.

Of *course* he would. Because the guy made a living of running *into* storms.

Which was almost as bad as her profession, so maybe they were actually right for each other.

And that thought had simply fallen through her, turned her silent.

Truth was, she'd never felt so in sync with someone as she had with Jonas, soaring over the mountains. He loved it like she did and...

And maybe that's why she'd made promises to him. Okay, not a promise, really, but she had agreed to teach him to paraglide.

Which meant *he* was planning on sticking around.

Oy.

He'd offered to drive, and she'd let him, trying to do some research on the kind of bomb that might have been attached to his dirigible. She studied the pictures on his phone and compared it to some of the bombs she'd dealt with.

What she didn't know was the trigger, although she guessed it might be—

"You're very quiet over there." He drove with one hand on the steering wheel, atop it, tapping his thumb as if also thinking. In fact, they might not have said a word to each other for the past thirty kilometers.

Which felt okay. Easy. Like he understood the weight of his earlier words.

She could appreciate a man who didn't have to fill all the silences.

"What if the trigger is an altimeter? It detonates as soon as the bomb reaches a certain height."

"Someone would have to control it, because the dirigible is designed to stay aloft." He nodded, however, as if letting that thought sink in. "That makes sense, because if they hacked the radio frequency and the RFID, then they would have the ability to direct it, even hover it above the city, or village or wherever they wanted to deploy the caesium-137."

"By the way, did you take your blue pill today?"

"I did, doc. And you?"

"Yep. Not bleeding from my eyes." But maybe her heart felt a little less heavy. As if he'd gotten inside it, started to dissolve the hard case around it. "So, what's your plan?"

"I programmed into the software a back door—another way to connect with Sally if the main FM radio receiver went down. It's on an AM frequency, which has greater range than FM, and I can initiate an automatic descent."

"And once it lands, I can disable the bomb."

"That's the hope."

"So, what's the rest of the plan? How are we going to find Sally?"

"I have her last known location. We'll track her down."

"And then what?"

He went silent. Looked at her. "That's all I got."

She stared at him. "That's all you've got?"

"I figured I'd—we'd figure it out as we went."

Silence as his words churned through her. "Jonas, I never figure it out as I go. I always have a plan. If I don't know exactly what kind of bomb I'm dealing with, if I don't know what the trigger type is, if I don't know how to reach the trigger and neutralize it then...then I don't go in. I..." She looked out the window. They were driving through villages, past farmhouses and fields, the country slowly giving way to forest. "You can't just live your life without a plan. Even if it's a..."

"One-meter plan?"

"Yes." She turned to him. "I might not want to look too far ahead, but the part I can see...I know what I'm doing."

"And if it doesn't work out the way you plan?"

She opened her mouth, closed it. Drew in a breath. "I..."

"You run. You hide. You blame yourself."

"Ouch. Maybe I should get out and walk from here."

He looked at her. "I didn't mean it that way. But you're the one who told me that Rokko's death was your fault."

"It was."

"No. It was because of the fire and circumstances and things way beyond your control."

She folded her arms over herself.

"The fact is, life is a storm. It's unpredictable and mistakes are made and you can try and control your one meter, but really, one day you simply wake up and your life has been ripped apart."

She stared at him, frowning. What—

"And then you stop wondering how to control it and just try and get past it. Or through it. Or...survive it."

"Jonas?"

He drew in a breath. "My grandpa, the one who loved storms, was killed by a tornado."

"Oh no."

He nodded, his mouth tight. "He was driving home from Florida for my graduation from high school and just happened to drive through a town in Missouri right about the time a storm hit it. He tried to get to cover with grandma—they hid in an underpass. Which I could have told him was a bad idea, but anyway...

"One minute he was there, the next he was flung from his car. Grandma was trapped in the car and had to wait two hours before help came. Grandpa was killed almost instantly."

"I'm so sorry."

"Thanks. It changed everything for me. Up until then, storms were fun to chase and a sort of thrill. I'll never forget standing by my dad at Grandpa's funeral. I don't know why, but I sort of felt like it was my fault. Of course it wasn't, but my dad must have figured that out, because he put his arm around me, and I'll never forget what he said."

She stayed silent.

"He quoted a verse from Isaiah. 'As the heavens are higher than the earth, so are my ways higher than your ways and my thoughts than your thoughts.' And then Dad said that God is in the storm. That though the winds blow and my life feels torn apart, if I can just trust Him, I'll discover Him at the center."

He tapped the brakes as they came into a village, the sun turning the red roofs to fire. "There's a story in Matthew about Jesus sleeping in a boat while a huge storm comes up. And the disciples are terrified, and they wake Him and say, 'Save us, we're going to drown.' And He responds by saying, 'You have such little faith!' And then He calmed the storm."

"I know this story. My grandfather told it to me."

"I always hated that story because I felt like Jesus got angry with them for being afraid. But what He was saying is 'I'm aware of you and your storms and your dangers, even when it feels like I'm "sleeping."'" He finger quoted the word with one hand. "I had thought that God simply blinked, or didn't care that my grandfather died. But my dad reminded me in fact, my grandfather had to be in exactly that place at that time for this to happen."

"So, God made it happen."

"Or allowed it, depending on your theology, but either way, He knew it would happen."

"And didn't stop it."

"Nope. Just like He doesn't stop a lot of storms, tragedies, and..." He looked at her. "Bombs that go off in our lives."

"He should."

"Maybe. But how many times do we discover that the storm saved us from something else, or made us stronger—"

"Or made no sense at all."

"Yes, there's that. To us, it makes no sense. But that's when we just have to stand. Believe that God is with us in the storm. Even if it feels like He's sleeping."

"I don't know. It feels like God should save us from tragedy."

"It does. Yes. From our perspective, always. But while I can't see past one meter, He can. And His purposes and thoughts are much greater than mine. So...I trust Him in the storm. In fact, I even run into them. And there, I expect to see Him already at the center."

He looked over at her, then switched hands and reached across the console to touch hers. "So no, I don't have a plan. I have faith, and hope and my meager skills. And you."

He squeezed her hand.

And probably she was crazy, but she squeezed it back.

She still preferred a plan, however.

They were coming into a larger town. She read the sign. "Ilirska Bistrica. It was a defense city during the Ten-Day War. They blocked the Yugoslavian army from reaching the interior of Slovenia."

"According to the GPS, we'll cut east after this town. No highways, so we'll just have to find a road that heads into the forest."

She pulled up her cell phone and widened the map. "There's a service road up ahead. It looks like it heads to a tiny village. Or maybe just a cluster of houses, but it leads up to Snežnik Mountain. Turn here and cross over the railroad tracks."

He turned left and onto a side street, and she directed him through a small neighborhood, a row of whitewashed townhomes with red clay roofs and tiny green yards. Two blocks later, they'd left the neighborhood, taking a half-paved road into the forest. He cut down his speed, and they wove into the hills, the old mine, and after a switchback, they came to the small community, a cluster of houses.

"Where now?"

"According to your GPS pin, we keep going." She pointed to a dirt road that continued past the houses.

He drove past the houses, onto the road.

"So, what happens if we simply drive into a party of Russians—"

"I'm very good at driving. I've mentioned that, right?" He slowed as they came to a large quarry, the pit deep all but abandoned. The quarry seemed almost a mile around, some one hundred meters deep, a barren wound in the land.

"The GPS is pinned here," she said as he came to a stop.

"It's not a bad place for a dirigible to go down." He pulled over and got out. Grabbed a pair of binoculars from his pack in the back seat. Then he stood behind his car and scanned the area. "There are fresh truck tracks up the hill."

He passed the glasses to Sibba.

"It looks like they disappear on down the service road." She handed him back the glasses.

"Let's go."

She got in. "I feel like I'm in an episode of *Strike Back*."

"What?"

"It's a British show—about this team of MI-5 types who follow trouble around the globe. They're always chasing bad guys..."

"Except they have guns and grenades, and we have..."

"Sandwiches."

He glanced at her as he pulled around the quarry. "They were good, too."

She grinned at him, perfectly on board with ignoring the possible danger they were driving into.

He went quiet as they rounded the quarry, however, and turned onto the road.

Ahead, maybe a hundred meters, she spotted the truck she'd seen outside the village parked in front of a large metal garage.

He did too, because suddenly he was pulling off the road and driving right into the forest.

"What are you doing?"

"Hiding."

Yes. Good.

He got out, the binoculars around his neck, and grabbed his backpack.

She reached for her kit.

"Leave it."

"What?"

"Here's the plan."

"Finally."

"It's not brilliant. But we sneak through the forest up to the shed. Take a look. If Sally is there, I try and connect with her and shut her down."

"Good enough for me. And if you can't?"

"Then...we get out of here and call the right people."

She looked at him. "Really? I thought I was here to shut it down."

"Yeah, I've been thinking about that." He stepped up to her. "It might have been an impulsive, desperate move to see you again."

Her mouth opened, closed. Oh.

Oh.

She grabbed her kit anyway. "Listen, if the Russians are in control of a dirty bomb, then I can't let them deploy it."

"Sibba—"

"No. You might have brought me because...well, whatever reason, but I came along because this is my job, Jonas."

He stilled, his mouth a grim line. "We'll see."

"What does that mean?"

But he just took her hand and pulled her into the forest.

Beech, spruce, and chestnut trees rose to clutter the canopy, but the ground was mostly old needles and scrub as they hiked through it. He finally dropped her hand and then motioned her to crouch as they came to a clearing.

The two trucks she'd seen were parked in front of a massive metal garage. Next to it were a couple outbuildings that looked like offices, populated with a handful of men.

The door to the garage hung open, and Jonas studied it a long time. "I see Sally, so they haven't launched her yet."

But just as he spoke, a man climbed into a truck and backed it up to the building.

They watched in silence—she could almost feel Jonas's horror—as the men loaded the dirigible onto the back of the truck.

"Can you send the kill signal?"

"I'll try."

He pulled out the radio transmitter from his pack. Turned it on. "She's not receiving. It's possible they replaced the entire system."

She put a hand on his arm. "Look."

They'd backed up another truck to the open space. Then even she went cold when another dirigible was loaded onto the second truck.

"Is that...what's her name?"

"Farah? No. It looks like a copycat."

"Which means they, what—stole your design?"

He looked at her, swallowed.

The man in the first truck drove to the edge of the parking lot and got out. Walked to the building, where he joined the other driver and the group of men.

They went inside, and Sibba got up.

"What are you doing?"

"If this is an altimeter fuze, it's a variation of a proximity fuze—my guess, after looking at your pictures, is that it operates on a GPS, correspondent to height. So, as long as it's on the ground, it isn't armed. I can defuse it without triggering the explosion. Which means I need to go now."

"Sibba—" Jonas hissed.

"It'll take me two minutes," she whispered back. She cut across the forest, her gaze on the truck.

But in her head, she was doing the math. As long as the Russians hadn't changed the electronics to detonate if she short-circuited the fuze, she could pull the fuze and be out of the truck in a minute.

She climbed aboard, the burn of Jonas's gaze on her neck.

Inside the truck, the darkness blinded her, but she felt around the dirigible and then lowered herself to the ground. Pulling her penlight from her kit, she shone it on the mechanism below.

Yes. A simple fuze, on the underside of the bomb, a diode no more than the size of her pinky finger, probably battery operated. She could use liquid nitrogen to freeze it, then pull it out.

Feeling around in her kit, she found her insulated bottle and pulled it out.

Voices.

She glanced out of the back, between the slits in the canvas cover, and spotted the driver headed back her direction.

Oh, Jonas was going to murder her.

Quick, quick—she sprayed the nitrogen on the fuse as the driver got into the cab.

Twenty seconds to freeze through, and she could pull it.

The truck started up, the engine running beneath her.

Hurry!

She pulled out her wrench to tug the fuse out.

The truck lurched into drive, and suddenly the dirigible wobbled.

Oy! She rolled toward the edge of the truck just as the massive balloon banged against the side.

She shuddered with the impact, but she wasn't hurt. Instead, it trapped her in the pocket of its arch, the bomb casing at the bottom now out of reach.

And then the truck bumped down the dirt road, away from the camp.

Away from Jonas.

And her, without a plan.

He wasn't a superhero, not a Navy SEAL like Fraser—or Ned, for that matter—but Sibba was in that truck.

Jonas didn't even have to think.

As soon as the driver walked past, heading for the driver's seat, Jonas took off for the truck.

Get out, Sibba! Get out!

In a second, the driver had fired up the engine, wrestled the gears into place, and with a cough, the truck lurched ahead.

Jonas turned and ran at an angle through the forest, toward the road.

It lumbered onto the drive, and the truck hit a rut, jerking the entire truck to one side. He heard something in the back slam, but maybe it was just the old shocks.

The rut did slow it down, just enough for Jonas to break through the forest, a step behind it, and leap for the back hatch.

His feet landed on the fender, his hands on the tailgate, and for a second he debated—stop the truck, or help Sibba—

Then he heaved himself over and rolled inside.

"Sibba," he hissed, but didn't see her. Instead, the dirigible had cocked to one side, the entire beast of a balloon leaning against the ribs of the truck. The truck jerked, and he fell against the side, grabbing a rib.

Spotted Sibba's feet.

Oh no—he knelt, grabbing them. "Hey—are you okay?"

"I'm trapped! I'm fine—there's room for me, but I can't move it off me."

He put his weight against it, but with the jerking of the truck, he couldn't dislodge it over the hump where the bomb—oh, perfect—lay wedged underneath it, trapping it on its side.

"I'm going to pull you out." He grabbed her feet, and she helped by wiggling her body, and even as the truck jolted along, Jonas was able to work her free.

She got to her knees, breathing hard, her hat gone, her hair free of her usual braid. "I tried to freeze the trigger, but the truck lurched before I could finish. It's not disabled."

"Let's see if we can get to it on the other side."

He scooted with her toward the assembly. The bomb had been attached to the bottom housing, next to the black box. "I don't see the container of caesium-137."

"It's probably inside the container." Sibba had crawled up beside him. "The problem is this—" She pointed to the end of the bomb, and specifically a housing in the tail fin. "That's the fuze."

"What is it?"

"A small diode that, when the altimeter reaches a certain height or distance to the ground, is released electronically and the connection to the trigger is made. It's battery operated, so I thought if I could freeze it, I could remove it, but the housing was crushed against it when the bomb fell. There's no way I can fully freeze it now."

He looked at her, and a beat passed. "You can't disarm it."

"No. Not like this."

"Will it arm itself when it reaches altitude?"

"Can it still fly?"

"Float, and..." He ran his hands over the balloon. "It seems to be intact. All it needs is helium."

"Can you release the gas? Keep it on the ground?"

"The skin is made out of Kevlar. No. It's not easily punctured."

"Try." She pulled a knife from her kit.

He looked at her. "Kevlar is stronger than steel. Your little pocketknife is not going to make a dent."

And right then, the truck jerked again, slamming them against the rail. Thankfully, Sally only shivered, not moving.

"Then what are we going to do, Mr. No Plan?"

"We have to stop this truck."

"How?"

"I'm going to take out the driver."

"You and Bravo team?"

The truck swerved.

"No. Just me. But I could use some help."

She lifted her little knife. "This is the extent of my combat skills."

"But you look pretty."

Then, and he had no idea why, he leaned forward and kissed her.

He meant it as something quick and—okay, he didn't know how he meant it, really. Just followed the urge to grab her by her jacket collar and touch his lips to hers and maybe, just for a second, tell her that—

What? He loved her?

Three days. He'd known her for three days.

But yeah, maybe. Because with everything inside, he knew she was the *more* he'd been looking for.

He leaned back, met her eyes.

"What was that for?"

"Not sure. I'll figure it out later. Now, I want you to go to the end of the truck and peek your beautiful face out of the back. Wave your arms. Get his attention."

"And what are you going to do?"

"Something stupid, probably."

"I am not a fan of your planning techniques."

"I know." Then he smiled and worked his way to the front of the truck, where the fabric met the ribs.

She, meanwhile, headed to the back. "When—"

"Now." Please, let this work.

Please, Igor, see the beautiful woman waving at you.

He climbed up onto the wall of the truck bed, peeled back the canvas, and worked his way out of the rib.

Sibba hung out of the back, shouting.

Attagirl.

But really, what. Was. He *doing?*

He crouched on the foot bed of the door, and before Igor could look his way—or maybe he already had, Jonas couldn't know—he flung the door open and swung inside.

"Shto!"

Jonas kicked the man in the face. The truck swerved, and he did it again, hard.

The man's nose erupted, and he howled, again swerving. They scrubbed the woods, and a branch slammed against the windshield.

Jonas kicked again, this time to the man's ear, and his head hit the passenger door.

Then Igor snarled and turned toward him, words littering out of his mouth.

Jonas was about to kick him again when the truck squealed, and Igor jerked the steering wheel hard. The truck swerved hard, bumped over the edge of the dirt road and into the forest.

They hit the tree head on. Jonas slammed into the dashboard, onto the floor as the windshield shattered around him, glass pinging on the driver's seat. Jonas covered his head.

The truck shuddered, and Jonas scrambled to his feet.

Igor was unconscious, blood streaming down his face.

Jonas practically fell out of the passenger side—"Sibba!"

"I'm fine!" She swung out of the truck. "I'm fine. And so is the dirigible!"

Shoot.

"C'mon." He grabbed her arm, then pulled her around to the driver's side. Opened the door and grabbed Igor. He yanked him out to the ground. Pressed fingers to his carotid artery. "He's alive."

He turned to Sibba. "Stay here."

Then he climbed into the driver's seat.

"What are you doing?"

"I'm going to destroy the dirigible."

She stepped back as he put the truck into reverse, gunned it. The wheels spat up loam, dirt, and mud, and Sibba stepped back. But the truck eased away from the damaged pine tree.

He opened the door. "Get your car!"

"What are you going to do?"

"Drive."

He gunned the truck down the road, the gears whining as he put it into second.

Ahead, the road turned and curved around the empty quarry. Which would make a perfect final resting place for the caesium-137.

At least this batch.

The truck had reached the rip-roaring speed of twenty-five, the radiator steaming, the front windshield dangling in massive, lethal pieces and blowing in the wind.

He glanced in the driver's mirror, but it had broken. The other, too.

Please, Sibba, stay safe.

He broke free of the klatch of forest. There, straight ahead, some fifty feet, the quarry opened up like a giant yawn, raw and broken and lethal if he didn't get out of the cab. He gunned it, then shoved the truck into neutral, hoping the momentum would take it.

Then he opened the door, stepped onto the running board, and waited.

Just in case.

But the truck kept moving, the momentum pulling it forward, and just before it reached the edge, he jumped.

Jerked.

He turned—his denim Vortex shirt was caught in the metal debris of the mirror strut.

Aw—but he had another shirt underneath.

He ripped the buttons of the denim shirt, slid out of the arms, and jumped.

Hit the ground and rolled.

The truck sailed over the edge.

He was climbing to his feet when he heard the vehicle slam into the ground. Ran to the edge.

It lay upside down like a bug, the dirigible certainly flattened, the wheels spinning.

Sorry, Sally.

Then he turned and ran down the road, back to their car. He'd sort of thought that Sibba might be behind him, coming up fast to pick him up, but as he drew closer—

The car was empty.

Still secluded in the forest.

A shout ripped through the forest, something in Slovenian, and he ran back to the road.

Stilled.

Sibba struggled with a man who had her around the throat.

"Hey!" He took off. No plan, just impulse—

Until the man raised a handgun, jerking her hard off her feet and shouting at him.

"Stop!"

Russian or not, he got that. And the part where the man motioned him down to his knees. Not that he had a lot of choice—two more men appeared, running down the road toward him.

He put up his hands, sank to his knees. "Let her go!"

It's what they said in the movies. But no one listened to him as the two men came up to him.

One landed a punch across his face. He tasted blood, even as he jerked back. He didn't even have a chance to rebound before the other kicked him in the gut.

Then he was wheezing and fighting for breath as they hauled him up.

And with everything inside him, he wished he'd chosen a different profession. One that had a little more oomph.

Especially when they shoved him against the truck—the one with the copycat dirigible—and slip-cuffed his hands behind his back.

Next to him, Sibba got the same treatment, grunting as they cuffed her.

"Leave her alone."

She met his eyes, anger in them along with something else.

Fear.

And that just undid him.

"It'll be okay," he said as they were dragged to the back of the truck. Then one of the men opened the gate and shoved her inside.

The other motioned for Jonas to join her.

He stepped on the tailgate, and the man pushed him in. He skidded to his knees on the deck. Then they shut the tailgate.

And there they sat, in the shadows, with the as-yet-unnamed dirigible.

And a bomb.

"I saw this ending differently," he said.

"In your plan."

"Maybe in my dreams."

She sighed. Looked at him. "Me too, Weatherman. Me too."

Then she leaned her head against his shoulder as the truck lurched forward.

TEN

"I'm sorry I got you into this."

The voice came from the semidarkness, soft beside her, and Sibba took her gaze off the slit of sunlight in the back of the truck and looked at Jonas.

He was beat up. His cheek bruised, and blood on his lip from his nose, which had stopped bleeding, finally. She didn't think it was broken, just bloodied.

Either way, "This isn't your fault."

"I followed you to the mountain."

"I ran after the bomb in the first truck."

"I should have just grabbed you and gotten into the car."

"You had to dispose of the bomb."

A sigh. "I don't know why I have to run into danger instead of running away. I mean, a smart person would have said, 'Hey, Jonas, run away and wait for the superheroes.' But no. I had to punch the core, and now here we are, in the hands of terrorists, about to be shot, or blown up, or if they are Russians, maybe sent to a gulag. I've never been to a gulag. Read about it. Solzhenitsyn. Not a great place, from what I read. But it could be better than being shot. Or blown up. Or exposed to another bath of nuclear waste—yeah, that's my favorite option."

She smiled despite herself and leaned her head on his shoulder. Wow, she liked him just being here, with her. Something solid and sure in the darkness. "I should have just run, but I saw you trying to get out of the truck and—" She drew in a breath. "It scared me."

"Scared me too. My shirt got stuck."

"I liked that shirt."

"Me too. It was my lucky shirt. Or maybe not so lucky." Another laugh. The sound of it cycled deep inside her.

Wow, she loved—

His laughter. His *laughter*. And wit, and sarcasm, and...yes, she loved those things about him. But she barely knew him.

She couldn't love him.

Although, seeing him struggle to get out of the truck had sort of rooted her to the spot, terror immobilizing her.

She hadn't been that afraid since—

"Sib. Are you okay? You're making funny noises. Are you crying?"

She lifted her head. "No." She didn't think so, or... "I don't know. I just..." She turned to look at him. "I don't know how to do this, Jonas."

"Do what?"

She considered him, his brown, now dirty hair, mussed, and his layer of whiskers, and how, with his hands behind his back, it only bunched up his shoulders, and he might be tied up, but he still seemed fierce and rugged, and she could, for a moment, feel the taste of him on her lips, right before he took off to dispose of the truck.

"Be with you."

"Be...with me? Like—"

"Like, past today. Past this moment. Tomorrow."

"And the day after—"

She sighed. "Yeah."

"Do you want that?"

A beat. "Yeah." Her voice emerged small, broken. "And that's what scares me the most."

"Aw, Sibba—"

"No, listen. See, I'm not lucky. I'm careful. If I was lucky, my parents would have survived, and my best friend Maja wouldn't have been blown up right in front of my eyes."

"She was?"

"We were ten and on a club trip to watch the Purples in Maribor."

"The Purples?"

"It's a futbol club. She and I played in the local club from Cerkno, and the coach brought some of the players out to watch the game. It was overnight, and we stayed at a hotel near a shopping center that was under construction."

She glanced out the back. Night had begun to fall, the shadows deepening along the dirt road. The truck groaned, jerking and fighting its way through the mountains.

Maybe she should jump out, run for help.

She looked back at Jonas. "The Purples won, and we got back to the hotel really late. Maya and I thought it would be fun to play in the parking lot under the bright lights, so we snuck down. We were kicking the ball around, and I accidentally kicked it past her. She went after it into the construction site."

A beat fell between them, and he didn't move. Just studied her face.

"The whole place exploded. Just—boom. I didn't know it, but that area was known for unexploded ordnances. It was bombed more than twenty-five times by the Allies in World War Two. I don't know how, but Maya walked right into one of those. I'm not sure if the ball armed it, or how, but...she was gone in a split second. I was standing near a building, or the explosion would have killed me too. As it was, I was alive, but seriously injured. I ended up in the hospital for a month. Scared my grandparents to death."

"I'll bet," he said softly. "And that's why you got into EOD."

"Mm-hmm." She drew up her knees. If she could get her hands in front of her, she could get out of these zip ties.

"And why anything beyond tomorrow..."

"No, Jonas. Anything beyond today. This moment."

"How about this moment?" Then he leaned forward and kissed her.

What?

And sure, he tasted wrecked, like the fight he'd been in, but she didn't care.

Not even a little. Because suddenly it all broke open, the terrible wall that she'd constructed in front of her heart, around her life, standing between herself and—well, everything. Hope. Faith. Joy.

A happy ending.

Jonas.

She might have made a sound with the tearing, might have even cried, but she leaned in and kissed him back with everything in her soul. Even let him deepen the kiss, although he couldn't put his arms around her.

Yes, she wanted every single tomorrow she could have with this man.

He leaned away, breathing hard, his eyes in hers. Shiny, even if she couldn't make out all the layers, the beautiful colors. "Sibba, I...I am—"

The truck lurched, and he nearly fell against her, caught himself. She looked out the back as it came to a stop.

Nothing but forest.

She leaned back, fighting to get her hands over her backside.

"What are you doing?"

"Getting free."

"Wait until we get out. It'll be easier." He lowered his voice now that the truck had stopped. The truck door closed. Footsteps.

"You do this a lot?"

"When Fraser was in quals for SEALs, every time he came

home, he'd teach us some cool tricks. Like getting out of zip ties, and breaking holds, and pressure points for pain—that wasn't fun. Anyway. Let's get outside. First chance we can, we'll run."

She wanted to ask about the bomb—hello—and maybe how they didn't want to leave that behind, but the back end opened, the canvas flipped back, and a torch shone on them, blinding her.

Squinting, she couldn't see the man who grabbed her and pulled her out of the truck. She barely got her feet under herself before she hit the ground.

Jonas was already out, on his feet. "Easy, buddy," he said to her captor, who jerked her up.

Probably she wouldn't translate the words he said to Jonas. Not that she understood Russian, but some of the words sounded the same. Like the curse word he'd just spat.

She stumbled over to Jonas.

"We're on a cliff," he said quietly.

"I see that." More than a cliff, they'd stopped on a bald spot above a small village, the lights just beginning to wink against the growing darkness. Maybe a handful of houses, all tucked in a valley between two pine-covered mountains.

"They're going to dose the town with the caesium-137," she said.

"My guess too." His gaze was fixed on the four men hauling out the dirigible from the truck. It wasn't as big as Jonas's, so maybe not as heavy, but she clearly made out the bomb affixed at the bottom.

"Where's the radio receiver?" She remembered seeing the black box on the bottom of his dirigible.

"I don't know. Inside the housing?"

"Stoy! Shut up." This from one of the men.

That she didn't have to translate.

The dirt road seemed to end here, at the top of the hill. The clearing itself was maybe ten meters by twenty meters wide, with dark, shaggy forest behind them and down the road. The sun had fallen, just enough remaining over the sea to the west. The air had cooled, and she shivered.

A buzz in the air, from the forest, sounded like the night closing in.

What had she been thinking, running after that truck—

"They'll have to carry the dirigible over to the cliff to launch it," Jonas said softly. "When they do, lean over and jerk your wrists down and out, hard. If it doesn't work the first time, try it again."

She nodded, almost imperceptibly.

"We'll take off into the forest. It's getting dark—they won't find us—"

"What about the bomb?"

Silence, and she glanced at him, even as the men finished pushing the dirigible to the edge of the truck.

He was watching them, something unreadable in his eyes. Anger, maybe. Or…

"You're not going to let them launch it, are you?"

He blew out a breath and then met her eyes. The look he gave her was almost pained. "I…I don't know what to do. I can't let them use my device to kill people. And yet…I can't drag you into…whatever happens. I can't live with that outcome."

Oh, Jonas. "I get it. I really do. But there are innocent people down there—"

"I know."

"You and I are both…well, this is what we do. I disarm bombs, and you certainly don't run away from danger, so…" She lifted a shoulder. Offered a smile. "If we were going to take it down… what would we do?"

"It won't arm if it can't leave the ground, right?"

"Yes."

"If you'll remember, the dirigible has an inner shell of metal that forms the frame. To get it to fly, they need helium. I saw four tanks in the back—my guess is that they're planning on filling it here. That could buy us time. If I could get to the tanks and somehow dispose of them—"

"What are you going to do—throw them over the cliff?"

He gave her a look. "I like that idea. What if the entire truck went over the cliff?"

"Not again."

"If it ain't broke—"

"Jonas, what if you can't get out this time?"

"I'll get out."

Right. "Couldn't they just push the dirigible over the cliff?"

"Sure. And it'll fall like a brick. It weighs nearly a hundred pounds."

It did look heavy, the way the men struggled with it. And she remembered being trapped.

"But on the way down, will it arm and explode?"

"I don't know."

Too many what-ifs.

"So, how do we do this?"

"I'll do this. You get free and get to the woods. Wait for me."

"Jonas—"

"For cryin' out loud, Sibba. I can't watch someone else I love die because of me!" He didn't yell it—it emerged more of a hiss—but it had the effect of a sledgehammer to her chest.

Love?

She couldn't breathe.

Love.

Yes.

She looked at him, nodded. "But you better make it out of that truck."

He winked.

Oh no. Just like on the mountaintop. She gave him a look.

"Now, Sibba. Get free!"

The men had moved around the front of the truck. She bent over and yanked her arms down and out—

It worked. What? She stood up.

Jonas was sprinting for the cab of the truck.

Run—*run*—

But her feet wouldn't move.

Jonas opened the door. Swung himself into the cab.

In a second, the truck had jerked into gear. Coughed.

She turned and fled to the darkening forest. It embraced her, the shaggy arms of the pine reaching out to hide her, and she fell into its grip. Turned to watch as Jonas gunned it—

The truck didn't move.

What?

It had gone a meter, maybe, before Jonas tumbled out onto the ground and the truck shuddered to a stop.

One of the Russians rounded the front of the truck, his handgun out.

Pointed it at Jonas.

No!

The shot punched the air, and she crumbled, unable to breathe as Jonas's body jerked.

Honestly, he just hoped he hadn't shot his brother. Ned exhaled, his shoulder hot after the recoil of his M4A1.

"Target down," Sonny said into comms.

Around him, voices lifted, but none of them belonged to his team, and Ned located his next target. Terrorist number two, with the wool hat, holding a handgun—

"I got him," Marsh said, and a second later, with a pop, the man left the earth.

"Sit tight," Trini said, and not for the fourth or fifth time, because he'd been saying that for the past two hours as they'd tracked Jonas's and Sibba's cell phone GPS signals through the Slovenian forests.

They'd had to leave their Slovenian spec ops-slash-babysitters behind when they'd crossed into Croatian territory. But according to Ina, and especially the agent that had shown up on the doorstep of their ultra-secret TOC—a woman named Ziggy with dark brown hair and a look in her eyes that said don't ask questions—they needed to stay hot on this target until it was neutralized.

They'd piled out of two SUVs a half klick away when the pin stopped moving, then hiked through the forest, blending into the shadows as their cover increased.

Ned had flicked on his NVGs when they reached the campout at the cliff.

Everything inside him turned to ice when he recognized Jonas, standing beside a woman, his hands behind his back.

That's when Ned got his first personal "sit tight."

The second happened when Jonas did a MacGyver—or a Fraser, because Ned remembered his big brother teaching them the get-out-of-flex-cuffs move years ago. He'd wanted to tackle him as he'd run for the truck.

Sit tight, Bull, Trini growled.

Ned had hunkered down, his body a knot when the woman ran into the forest, nearly into the embrace of Marsh, who hid nearby, trying to get a bead on the terrorists on the other side of the truck.

Sit tight!

And then Jonas had jumped in the truck, and all Ned could think was something crazy—like, he was going to run over the dirigible. Or maybe the terrorists—not a terrible idea, really. But what *was* terrible was where the truck would go after the assumed running over.

As in, space.

Nothing below it but a sheer drop according to Cruz, who ran the drone.

And yep, that's exactly what Jonas was going to do as he put the truck into gear. Big brother was taking out the bad guys.

His way.

Except—not. Because someone entered the cab, and Jonas came out and then—

"Take it." Trini voice, soft in Ned's ear, and he squeezed the trigger, head shot.

Boom.

But Jonas was down too.

A second ticked, another—he *hadn't* missed, Ned was sure of it. But maybe a ricochet that he hadn't seen—

Jonas rolled, and then to Ned's horror, got back into the truck.

C'mon, bro!

Another terrorist rolled out beside the truck, his gun aimed at Jonas.

Ned neutralized him, a neck shot. And now Jonas hit the brakes.

Because, aw, his girlfriend had come out, running for the truck.

"Go—go!"

He and Sonny deployed out of the woods, fanning out, and twenty feet away, Mac and Marsh did the same.

The woman had reached the cab, and Jonas opened the door. Caught her up.

And now Ned realized why Jonas had braked.

Headlights illuminated the last terrorist, who stood with his gun against the case of what looked like a missile.

Or a bomb.

"Stop!"

He glared at the headlights. A young man, skinny, unshaven, and desperate.

One shot.

"We want him alive, Mac."

Two clicks into the mic, affirmative. Then the shot, and the terrorist crumpled, screaming, holding his leg.

If Ned was to hazard a guess, broken tibia or fibula. Maybe both.

Ned ran forward, relieved the terrorist of his weapon while Sonny grabbed him by his shirt and pulled him away from the edge of the cliff. *And* the dirigible. A four-foot-high, six-foot-long zeppelin with a casing on the bottom. Impressive.

"Don't touch it!"

He turned and spotted who he assumed was Sibba Kovac headed toward him. In his eerie green light, he made her out as maybe five-seven, tawny-brown hair down. "Don't. Touch it."

He held up his hands and backed away. "Ma'am, you're the one who shouldn't touch it. It's—"

"I know what it is, Mr. Spec Ops, and you're the one who needs to listen to me."

He flipped up his NGVs. "I don't think so, ma'am."

"You better think so. That dirigible is armed with a dirty bomb, and the only person who can disarm it is this woman, right here."

Jonas. And in the dark light, he didn't recognize Ned, which, of course. Why would he?

Who would expect their brother to show up and tag the guy who was about to kill them? And that just made him smile.

"Really. And you are?"

Jonas's eyes narrowed. "Wait."

Ned grinned. "You'd be dead if I hadn't shown up."

"Ned?"

"Bro."

Jonas walked forward and yanked Ned into a one-armed hug. "Seriously." He stepped back, pounded him on the shoulder. "For a second there, I thought I was the one shot."

"You almost were. And then you get back in the truck? What were you thinking?"

Around them, Sonny had administered some first aid to the wounded terrorist, and Cruz landed the drone, capturing it and picking it up. Trini came up, his NVGs also flipped up.

"Sit rep."

He directed the question to...Sibba?

She raised an eyebrow.

"I know you work EOD for the Slovenian government."

"It's a civilian position."

"Now. But I also know you served for four years on secondment to the Royal Civil Engineers and four for the Slovenian Army, so you know what I'm asking."

She sighed. "Yes. Sir. What we know is that a fifty kilogram bomb went off just outside Poče, releasing a canister of caesium-137—we don't know how much. Thankfully, the storm that came through washed it into the ground and disseminated it into the air, and it was such a small amount that we managed to stay largely unaffected."

Ned glanced at Jonas during this, a part of him growing cold. What—

"How?" This from Marsh.

Jonas looked at him, blinked. "Ford?"

"Hey, couz."

"You two are on the same team?" He pointed to Ned, back to Ford.

"That rule is just for siblings, although, sheesh, it's like having a kid brother for all the trouble he gets into."

Ned looked at him. Ford grinned.

Although, in their kit, they did look like brothers.

"How what?" Jonas asked.

"How did they deploy it?"

"An altitude bomb," Sibba said and walked over to the dirigible. "Torch, please."

Ned slapped one into her hand. She got on the ground and examined the device on the bottom. "It looks intact. I think I can pull out the trigger."

"Maybe take the caesium-137 off first," Trini said.

She looked at him, then nodded. "Did you bring anything to put it in?"

"As a matter of fact..." He turned and motioned to Mac, who'd carried with him a container in his pack. "We were briefed by your friend Ina. She and the rest of the Slovenians had to stay at the boarder."

"We're in Croatia?"

"About three klicks in."

She nodded and turned to the bomb. "Okay, help me roll this over."

Jonas and Ned pushed the dirigible over, and she examined the bomb.

"This is the weather balloon you were jabbering on about in Geneva?" Ned said to Jonas.

"*Dirigible*. And I had six of these. I'm down to one, somewhere in northern Slovenia. This one is a replica of my original design. Although, I don't know how they got their hands on it." He drew in a breath. "Or maybe I do. They hacked my computer at my lab and pulled off the radio frequencies. So probably, they took everything else too."

"Like—"

"My designs, all the radiosonde information. And I don't know. Family pictures?" He smiled.

Ned didn't. "They know where we live?"

Jonas frowned. "I...maybe. But I don't think—they were after the dirigibles, Ned. I promise."

Ned's mouth made a tight line. "Perfect. First Shae, and now I have to worry about the family."

Jonas gave him a look. "What aren't you telling me?"

"Nothing. It's a long story."

"His fiancée broke up with him," Sonny said.

Ned looked at him. "Really? You couldn't have kept that to yourself?"

"It's your *brother*."

Jonas's gaze settled on him. "You and Shae broke up?"

Ned glanced down at Sibba. "Should we get back or something?"

She looked up. "As a matter of fact, yes. And I could use a screwdriver to open the casing."

Trini asked, and Marsh appeared with a small toolkit. She took it.

"Now you guys get back." She gestured with the tool.

"Why?" Jonas said.

"Because...I don't know. These guys didn't look like the brightest bulbs on the tree, and maybe they screwed up on the wiring, and one wrong move—"

"No way are you doing this," Jonas said.

Ned cocked his head at him.

"Yes," Trini said. "She is. We have no other EOD from Slovenia here, and to get the Croatians read in on this will take days and more red tape than I want to deal with." He turned to Sibba. "Can you do this?"

"Absolutely. I'll remove the caesium, then disarm the bomb." She looked at Jonas. "Okay?"

He folded his hands over his chest.

"It wasn't really a question."

"I know."

She sighed. Stood up. "Jonas. This is what I do."

His mouth tightened. Then he nodded.

"Now, go stand over there, and please don't follow me."

Her eyes met his, and her gaze didn't move.

Ned grabbed him by the arm. "Let's give the lady some room."

Jonas let Ned walk him back behind the truck while Mac delivered a lead-lined case to the edge of the perimeter.

Not far away, the terrorist, shot with morphine and slapped with a splint, his hands zip-tied, sat up watching the procedure.

"So, you and her—"

"Zip it, Ned."

Ned smiled.

"Unless you want to catch me up on you and Shae?"

Right.

Jonas's gaze softened. "Sorry."

He drew in a breath. "It's just a misunderstanding. I'll clear it up as soon as I see her again."

Sibba had removed the bottom of the bomb casing, and now removed the container. "I have the caesium."

Mac held the lead-lined container.

Yeah, Ned bet that had been fun to carry from the SUV a couple klicks.

"I'll bring it to you," Sibba said. She got up, turning away from the bomb.

And that's when Ned noticed that Jonas was looking *away* from Sibba.

At the Russian.

Who, despite his pain, his bonds, and his splint, had turned over, pulling himself into the fetal position.

What—

Jonas took off running for Sibba.

What! "Jonas, get back!" Ned ran out after him.

"It's armed! It's already armed!"

Jonas tackled her—

Ned took one more step.

And then the world lit up, fire and smoke and shrapnel and heat—

Jonas!

The world turned to black.

Buzzed.

Then the world turned gray and woozy as he opened his eyes.

He wasn't dead, he wasn't—because he could hear the shouting, the thunder of footsteps reverberating in his ears. But they came through as if he might be underwater, the sound muted, watery. His eyes burned, his face gritty.

He rolled over, tried to catch his breath.

Then, like a snap, the pain washed over him, the shouts vivid and bright.

Marsh was standing over him.

"You're okay, you're okay." Marsh ran his hands over him. "Don't move. You've got a piece of metal in your leg."

And now, yeah, Ned's leg started to burn, fire right through his calf.

"What happened?" His voice sounded far away, wounded.

"The bomb went off—the dirigible just—disintegrated." Marsh was working off his helmet. "Metal everywhere. Good thing you got out from behind the truck. The windshield is in a thousand pieces, right where you were standing."

And then he remembered—

"Jonas." He made to sit up, but Marsh pushed him back. He'd never known Ford well when they were growing up, his cousin about five years older than him. But he'd liked him. Thought he was cool.

Now, Ford looked downright dangerous. "Yeah. He's..." He glanced over his shoulder. "Trini is with him. And Mac."

Mac was their team medic, the guy who kept people alive until they could get to some help. Or tried to.

"Cruz is calling for an CASEVAC."

That bad...

"Don't you worry, buddy. We'll get you out of here."

"What about the caesium?"

He tracked Ford's gaze to Sibba. She stood, bloodied, broken, wide-eyed, clutching the lead canister. Intact.

"I think—I hope we're in the clear with that."

He searched again for Jonas.

"Eyes on me, Bull."

Aw.

"I'm packing your leg now, so this is going to hurt."

He closed his eyes.

It didn't matter. "Just don't let Jonas die."

"That's not up to me. But yeah, now might be a good time to start praying."

ELEVEN

If she closed her eyes, Sibba was still back on the cliff, watching one of the SEALs struggling to save Jonas's life.

How stupid could she be? Rookie mistake—to not check if the device was already armed.

To check the fuze.

To see if it might have been booby-trapped.

She'd been so focused on the caesium-137 she hadn't seen the bigger picture.

Hadn't seen the fuze brighten when she removed the lead casing, ticking down.

How Jonas had figured it out, she couldn't know. Just that in a second, he was there, tackling her. His body over hers.

Taking the hit of the bomb. A thousand shards of metal from the dirigible's interior exploding like an IED.

He'd moaned as they'd rolled him off her, and then she'd scrambled up, clutching the leaden caesium container to herself, forgetting for a long moment anything but Jonas.

So much blood. She should have been bathed in it, but he'd taken the brunt of the explosion in his legs and back, so really, just the back of her legs had caught his blood.

He passed out after they pulled him off her, and that's when she really got scared. Blood dripped from his mouth, so they'd had to clear his airway before they could administer oxygen, but with the injuries to his back, it got complicated. Metal shards from the skeleton of the dirigible impaled his body, big and small, the largest being lodged in his back, so terribly near his heart, his spine, his lungs that the medic SEAL—she heard him referred to as Mac—feared removing it.

So they'd sat him up and tilted his head back, and Mac somehow inserted an endocrine tube down his throat, got him breathing.

Then they put him on his side, rolling him onto a piece of canvas and securing him.

Sometime around then, one of the other men came up to her and relieved her of the radioactive waste, putting it into another lead container. That's when she noticed Jonas's brother (really? that craziness hadn't escaped her), but now the man writhed on the ground, a piece of jagged metal protruding from his leg too.

She noticed a woman nearby also, standing back, on the phone. Hopefully calling in help.

Jonas woke up then and started groaning, and Mac shot him with morphine. Sibba just held herself. Mac started shouting for more help then, and a couple more SEALs showed up, cutting off Jonas's shirt, packing gauze around the bigger shards, removing others, the wounds sealed with glue.

So. Much. Blood.

It seemed to embed her soul, even six hours later as she paced the lobby of the surgical wing of the Sigonella Air Base Hospital in Italy. She shivered in a pair of loaned scrubs, her feet bare, her hair wet.

The massive windows looked out on the rolling countryside of Sicily, where the sun was just rising, casting gold across the Air Force operations center in the distance, where US planes flew sorties into the Middle East and northern Africa.

And where the Black Hawks had landed after evacuating

them out of Croatia late last night. Or maybe early this morning—she'd lost track of time.

She'd had a little tussle with the big man in charge when the birds arrived, because sure, she had the caesium-137 and answers, but most of all, she wasn't letting Jonas out of her sight.

In the end, the fact that that they'd gotten her a pass onto the base at all was only because she had her own injuries. Just a couple of scrapes, but they'd run a concussion protocol on her and had stitched up a gash in her leg.

She ran her hands over her arms. Glanced at the man who was Jonas's cousin. He'd introduced himself after she'd been patched up, examined, and okayed for release.

Apparently, he was now her keeper. Ford Marshall. He wasn't particularly tall, maybe just over six foot, but he had a cowboy look to him with his tanned face, tawny whiskers, and blue eyes. Wide shoulders, lean body, he now wore a clean pair of BDU pants and a white T-shirt with his dog tags leaning out from his body as he braced his elbows on his knees, his gaze on her as she paced.

"He's going to be okay."

"You don't know that," she said. "And what about his brother, Ned?"

"He's already out of X-ray, being stitched up. The metal nicked the bone but didn't break it."

"And the impact—does he have a TBI?"

"No. No concussion. Just bruised."

"No internal bleeding? Because—"

Ford held up his hand and rose from the chair. "Listen. We're all okay. The radiation from the caesium-137 didn't leak—mostly because you protected it from the blast. And Ned is going to be fine—frankly, he needs some time off to sort out some personal issues, so this might be a blessing."

She blinked at him. "A blessing."

"I'm just saying that you don't know the bigger picture—and in Ned's case, this could be a good thing."

"It is never a good thing when a bomb goes off."

He drew in a breath. "No. But we often only see the fallout, not the long-term effect. You stand in the place of disaster and all you can see is...disaster."

She shook her head and walked to the window. "Jonas was there because I did something stupid."

Silence. Then, "My guess is that he wouldn't see it that way."

She closed her eyes. Given their conversation yesterday, maybe not.

Her hand found her lips, pressed, remembering Jonas's touch. *Please, God, don't let him die.*

The bubble prayer seemed at once out of place and like a long awaited ache relieved.

She opened her eyes, shook her head.

But Jonas was there anyway. *God is in the storm. Though the winds blow, and my life feels torn apart, if I can just trust Him, I'll discover Him at the center.*

It didn't feel like God was in the center.

It felt like He was asleep, in the bow of the boat.

Footsteps down the hallway turned her. But her hope fell when she spotted Ford's boss, Trini. He'd changed into clean green BDUs, his name on a patch, a trident pinned above it, a force of command and power.

She couldn't believe she'd stood up to him.

Now he gave her a smile as he came up to her. "How are you doing?"

"I'd be better knowing how Jonas was."

"All I know from the staff nurse is that he is out of surgery."

"Am I allowed to know if he's going to live?" Oh, she hated the tears that suddenly burned her eyes, but—

Trini put a big hand on her shoulder. "You were incredibly brave. And by the way that Jonas risked his life for you—yes, you're on the list of people who will be informed."

Oh. "Thank you."

"Has Ford finished getting your statement?"

She nodded. Mostly, he'd pushed record on his phone and she'd unspooled the entire story of the past three days, leaving out the paragliding, her grandfather, and the secret partisan hospital, but keeping in everything that she remembered about the men who'd chased her, as well as the location and set up of the warehouse where they'd found the dirigibles.

"What happened to Jonas's other dirigible?"

"The Slovenian Air Force shot it down." The answer came from a woman with long black hair pulled back in a sleek ponytail, wearing a pair of cargo pants and a black T-shirt. She looked Greek, or maybe Italian, with dusky skin and golden-brown eyes, and her accent suggested European too. She held two cups of coffee. One she handed to Sibba. "It's tea. I figured, you know, not American." She held out her hand to Sibba. "I'm Ziggy."

Sibba liked her. "You with the Navy?"

"No."

A beat. Oh. That's all she was getting. "Can you tell me what happened to Jonas's black box?"

"That was recovered." She didn't offer any more. And maybe the weather pattern information that the dirigible had collected didn't matter anyway.

Who cared about predictions when they had today's storm to contend with?

"Do you know where the caesium-137 came from?"

Ziggy glanced at Trini, then back to her. "We have some ideas. It's an ongoing investigation."

"Who were those Russians?"

"We're still interrogating the man we apprehended. But we think they're working for a rogue Bratva group."

"Isn't all Russian Bratva a rogue group?"

Ziggy smiled at this. "Point."

"I'd like to help."

"I think we'll probably take it from here," Trini said. "But we are grateful for everything you and Jonas did. As civilians, you put your lives out there for others. That's no small thing."

"It was Jonas. He was the one who said we had to find the bomb. Although, we were going to just contact someone he knew—" She looked at Ziggy. "You, maybe?"

Ziggy nodded. "My organization."

"Which is?"

Ziggy smiled. "Are you hungry?"

Oh. She sighed. "No. I just can't believe this is happening."

"Consider this. If you hadn't engaged and gotten caught, they would have deployed the dirigible into Croatia and dosed another village. And who knows what the fallout would have been."

For some reason, Jonas tiptoed into her head again. *As the heavens are higher than the earth, so are my ways higher than your ways and my thoughts than your thoughts.*

Maybe.

They all looked up when a couple doctors appeared, a man and a woman both wearing green scrubs, surgical caps. "Master Chief Terrell Baptiste?"

"That's me," said Trini.

"How is he?" Sibba said, stepping in.

"She's cleared for information," Trini said, nodding, his mouth a grim line.

"Lieutenant Commander Syme," said the female. "And this is my associate, Lieutenant Clifton."

The man nodded at them.

"So, most of the shrapnel were penetrating wounds—we were able to stitch those up. The one near his spine nicked his lung but managed to miss his aorta. A couple millimeters closer and..." She shook her head. "As it is, he had some internal bleeding and lost a lot of blood, but we were able to get a handle on it. He's back in his room, but not quite awake yet."

Silence, and Trini ran a hand across his face, Ford folded his arms together.

"Where's his room," Ziggy asked.

"It's down the hall, but the nurse will come and get you when he's awake. Until then, we're making plans to send him stateside."

Sibba stilled. "Stateside?"

"Yes. When we tested his blood, we discovered a trace amount of radioactive poisoning in his system. We want to send him to Mayo Clinic in Minnesota, make sure his system is clear while he recovers."

Yes, that sounded right. "Of course."

"The next twenty-four hours are the most critical." This from the Lt. Clifton. A younger man, blond hair, stocky. "He's lost a lot of blood, and he needs to start breathing on his own. And there's always the threat of septic shock after a puncture wound, so…"

"Thank you, Lieutenant Commander," Trini said.

Sibba watched the docs leave, their cloth-covered feet making *pfft* sounds against the linoleum.

"We'll arrange for a flight back to Slovenia," Trini said. "Unless you want to go with him to Mayo—"

"No." The answer came faster than she wanted. But she couldn't leave her grandfather. Still, it shook her how much she wanted to say yes.

To follow Jonas home. And into tomorrow.

She turned and walked again to the window, unwilling to elaborate.

Ziggy, however, came up beside her. Cradled her coffee cup in one hand and folded her arms. "Ina told me about your grandfather."

Sibba looked at her, tried to keep panic from her face.

"I know his farm was the site of the bombing. His soil is probably tainted."

Oh, that. Sibba nodded. She hadn't even thought of the fact that Dedi couldn't return to his farmhouse. Or at least, not to work the land. Maybe even drink the water.

"And"—Ziggy's voice dropped—"I know he's American."

This time Sibba stilled.

"I wasn't poking around—it was in your dossier I received after they sent me to Ljubljana."

They. The unnamed agency.

"I did a little more digging...I also know he can't return to America."

Sibba glanced over her shoulder, but Trini had left, and Ford was now on his phone, his back to them, across the hall.

"Would he like to?"

Sibba met Ziggy's eyes. "Is that possible?"

Ziggy considered her a moment. "Maybe."

Sibba drew in a breath. "I mean, without going to jail."

"I know what you meant. And...maybe."

Sibba's mouth tightened. She shook her head. "I can't take that chance. And...I can't leave him. He's all I have."

Ziggy cocked her head at her. "Is he? Because it didn't look that way on the mountaintop." Then she raised a cup to her and walked away.

But a partner, in love, walks the road with you. Helps to make sense out of the life we live. Gives it meaning.

Her eyes filled.

Not if she had to watch him die.

She turned around. Ford was still on his phone, Ziggy and Trini gone.

Sibba threw away the tea and headed down the hallway to Jonas's room.

HE DREAMED HE HEARD HER VOICE. THE SOFT ACCENT, the touch of her hand on his arm. *I don't know how to do this, Jonas.*

No, she said that before. In the truck, before the chaos. Before they'd tried to stop a bomb.

Before they'd failed.

Sibba!

His voice always shattered the cycle before he found himself again in the truck, her gaze on him. I *don't know how to do this, Jonas.*

Him either. But even as he'd sat there, listening to her, he knew he wanted to figure it out. *Would* figure it out. Which was why he'd kissed her. And that memory, too, lingered, the taste of her on his lips, the sense of time slowing.

Calm, in the middle of the storm.

Then it would end too soon, and the chaos rushed in—

"Sibba!"

In his head, it came out a scream. In reality, his own whisper wakened him, and he found his eyes opening into brightness.

Pain.

Every breath burned through him. He moaned, and the tenor of his own voice shook him.

"Mmm—"

"Hey. You're okay. Just take a breath." Ned appeared over him.

He lifted a cup of water from somewhere and now put it to Jonas's lips. "Take a sip."

It helped unglue his tongue from the top of his mouth.

"Feel better?" Ned was unshaven, a nick on his cheekbone, but otherwise his kid brother seemed unhurt. Although, not a kid anymore—something Jonas had noticed back in Geneva, but really, now, as he remembered—

"You killed someone."

Ned raised an eyebrow. "Um..."

"I mean—you saved my life."

"I tried to. And then you went and tried to lose it all over again."

He closed his eyes, leaning back into the pillow. "My chest hurts."

"Your lung collapsed on the ride over here, and then your heart stopped, so that was a fun thirty seconds."

Jonas opened his eyes and looked over at Ned, who'd sat back down. "Where is here?"

"You're in Italy. Sigonella Air Station. They have a hospital for the spec ops guys, and you got in by the skin of your teeth."

"I'm not spec ops."

"The way you practically jumped on a bomb to save someone—I don't know, Ford, what do you think? Honorary Frogman?"

Ned had looked across the bed, and now Jonas turned his head.

Yeah, he hadn't dreamed it. "Ford."

"Couz. You scared us all good." He reached out and thumped his shoulder. "Thought I was going to have to call Aunt Jenny and Uncle Garrett and tell them that their *least* favorite son had done something stupid—"

"Favorite."

"I dunno. At least Fraser and Ned are SEALs."

"I think Creed might be the favorite," Ned said, but he wore a smile.

Probably. Jonas leaned back into the pillow.

And then—wait. "Sibba." He looked at Ned. "Is she—did she—"

"She's fine. A few nicks and bruises, but yeah, last time I saw her, she was upright and maybe a little upset, but physically she was fine."

"Upset?"

Ned sighed, looked at Ford, back to him. "You don't remember?"

He gave him a look.

"Yeah, I didn't think so. I mean, you were pretty out of it, and we weren't sure you were going to make it through the night, so I thought that's why she was crying. But..." He made a face. "I think she was telling you goodbye."

I don't know how to do this, Jonas.

"What do you mean *goodbye*?"

"She left for Slovenia." Ford, his voice soft.

Jonas took a breath, groaned. Note to self...no breathing. "When?"

"Yesterday."

Aw, Sibba.

"Sorry." Ned said. "I don't know what went down between you two, but...for what it's worth, she was crying pretty hard when she left here."

Crying pretty hard.

Now the ache in his chest had nothing to do with his lungs. Because he got it. Oh, he got it.

"I was dying."

"Sort of. It was touch and go," Ford said.

"She's watched too many people she loves die." Now his throat burned. "And probably, me running into the bomb to save her life just...bottom line is, I get it."

Ned raised an eyebrow.

Yeah, it was just words.

Because, wow—he'd thought he meant something to her. More than something.

He thought she'd seen their today, and tomorrow, and everything all the way to the horizon.

At least, he had.

He closed his eyes and willed himself not to do something embarrassing like break into tears.

"You okay, Joe?"

"Yep." Which sounded not in the least okay. But he opened his eyes. "We only knew each other a couple days, so...you know."

Ned studied him, his eyes narrowing. "Right. Sure."

"So, she's back in Slovenia? Safe?"

"According to Ziggy," Ford said.

"Who?"

"The contact that—"

"Logan sent. Right."

Ned frowned. "Who's Logan?"

"He's a friend of Fraser's boss, Ham," Jonas said. "I called him for help after we found the caesium-137. I didn't know what else to do."

"Good call. Although I have to say, I nearly had a heart attack seeing your name on the BOLO list." Ned looked at Ford. "Our family is from Minnesota. We don't get involved in international plots and spy novels. And we don't chase down terrorists in the Russian mafia."

"That's who stole the caesium?" Jonas said.

Ned lifted a shoulder. "But it sounds like a good spy novel, right?"

Right. Probably his security level didn't go that high.

"Have you heard from Creed, by the way? Last I saw him, he was on the run with some princess."

Ned just looked at him. "How did you know that?"

"I saw Fraser in Lake Como. He was with her bodyguard."

A beat. "I take it back, Ford. Apparently, we are all about international plots and spy novels."

Ford laughed. "Please, let's not get started about family drama. And by the way, my fiancée, Scarlett, works for Hamilton Jones. I knew that Fraser was affiliated—he was on an op that Scarlett helped out with this summer. And Coco works for Logan, so, small world."

"I officially tap out of the spy game," Jonas said. He wanted to reach up to rub his chest, but his wrist hurt. Only then did he realize it was in a cast. "Did I break my wrist?"

"Probably when you landed. You must have braced your fall after you tackled her."

Yeah, maybe. He couldn't remember anything but—wait. "That Russian knew it was going down. As soon as she extracted the canister of caesium, he rolled over into a ball—he knew it was going to blow."

"I wondered how you figured it out," Ned said.

"If you hadn't, she would have been killed," Ford said. "Standing up like that—she would have been blown right off the mountain. And maybe the canister destroyed too." Ford nodded now. "So yeah, honorary Frogman." He smiled, folded his arms over his chest.

"No. I'm not the tip of the spear like you guys. I...was just in the right place, right time." He shook his head. "Too bad I'm the wrong guy."

"Right guy from where I'm sitting."

He looked over and a large man had come into the room.

Both Ned and Ford got up. "Chief."

"Master Chief Terrell Baptiste," he said. "But you can call me Trini." He stood at the foot of the bed. "Welcome back."

Jonas nodded. "Did you happened to track down my other dirigible?"

Trini nodded. "Sorry. It's...gone."

"Good. Then they can't use it to do any more damage. Although, they have my plans, so—"

"You just get better. We're on this. Although, Ned will be taking the trip home with you."

Jonas frowned. "Home?"

"Mayo. They just want to make sure you're all good."

"I think you should make sure they examine his head, get a full scan to see if there's anything inside there," Ford said. "Because who runs *toward* a bomb?"

Ned looked at Jonas. Smiled. "This guy."

Jonas shook his head. "Not anymore. I just want to get home."

And maybe figure out how to stop blowing up his life.

TWELVE

"Jonas, I'm not trying to be nitpicky, and Lord knows I love you, son, and you're a grown man, but the fact is, you probably need to wash that bathrobe, and along with it, yourself."

His mother, Jenny Marshall, slid a plate of pancakes across the island toward him. She wore a pair of jeans, a white shirt, her blonde hair pulled back with a headband. "It can wait until after breakfast, but not much longer if you still want to abide in this home."

He laughed. "Wow. Ultimatums much, Mom?" Jonas drew the plate to himself. But he smiled, because yeah, she was probably right.

Six days after arriving home—after a short stop over at Mayo Clinic—and he was just starting to feel like himself. Himself, with a few tender places inside. His lungs hurt less now to operate, though, and the terrible hole in his back had stopped screaming every time he moved. His arm, too, was on the mend.

It could simply be being at home, however. Back in his bedroom that overlooked the acres of harvested vines, the familiar creaks of the house at night, the aroma of his mother's cookies, a fire in the hearth in the great room. Nothing had changed in years, and he needed that more than he'd realized.

He reached for the syrup. "Give a guy a break. I did nearly die."

"So did Fraser, and Creed, but you don't see them lying around here in their pajamas." She set a plate down in front of Creed, who was still sore after being shot. Jonas had a hard time getting *that* into his brain. Or the fact that their home had been attacked.

And that Fraser had nearly lost his hand in the fight. So yes, his mother might sound like she was teasing, but he knew there was probably a place inside her that was still shaking. At least Iris had called her to check in. Still on the road in Europe reffing for the European League of Football, but apparently she hadn't come across any Bratva thugs that wanted to kill her, so that was a win.

"I think a pair of track pants counts as pajamas," Jonas said, gesturing to Creed.

"I showered," Creed said, pulling the plate to himself. "Thanks, Mom." He took the syrup from Jonas. His brother had put on a little weight since Jonas had seen him only a few weeks ago in Switzerland. And he hadn't shaved. Look at that, the guy was growing a real beard. He hadn't really seen Creed as an adult. More the kid his parents had taken in and adopted. And yes, he liked Creed—saw him as a brother. But he'd always been, well, a kid.

And then he went and rescued a princess after she witnessed a murder in Switzerland. In fact, his entire story of his escape from Europe seemed like something out of a thriller.

He glanced at Creed now. "You only showered because you have a cute girl living here that you have a wicked cr—"

"Hi, Imani," his mother said as she looked past Jonas and Creed to the girl coming down the stairs. Jonas glanced over his shoulder, saw her smile at Creed.

The fact that he'd brought the princess home was pretty

significant proof of his crazy story. Her *and* her bodyguard, the proper Englishwoman named Pippa Butler that he'd met in Italy.

Look at that. Apparently big brother had listened to his advice. Or maybe God just intervened despite Fraser's hard head. Whatever—he was glad to see her, even if she'd corrected him twice the first day he arrived when he'd addressed Imani as…well, Imani.

Instead of Her Royal Highness Princess Imani of the House of Blue.

Whatever. Imani had finally stepped in and told him to call her *Imani*. Pretty girl, dusky skin, black hair, golden-brown eyes. Creed had it for her bad, the way his eyes lit up around her.

Jonas was trying to forget how that felt, to feel his entire body light up when Sibba walked into the room. But the fact that Sibba had just…walked away…

He was starting to breathe through that too.

A little.

Okay, not really. He couldn't get his mind off her smile, her laughter. Her attempts at humor.

The soft noises she made when he kissed her.

"Pancakes, Fraser?" Their mother turned back to the griddle on the stove.

Jonas hadn't heard his brother emerge from the study, aka, security central. Because of Imani—and the threat still out there—Fraser had turned the Marshall Fields Winery into a sort of compound, complete with cameras and proximity alarms and bright lights around the perimeter of the house that probably could be seen from space.

"Sounds good, Ma," Fraser said and sat down on one of the other stools. Fraser wore an intricate cast on his arm, and apparently, was regaining some feeling in his hand after the high-tech surgery he'd received.

Still, Fraser, Jonas, and Creed were a sorry trio, all three of them wearing casts. Three bumblers trying to cut their pancakes.

Oops, not Fraser, because Pippa—who seemed to have taken

that leap to more between her and Fraser, the way they smiled at each other and stayed up late talking, or even sitting pretty close on the sofa—came up and cut his pancakes for him.

And Fraser didn't even stop her. So, what was *that* about? He even grinned at Jonas, winked.

Okay, he was a little jealous, he could admit it.

It didn't help that Jonas sort of reverted back to his teenage self when he returned home, that old rivalry between him and Fraser sparking—who got the bigger pancakes, who got out of mowing the lawn or cleaning out the winery.

Apparently not Ned, who was right now outside with his dad, driving the flatbed in from the back forty, hauling in pumpkins for sale.

Of course, Ned was the only one with two working hands, although he did have a wicked bandage on his leg. The Navy had granted him some well-earned PTO, and he'd happily jumped on the plane with Jonas for the trip stateside.

Although, according to last night's moment when he'd nearly thrown his phone across the room, Shae still wasn't taking his calls.

Which felt weird to Jonas. He liked Shae. And any woman who followed her SEAL boyfriend from one training assignment to another felt like a woman who might pick up the phone to sort things out.

So maybe Jonas was a little worried too.

Jonas slipped off the stool in the kitchen and walked over to the coffee pot.

He liked having his mom at the helm. He leaned over and gave her a kiss. She smiled. Patted his cheek. "I like having all my boys home." She kissed him back. "Although I would prefer them all in one piece."

He hadn't told his parents the whole story of the bombing in Slovenia—no need to scare them. But Fraser knew, thanks to Ned, and they'd had a sort of powwow in Fraser's room last night, where Fraser quizzed Jonas on everything that had happened since he'd last seen him in Italy.

Before his world imploded.

"So, you think this Petrov group"—Fraser had looked at Ned when he said it—"stole the caesium-137, along with the plutonium, in Geneva, and then used the caesium-137 to set off a dirty bomb in Slovenia."

Ned had probably given away a few high-security-clearance secrets, but Fraser seemed to know at least part of the story, thanks to Creed's adventure.

"Why Slovenia?" Fraser said.

"Maybe it wasn't about Slovenia as much as that's where your dirigibles were," Ned said. "Maybe that was the connection. Did you post any articles on the web about it?"

Oh... "Yes. I was trying to keep the Vortex.com blog going, so I put up some early pictures of my prototype last summer. That's how I got my grant."

"Why did *you* choose Slovenia?" Ned asked.

"I first started in northern Italy—they have the most lightning strikes anywhere in Europe. And then I followed the storms to Slovenia. They have the most intense storms of all of Europe."

"Still chasing storms." Fraser sat on his bed, leaning back against his headboard. It felt so incongruent to see his huge body on the thin twin bed, but he guessed that Fraser had slept in worse places.

Like in captivity in Nigeria. To Jonas's eye, Fraser looked calmer, more at peace than he'd been in Italy. Something had settled in Fraser's soul, maybe.

"No. I'm done chasing storms," Jonas had said. He sat backward in the desk chair. "It gets people killed."

Silence, and then Fraser gave a tight lipped nod. "But your research saves lives."

"And you love storms," Ned said softly. "For as long as I've known you, you've been drawn to the chaos."

"I was drawn to the power. And driven to try and understand

them. And yes, they are weather patterns, logical, with cause and effect. But maybe I've been blind to the dangers."

Silence, a pulse of understanding, maybe, from his brothers.

Then, from Fraser, "I'm sorry I wasn't here after your accident."

"You were deployed. I get it." He looked at Ned. "I didn't expect either of you to rush home because I had a car accident."

"You nearly died. And your friend—"

"Geena."

"Yeah. I can't imagine lying there, listening to her suffer."

His jaw tightened. "Yeah. A lot of praying that night." In fact, he'd sort of felt like someone—an angel, or Jesus Himself—had been there, keeping them both alive.

Weird. He'd never shared that with anyone. Then, "I think there is something to the idea that suffering reveals who you really are. And what you really believe."

Fraser had nodded then, his eyes holding a depth to them as he met Jonas's.

"How is Geena?" Ned said.

"I don't know. Nixon came to visit me in Slovenia about a month ago. He says she'll walk again, but...who knows."

His throat tightened then, and he looked away. Truth was, he should have checked on her when he returned to Minneapolis, even in his sorry state.

"You blame yourself," Fraser said softly.

"Who else is there?" Jonas looked at him, and Fraser didn't flinch at his tone.

"Um...life? Circumstances?"

"I made a mistake. I misread the storm—"

"Sheesh, Joe. You're not God." Ned was holding up a wall with his shoulder.

Jonas looked at him.

"I agree with Ned. How could you know?" Fraser sat up, his feet off the bed. "At some point you just have to follow your instincts." He put a fist to his chest. "The ones God gave you."

"And if those instincts get people hurt?"

Fraser shook his head. "I agree with Ned. You're not God. You can't predict every path a storm is going to take."

"Listen, I know that. I just can't—"

"Forgive yourself."

Jonas looked up at Fraser.

"I get it. You don't know how many times over the past four months I've rewritten the op in Nigeria in my head. I finally had to come to the fact that it played out the way it played out and I can't change that. But I can forgive myself for screwing up. And I can also believe that God hasn't abandoned me just because my life blew up. Feelings aren't facts. The truth is that God loves me. And is up to something good in my life. Something you pointed out to me just a few weeks ago, bro."

Right. That shadowy night in his sister's flat in Lake Como flickered in his mind. He'd said something similar to Fraser. "It's a little easier to remember that when you're not in a cast."

"With a hole in your lungs?" Fraser said nodding. "Yep."

Jonas ran a hand behind his head. "I just can't help but feel that maybe I could be less...reckless."

"Jonas. You're the least reckless person I know," Fraser said.

"Um," Ned interjected, "I'm just going to say that a guy doesn't throw himself in front of a bomb without being reckless—"

"That wasn't reckless. That was courage. It's nothing less than you or I would do."

Oh. Jonas looked at Fraser. His big brother met him with a smile. "But it was crazy."

"Or love?" Ned glanced at Jonas.

Jonas lifted a shoulder, looked away.

"Have you heard from her?" Fraser asked.

"No. And I don't expect to."

Silence.

"Maybe you should—"

"Nope." Because in his head, he kept hearing *Please don't follow me.* So, no. "I don't want to bring her any more trouble."

"Seems to me like she's a woman who doesn't flinch at trouble," Ned said.

He considered Ned, who shrugged. Then, "No. But she walked away for a reason. And that reason was me. And the fact that I nearly got us both killed."

"You can't live in the regrets," Fraser said. "It's unproductive and keeps you in the past. You need to focus on the now."

"Except, I don't know what now looks like," Jonas said. "I have nothing left. Vortex.com is shut down and my grant has been canceled, and it seems like my prototype is going to get people killed—" His mind briefly went to Tarek. He stared at his cast. "I don't know what to do from here."

"Maybe you're not supposed to do anything right now." The voice came from the doorway. He hadn't seen his father, Garrett, come in.

"Sorry to intrude. I was headed to bed and couldn't help but overhear. But I'm going to throw in the dad card here and say this to all of you." He took a breath. "Sometimes, all you're called to do is stand."

"Stand?" Fraser said.

"Yep. Be. Believe. Hold on. *Stand.* Our best hope in the middle of confusion and chaos is not to try and solve our problems ourselves but to simply remember whose we are and who we hope in. You stay rooted in the middle of a storm—darkness, confusion, chaos—by putting your focus on the One who is stronger than the storm."

Silence.

"It doesn't mean you stop fighting. But maybe your fight is to simply trust." He put his hand on Jonas's shoulder. "We taught you boys—and Iris—to meet your problems head on and not close your eyes to trouble, and looking at you, maybe we taught you too well."

He gave Jonas's shoulder a squeeze. "Just make sure that you fight the battle God has given you, and not one of your own making."

His father's words had lingered with Jonas all night, and even now, as he finished filling his coffee and headed back to his pancakes.

A battle of his own making.

Outside, Ned had finishing hauling the flatbed of pumpkins and now came in the back door. He stripped off his jacket, stepped out of his boots, but still wore his hat as he limped over to the counter.

"Pancakes, Ned?" his mother asked.

"Nope." He set his phone down, and the expression on his face made even Creed put down his fork.

"What?"

"I asked Ford to stop by Shae's place in San Diego." He pulled off his hat, set it on the counter. "I know it was a little desperate, but the next step was me getting on a plane, so..." He set both hands on the counter, as if steadying himself.

Jonas didn't know why a fist formed in his gut. But seeing his brother's expression...

"She wasn't there. Hasn't been there, given the mail piled up in her box. The house is dark."

It took a second, and it was his mother who seemed to put the math together. "Are you saying that she hasn't returned from Europe yet?"

"I don't know. I called her uncle in Montana—sometimes she goes there. But it went to voice mail." His mouth tightened. "I don't know what to do."

"Well, son, if you think she's in trouble, you go find her."

The way his mother said it, it sounded so simple. Easy.

And right.

He nodded. "I think maybe I'm going to grab a flight to Montana. See if she's out there. Ask her uncle." He pocketed his phone. "Thing is, I have this crazy gut sense that she never left

Europe. That...maybe something happened to her after she left me at the hotel."

"She left you?" This from his mom.

"We got in a fight," he said. "Misunderstanding. Or...I don't know. I said some stupid things."

"You?" said his mom. But she walked over to him. "Listen. I know Shae loves you. And I'm sure you'll work it out. I've learned that in a fight, I need to ignore about fifty percent of what I'm feeling, about twenty percent of what I think I hear, and go with what I know. What the truth is. Otherwise, we get caught up in the destruction of the fight, and we end up much more wounded than we need to be."

She put her arm around Ned's shoulders. "He will keep in perfect peace he whose mind is stayed on Him, because he trusts in Him. That's where you should go when your thoughts lead you to panic. God *will* give you your next steps."

Giving his shoulder a squeeze, she then glanced at Jonas, then Fraser, and raised an eyebrow.

So maybe Dad had briefed her last night after he came into the room.

"Want me to ask Ham if Coco can pull footage from the hotel?" Fraser asked.

"Yeah, Ford mentioned his foster sister. I thought she was in Russia," Jonas said.

"She returned a couple years ago armed with some serious hacking skills. But she might be able to pull up CCTV, if they have any. Give me the details of the day and time and I'll text him."

Ned picked up his phone, headed over to the living room, and sat on one of the worn leather sofas.

But Jonas was back in last night's conversation. *Forgive yourself.*

Yeah, that would start with someone else.

He pushed off his stool, picked up his plate, and brought it to the sink. Rinsed it and put the plate in the dishwasher. Then he picked up his coffee.

"Where are you going?" his mother said.

"To get a shower." He finished his coffee and set the mug in the dishwasher. "And then I'm going to stop being a wuss."

"About time," Fraser said. "I've been waiting for that for twenty-eight years."

RUNNING SEEMED LIKE THE ONLY LOGICAL THING to do.

Besides, Sibba had to get out of the house, air her brain out. Stop reliving the moment when Jonas saved her life.

No, the moment when she destroyed his by walking away.

What. A. Jerk.

The wind snaked down from the mountains, through the wet streets of Cerkno where her feet slapped against pavement, her breaths forming in the air in front of her. She wore mittens and a hat, but just a lightweight pullover and running leggings, and still the sweat streamed off her.

Just keep running. And maybe she wouldn't hear the way he made that low rumble in his throat when he was thinking. Or see the flash in his blue eyes when she verbally sparred with him. Or his smile when he thought she was funny.

She wasn't funny.

She was stupid. What kind of person walked out on the man who saved her life?

The person who feared he'd someday lose it running after her again, thank you.

She had run through town, all the way out to the ski hill, some seven kilometers west. They were gearing up for the season, checking seats on the two six-seater lifts. She stood for a long moment in the parking lot, her hands on her hips, breathing hard, watching the clouds, the thermals. She loved skiing—right after paragliding.

No, what she loved was speed, the wind in her ears, the sense of being fully alive.

"I don't know how to do this, Jonas."

"Do what?"

"Be with you. Past today. Past this moment. Tomorrow."

"Do you want that?"

Yes. Yes, she did.

Or at least she'd thought so.

And then the jerk had nearly died saving her life—

Aw. She wiped her eyes—stupid wind. Drew in a breath and took off for home, the familiar slap of her feet drilling into her, setting a rhythm.

This was her life. One step at a time, one moment at a time. She didn't need more.

Whatever.

The sun had already broken in the east, was starting to dry the streets from last night's thunderstorm. It had only made her think of Jonas, of course.

She had to get the man out of her head. Three days, and he'd made such a place inside her soul she'd probably bear scars for a while.

But alone was better than...

She shook away the thought and turned up her street.

Slowed.

A car sat in her driveway to the townhouse. A rental, late-model Panda, and...her breath caught.

What?

Her breaths quickened, and everything turned hot.

What was—

She sped up, took the stairs two at a time, then hit her door, every cell sparking.

A woman stood in the family room talking to her grandfather, and as Sibba entered, her breaths betrayed her.

Along with, she supposed, the shock on her face. "Ziggy?"

The spy—or whatever she was—wore a puffy black jacket, a pair of green cargo pants, running boots, her hair pulled back, shiny and dark, and now turned to her with a smile. "Hey, Sibba. How are you?"

She almost looked around for Jonas and wondered if they could see the explosion through her, the sudden whoosh of darkness.

She was a fool. The man was not going to come after her. Not in his condition.

Not after she'd probably broken his heart.

Besides, he wasn't a fool. Her life hadn't changed. She still disposed of bombs for a living. Still lived in a tiny, one-meter box in her mind.

Okay, now the box had pretty big peep holes, but still— "I'm good. How are you?" She pulled off her mittens and put them on the table. "What's going on?"

Her grandfather turned to her. "Sit down, Sibba."

She started to walk toward the family room, and then slowed.

Wait. Ziggy held a package in her hands.

Sibba pressed her hand to her gut, remembering Ziggy's words at the hospital. *"I did a little more digging...I know he can't return to America."* Did...Ziggy hadn't done something to get her grandfather in trouble with the US, had she?

"What's going on?" She stood next to her grandfather.

Ziggy still wore that smile on her face. "I was in the middle of asking your grandfather if he'd like to go home."

Sibba placed a hand on his arm. "You know what that means. Don't joke like that."

"What if it didn't mean...what you thought?"

Sibba reached into the bag and pulled out shiny blue passports.

Sibba looked at them, then at Dedi.

"I'm not going to lie to my government about who I am," he said quietly. "So if those are an assumed—"

"Nothing of the sort," Ziggy said. Then she turned to Sibba. "Did you know your grandfather was nominated for a Medal of Honor during his service in Vietnam?"

She looked at him. "No. He left that part out."

"I didn't deserve a medal. And"—he looked at Ziggy—"I ran, if you remember."

"Here's how the story goes, Sibba," Ziggy said. "Your grandfather was a corpsman during the war." She looked at Dedi, her face solemn. "Which meant he ran into danger to save lives."

Her grandfather's expression remained still, save for the tightening of his lips.

"On April twenty-third, 1968, he was attending to two marines who were injured, trying to get them to a chopper for casualty evacuation when his rifle company was attacked by a unit of North Vietnamese Army. He not only evacuated those marines to the chopper but returned to aid other wounded marines."

"It was my job."

Ziggy held up a hand. "While he was attending to the wounded, a grenade landed near them."

Sibba stilled.

"He covered the grenade with his body to shield the wounded marines."

She stared at her grandfather.

"It was...impulse. Not bravery."

"It was bravery," Ziggy said. "And just because the grenade didn't go off doesn't mean it wasn't completely, absolutely heroic. And yes, maybe an impulsive move, but you could have jumped the other direction."

She turned to Sibba. "When he realized it hadn't exploded, he scooped it up and threw it away."

"It exploded," Dedi said quietly.

"Yes. And you were injured. But you'd saved the lives of those marines, and they didn't forget it. I have testimonies here of six marines whose lives you saved that day. One of those was a nineteen-year-old kid who just happens to be a US senator today, sir."

She pulled a piece of paper from the envelope. "And this, Hospital Corpsman Second Class, is a pardon from the president of the United States."

Silence, and in it, she saw her grandfather swallow, blink. Then, "What?"

"I asked my friend Logan Thorne to investigate it, and he found the Medal of Honor application and the details, along with the charge of desertion. He brought it to the president, who conferred with Senator Long as well as the judge advocate general of the Navy." She shook her head. "Unfortunately, the charges of desertion, since it was in the time of war, still stand. And you were convicted and sentenced, in absentia."

"Dedi—you can't go back to America—"

"But"—Ziggy held up her hand—"this allowed the president to take into account your valorous service, and in lieu of a medal... he has granted you a pardon." She handed over the passport. "And requested that you be issued a new passport, one that you can use to return to your homeland, if you wish."

Her grandfather took the passport and opened it. Ran his thumb over the picture. Closed his eyes.

Sibba's throat tightened, tears pooling. Then Ziggy handed her a passport. "Apparently, your father applied for a social security number for you when you were born."

Inside was a photo taken from her time in service in the Slovenian government.

She looked up at Ziggy, then at Dedi. "I...I don't know what... do you want to go back to America?"

He turned to her and put a hand on her shoulder. "I think it's time to stop running away and start thinking about what we're running to." He raised an eyebrow.

Oh, Dedi. She sighed. "I have nothing to run to."

"You have everything to run to," he said as he pulled her against himself. "You just need to open your eyes and see it."

THIRTEEN

After his time in Mayo Clinic, the smell of the hospital didn't feel quite so repugnant.

In fact, the Courage Kenny long-term rehab facility smelled of autumn spices—cinnamon, ginger, cloves—and Kenny G's easy sax played over the hidden speakers as Jonas got a pass from the reception desk.

Girded himself with a deep breath.

He hoped he wasn't making things worse—but frankly, maybe it was already as bad as it could be.

"You can't live in the regrets. It's unproductive and keeps you in the past. You need to focus on the now."

Fraser's words, but he was probably right.

Sometimes, the tinny taste of blood, the freezing rain, the roar of the tornado could make him curl into a ball. And he had the luxury of waking up and walking away.

He passed by rehabilitation rooms, with weight machines and tables and exercise balls and mats, to other rooms with recumbent bikes and stairs. Passed a person with a walker, in her early twenties, maybe, shuffling to the encouragement of a couple physical therapists.

She grunted as she moved the walker.

He nearly turned around.

But kept going and found the room at the end of the hallway. A bank of windows overlooked the gray sky—a storm hung in the nippy breeze. The trees were almost naked, and it wouldn't be long before the world would turn white.

In the room, a number of patients in workout clothing were strapped to machines, their physical therapists helping them maneuver.

He'd done his research, back when Nixon was giving him updates on the rehab devices—on the Lokomat, which helped people walk on a treadmill, and Ekso GT, a bionic suit that helped people walk.

He spotted Geena strapped into a Vector Gait, a ceiling-mounted dynamic body weight harness that helped support her weight as she walked. She wore a sports bra with a sleeveless Vortex.com T-shirt that revealed all her tribal tats. She wore a bandanna around her head like Rambo, and the cool dreads she'd started a year ago had been shaven, but her hair had come back short and silky brown.

Two physical therapists sat beside her, moving her legs. Nixon stood in front of her, holding her hands.

Jonas stood at the door, an anvil on his chest.

Jonas, don't let me die. Please—don't let me die. Her last words before she had passed out, before the brain trauma started to steal her away. Now, to see her upright, even smiling... Tears filled his eyes.

And still, he couldn't move.

He should leave. Now. Because—

"Jonas!"

Aw. She'd spotted him.

"C'mere!"

He started over even as Nixon turned, nodded at him, something in his brown eyes. Maybe respect.

He didn't deserve that.

"Wanna race?" Geena said, then laughed. Her speech was still a little slow, but clearly the accident hadn't stolen her spunk.

Nixon, too, laughed, and Jonas had nothing. This wasn't...funny.

"No."

"Aw, boss, you gotta calm down." She was sweating despite her humor, struggling for each step. Now, she stopped. Looked at her PTs. "Lemme go."

One man, one woman, and they both removed their hands.

Geena let go of Nixon.

And then she simply stood. Right there, on her own, for a full twenty seconds.

His heart hammered out every single second. Finally, "Wow."

She reached out again for Nixon, breathing hard. But looked at Jonas. "Tomorrow, I'll be dancing. You'll see." She winked.

With it, something released inside him. He lowered his head, cupped his hand over his forehead, and started to sob.

Shoot, but he just couldn't move. Couldn't stop—

"Oh. Um. Uh. Guys, get me out of this thing," Geena said.

"I'm sorry—" Ah, see, he was making it worse.

Nixon's hands landed on his shoulders. Then before he could step back, or maybe run away, Nixon pulled him tight to himself.

And Nixon was a big guy. His huge arms locked around Jonas's back.

Jonas ducked his head. Pressed his hands over his face. "Sorry—sorry—I got this—"

"No, you don't." Nix let him go. His eyes were wet too. "You don't got this, Joe. But God does. And that's how it's supposed to be."

Jonas looked at Nixon, then at Geena, now in her wheelchair. She came over to him, took his hand. "Boss."

He knelt down beside her. "I'm so sorry. I should have—"

"What? Stopped the tornado from turning? Chasing us down? Driven faster—oh, wait, I was the one driving."

He met her eyes. "Please forgive me."

A beat, and her chest rose and fell. "Please forgive me." Her eyes filled. "I should have gotten us out of there."

"I was the one who said to pull over—"

"Stop, please. Both of you," Nixon said. "I forgive you both for driving me crazy. I mean, I'm the one who has to go to Smashburger every day and bring this one her cold chocolate shake and double cheeseburger."

Jonas looked up at him. "You're right. Clearly, you're the one who is suffering here."

Geena laughed, ran her palm over her cheek. "I forgive you, boss."

He shook his head. "And, whatever—I forgive you too."

Then she leaned forward and put her forehead on his. "Good. Because by next summer, I'm going to be riding shotgun in the Vortex van."

Oh.

A beat, and she leaned back. "What?"

"I...the van is totaled. And...I'm not chasing storms anymore."

"Why not?'

He gave her a look.

"Seriously? Jonas—"

He held up his hand. Her mouth closed, and she sighed. "I get it. I think." She shrugged. "For now."

"Does it have something to do with that epic cast you're sportin'?" Nixon said as Jonas stood up.

"No. I fell."

A beat.

"Do you feel safe at home?" Geena asked.

He looked at her. Grinned. "Yes."

"What are you doing here?" Nixon said. "Is your gig over? Did you get what you needed?"

He stared at Nixon. Yes. Yes, he had. At least he thought he had.

"What?" Nix said.

"It's just...I..." He ran a hand behind his neck. "Actually, remember those women we rescued?"

"Women?" Geena said and cocked her head at Nixon. "Want to elaborate?"

He held up his hands. "Jonas did the rescuing."

"Of course." She shot him a smile.

"It was just one woman, but there was this other one..."

Nixon looked at him. "The tall one, with the brown hair."

"Yeah. Her name is Sibba, and...I sort of ran into her again."

A beat.

"Oh my gosh—you like her," Geena said.

He lifted a shoulder.

"Are you in love with this woman?" Nixon said. He crossed his arms over his chest.

"I...no. I mean, I only knew her for a few days—"

"Nix and I knew it was forever after the first date," Geena said, and took his hand.

Nixon grinned at Jonas.

"Okay, I mean, yeah. She was amazing, and smart and brave—really brave. You have no idea. And..." He nodded and let himself smile. "Maybe I was in love with her a little."

"Was?"

"Am—but it doesn't matter. I was injured." He pointed at his arm. "And while I was in the hospital, she left."

A beat. Then, from Geena, "Left? Like..."

"Like I was unconscious, and she walked out of the hospital without saying goodbye."

"Ouch." Nixon.

"Yeah. And I get it. She's...she..." He sighed. "The truth of it is that she disarms bombs for a living. And any minute, her life could go boom, and...that just sort of freaks her out."

Nixon blinked at him. Looked at Geena. Back to Jonas.

Then he started to laugh. And beside him, Geena had put her hands over her face.

"What?"

"Dude. She might just be perfect for you," Nixon said.

"What?"

"Don't you see it?" Geena said. "Her life could go boom—and yeah, that might freak her out, but it doesn't freak *you* out, right?"

"No. I mean, a little, sort of, but not enough for me to not want to be with her."

"Because you're not afraid of the storm, man. You see the danger and you say, Punch it, baby."

"That sounded a little violent," Jonas said.

"Sorry. I just meant—you're the guy, Jonas."

"The guy?"

"The guy who runs to the storm, not away. So why are you still here?"

"I'm...I wanted to say hi to Geena—"

"No, you idiot. Why didn't you go after her in Slovenia? Why did you let her walk away?"

"Well, I was unconscious, for one—"

"Wow, he really needs us," Geena said.

"No doubt." Nixon nodded. "Okay, I'm going to speak in small words. Simple sentences. Leave. Find Girl. Live happily ever after."

Jonas laughed. "What if she doesn't want me?"

"Don't be a wuss."

Now they both laughed.

"C'mon. I'm hungry. Did you say you had a Smashburger waiting for me?" Geena wheeled away. "You can fill me in on your torrid romance while you book a flight to Slovenia."

Nixon turned to him. "Better hurry. It looks like there's a storm coming." He gestured to the gray outside. "They say it's gathering over the Rockies. It's going to hit Montana, the Dakotas...might even shut down the airport."

"Who's the weatherman now?" He winked at Nixon and pulled out his phone. "Besides, I'm not afraid of a little storm."

"I'VE NEVER SEEN ANYTHING SO BEAUTIFUL." SIBBA SAT astride a bay named Marnee, in a western saddle, her hands on the pommel, staring across the vast horizon of the Benson Ranch in northcentral Montana. To her east rose the runnels and peaks of the Bears Paw Mountains, with Baldy Mountain peaking at the center, already tipped with snow.

Then the vast valley, still touched with patches of green, stretched as far as she could see, all the way to the far edge of Glacier National Park, where the Rockies rose brutal and glorious, rugged and snowcapped.

Stands of sturdy pine huddled here and there on hillsides, with rivers twining through the basin. It seemed a great sea of prairie land, the waves caught in mid drift, the yellow grasses swaying in the gathering winter breeze.

Here. Here was where they'd landed.

It felt like the land of milk and honey, and the breadth of it swept through her.

"Are you okay, Sibba?" Her uncle Marek sat on his own horse, having talked her into riding out with him to check on some cattle in a nearby pasture. He was a sturdy man, sandy blond hair, strong body, even in his fifties, and blue eyes that seemed to bear a twinkle. She imagined her father might have looked the same.

"Yes." She scanned the horizon again, the sky in the west turning to striations of amber and gold under a thickening layer of velvety magenta clouds. "It's so...big. I have never seen so far in all my life." She took a breath. "And it smells..."

"Like a ranch? Cow pies and grass and—"

"Perfect." She looked at him. Her uncle. The fact that he'd opened his home to her and Dedi, despite how large it was, still seemed...

Then again, watching two grown men weep in each other's arms, maybe it hadn't been such a sacrifice.

His saddle squeaked as he readjusted. "Yes. It really is." He looked at her. "Although, it's not without its problems." He nodded to the horizon. "There's a storm coming. And judging by the cloud cover, it'll be a doozy of a blizzard."

Cloud cover. "Those look like nimbostratus clouds," she said. "Low and thick."

He glanced at her. "That's right. I didn't know you knew weather."

"I know a weatherman. He taught me."

Knew. *Knew* a weatherman. Over a week since she'd walked away from him, four days since arriving in Montana...someday, maybe, the burning in her chest would stop.

Maybe.

She'd worn a jacket, a scarf, gloves, and a hat, but her legs chilled under a stiff wind that stalked the prairie. It riffled the mane of her bay. But she watched a hawk ride the thermals, high above.

"I'll bet there is some crazy paragliding around here."

He turned in the saddle. "My son is a paraglider. That's interesting."

She hadn't yet met her cousin Asher.

"There's a number of places around the state—the closest to here is off Centennial Mountain, about 5,800 feet. But you'll have to wait until summer."

If she was here until then. She hadn't exactly thought of sticking around permanently.

Although, the thought of returning to Slovenia had sort of put a noose around her neck. She didn't know why.

Maybe because, out here, she saw it.

Today. Tomorrow, all the way out past the horizon.

"We should get back before the storm sets in." He urged his horse into a walk.

"What about the cattle?" About fifty head milled around in a valley just below them.

"They'll be okay. Beef cattle acclimate to the cold. They've already grown their winter coats. When it snows, the hair catches the snow, and it forms a layer over the cow that acts as an air pocket. That pocket is then warmed for extra insulation. They eat more in the winter, however, so we drive out every day with extra feed and fresh straw and make sure the water barrels are free of ice. And that's why we leave stands of trees, cedar and pine and thickets. They go there for shelter."

Her horse followed his. "But that's why we have them in the closer field. If we need to, we can herd them into the barns."

"This is a closer field?"

He laughed. She liked it.

"Darling, we have over a hundred thousand acres here. And four different sections to our operation. This is a very close field."

Oh.

He clicked to his horse, and the gelding stepped up into a trot, then a canter. She kept up, enjoyed the familiar gait of the horse.

"Where did you learn to ride?" he said after they'd pulled up to walk, nearer the house.

"Dedi kept horses. I think his dad had them."

"Yep. Small farm in Minnesota. But he had a couple horses."

"You knew him?"

"My grandfather? Yes. He took me in when I came over from Slovenia—that was before you were born, before Luka was killed." He stopped at a gate, dropped his reins and got off. Then he opened the gate, and the horse walked through. Waited.

She followed and turned as he closed the gate. Returned to the saddle.

"Sometimes I wish I'd stayed, but...then I got nervous that if I returned, the government might find out where he was."

"They might have."

The massive timber home sprawled on one level across the land, with wide front steps that led to a main area. The double doors opened to a stone entry, then an expansive great room with a two-story rock fireplace. The kitchen angled off it, its own room with a large round table for twelve in an alcove of windows that went from floor to ceiling.

She hadn't seen beyond that—to the master bedroom suite, her uncle's office, and probably her aunt's office too. But she'd been impressed enough with the guest wing—four more bedrooms, each with their own ensuite and plush king-size beds.

So maybe she could stay awhile.

The wind whistled in her ears as they headed toward the barn. Funny that he hadn't taken her out in one of the four-wheelers that sat in the machine garage.

But maybe he preferred the quieter, simpler life.

Another way, maybe, that he was like the father she'd never known but only imagined.

"How did you manage it?" Uncle Marek asked now as he dismounted.

"Manage what?"

"Getting Pops...here. The pardon. I mean...I can't believe it. It feels like a miracle. At least a long waited for answer to prayer."

She dismounted too. Handed him the reins. "I didn't, actually. It sort of happened because of my friend, Jonas, who knew the right people, but even that." She turned, stared at the tumble of darkening clouds.

Heard Dedi's soft voice. *Into the middle of our darkness, God reaches out and saves us.*

"I think actually...well, *God* did it."

Uncle Marek just looked at her and smiled.

The snow came by the time they'd finished dinner—she and Dedi, and Uncle Chuck and Aunt Lyddie and their youngest daughter Henrietta, still at home. They called her Retti, and she had Grandmother's smile.

She liked Retti. Sixteen, smart, long brown hair, brown eyes.

Uncle Marek built a fire in the hearth, and he and his father brought out a chess board and sat at the kitchen table.

"Finally, someone to play with me!" he said, looking at Sibba. He'd shaved since coming to America, and something about his demeanor had changed. For the first time, she saw in him a younger man, one that fit the story Ziggy had told her.

A medal winner, at least in her heart, if not in reality.

But a freed man, for sure. Funny how having his sentence lifted and his past reckoned with gave him a redeemed view of the future.

"C'mere," Retti said, emerging from the kitchen. She hooked her arm through Sibba's and brought her to the massive window in the great room. Flicked off the lights inside and then turned on the outside lights.

A thousand tiny snowflakes drifted through the light, sparkling before they fell to the earth. The wind began to howl, and they swirled with the breath.

"Isn't it beautiful?" Retti stood with her hands in her back pockets. "I like to just sit here sometimes and watch the storm. It's so...big. And yet in here, it's warm and safe and...romantic."

Sibba raised an eyebrow.

"Do you have a great love?" Retti leaned against the back of the couch.

Sibba sighed. "I did. But...I was too afraid to...believe. And now it's too late."

Retti gave her a sad smile. "I believe it's never too late for hope."

Sibba nodded. Sweet girl. But even if she wanted to believe, her words when she left him were true.

She didn't know how to hope. To believe. To trust.

"I'm going to get us a couple blankets so we can sit on the porch. The sound of a storm is so amazing." Retti left her standing at the window.

Sibba stared out into the night, into the tempest of snowflakes. *It's never too late for hope.*

And then, like a whisper, she heard Jonas in the softness of her heart. *God is in the storm. Though the winds blow, and my life feels torn apart, if I can just trust Him, I'll discover Him at the center.*

She crossed her arms over herself.

Blessed are the poor in spirit, for theirs is the kingdom of heaven.

She turned, hearing Dedi's voice, but he was still in the kitchen.

Turned back to the window.

What does that even mean?

It means all the things. Grace and hope and love and...safety.

Yes. Yes, please. Because suddenly it all swept over her.

Maybe hope was simply reaching out for the hand of Jesus to hold her up.

She pressed her hand against the cold window. *Please forgive my unbelief. My anger. My pride.*

Yes, it had been exactly that—pride that she could control her one-meter box. Except, she couldn't even do that, could she?

Help me, God. Help me to have faith. To trust You.

To hope.

"Let's go outside."

She turned and spotted Retti standing in the entry, holding two massive quilts. "Outside?"

"Yes. To watch the storm. I promise, it's more beautiful than you can imagine."

FOURTEEN

So, this was probably a bad idea.

Because his GPS had quit on him in the storm, and his truck heaters were losing the battle against the howl of the wind, the ice that now formed around his windshield. He'd packed for the storm—warm boots, a parka, hat, scarf, gloves, along with an emergency kit that included candles and a sleeping bag. But he never thought he'd have to camp in the car.

Lost in unfamiliar country, and he hadn't a clue if Sibba would open the door to him.

Nixon's words sat in his brain, however, like an ember. *Find Girl. Live happily ever after.*

Easier said than done when she'd practically disappeared off the planet.

He'd been packing, his flight to Slovenia booked, when Fraser came into the room with a strange update.

I got a call from Ham. Who got a call from Logan. Who had sent a woman named Ziggy to Sibba's house.

Yeah, he remembered Ziggy. So that got Jonas's attention. But he'd stood there, holding a pair of socks, when Fraser dropped the bomb.

Sibba is in America.

Or at least, that's what Ziggy thought, because she'd left Sibba and her grandfather in Slovenia. But according to Logan, her passport had been used at Dulles International Airport, in D.C., only two days ago.

So, then, where was she?

Jonas had dropped the socks, set the half-packed bag on a chair, and headed down to Fraser's security lair in Dad's former office.

Started to scan through all their conversations in his mind and landed on the one that made the most sense.

More than anything, I want Dedi to see his son again, my uncle Marek.

So, he started his search there, with the name he'd seen on Henry's jacket. Benson.

Not a lot of Marek Bensons in America. He found a doctor at Harvard, in his thirties, and a director of athletics at a community college in Alabama, but with his darker skin, he didn't seem like a child of Henry Benson, of Danish and Slovenian descent.

And then he hit on the Benson Ranch, near the Bears Paw Mountains, east of Big Sandy, in Montana.

Found a picture of the family—four kids, most of them grown, one nearly Sibba's age. Marek might be a younger version of Henry.

"I'm going to Montana," he'd said to Fraser and got on his phone.

Except, the storm. It hadn't hit the Rockies, and sat there, pummeling the northland with snow and ice, and the airports across Montana had closed in anticipation of the blizzard.

He headed upstairs, packed his bag, and asked Fraser to borrow his truck.

"To drive to Montana?" Fraser had given him a *you're crazy* look.

"I'll get a rental—"

"You won't beat the storm."

"I can drive through the storm."

Fraser gave him a look. Then, "No. I'm not letting you take a tin can rental through the blizzard." And he tossed him the keys.

"Don't worry," Jonas said as he caught them.

Cocky words now as he crossed over the border from North Dakota and spotted the low hanging nimbostratus clouds hovering over the bleak northern prairie.

The rain came first, then turned to ice. When he headed north on 94, the snow hit. Gray blotted out the sky, the snow accumulating on the road, over the ice, turning it lethal.

He slowed but kept his headlights on low because the high beams only made the snow come at him at light speed. Instead, his low beams carved out a path through the darkness, this snow whipping across the blacktop to reveal, now and again, the edges of the highway.

The truck shuddered in the high winds, and a couple times, threatened to slide off the road. He slowed to a crawl, the heat on high, his arms cradling the wheel, hunched over to see through the layer of ice that was closing in around his windshield.

He passed Harlem and Chinhook, and debated stopping in Havre, at a hotel near Montana State University, but...

He wanted to see her. To tell her that she'd healed him, in a way. Being with her made him remember who'd he'd been. Who he wanted to be.

The storm chaser.

He cut south onto 87, drove past the lonely, snow-covered Havre City-County Airport, the bright lights still illuminating a frosty tarmac, a few planes covered in thick drifts of snow.

Then it was back to the darkness, the snow swirling against his windshield, the wind trying to smack him off the road.

He'd memorized the map to the Benson ranch. Big place, but the main house was just southwest of Big Sandy, on Judy Lane, then west on Merrick Road, and south again on Country Road 37, all the way to Benson Drive, which cut east to the house, about a mile farther.

At least, he hoped he'd gotten it right, because his GPS

winked in and out, and by the time he made the turn onto Judy Lane, passing the Big Sandy Airport, he'd lost the signal completely.

And then it was just his instincts. And hope.

Mostly hope.

Darkness had descended and blanketed the land, not a prick of light on the horizon as he headed west on Merrick. The wind snarled, the blizzard a tempest, the road completely obscured now.

So maybe this hadn't been his sharpest idea.

"Find Girl. Die in snowbank." He shook his head.

He glanced at his odometer. Maybe he'd gone too far. As he looked down at the offline directions he'd downloaded, darkness flashed against his lights.

A deer, or an elk, or maybe just Sasquatch stood in the glare, a snapshot, then darted away.

He slammed his brakes. The truck slid, spinning, and he fought the wheel, turning it one way, then back, and then—

He skated right off the road. And not into an easy ditch either, but the ground dropped away from the hardtop. The truck landed nose first a drift, its back wheels spinning.

Jonas sat for a moment, snow smashed against his windshield—still intact, thank you, God—and just caught his breath.

Nice. Just so. Perfect.

He put the truck into reverse and tried to back it out. The back wheels spun, the front wheels fighting for purchase.

After a couple tries, he opened the door.

He'd driven over a barbed wire fence, the churning wheels only tangling up the wire into his chassis.

Yep. That felt right.

He closed the door. Turned off the truck.

Sat in the darkness.

Tried not to hit anything, but yeah, he was just...done.

Done.

No matter what he did...he ended up here. Right here. In the middle of nowhere, the wind howling, slowly freezing to death. And he heard his own stupid voice to Sibba.

So...I trust Him in the storm. In fact, I even run into them. And there, I expect to see Him already at the center.

Wow, he sounded like a Sunday school sermon.

I got this.

No. No, he didn't.

But God does. And that's how it's supposed to be.

He leaned back, zipped his jacket up to his chin. Shoved his hands into his pockets.

Maybe that was the problem. Even in the storm, he put his focus on himself, his own abilities. His instincts.

His ability to read the forecast.

In fact, he hadn't been trusting God at all.

And the words of his father just sort of came in, sat down next to him. *You stay rooted in the middle of a storm—darkness, confusion, chaos—by putting your focus on the One who is stronger than the storm.*

He leaned his forehead onto the wheel. *I'm sorry.*

In fact, as he sat and listened to the howl of the wind, the snow slapping his windows, the immensity of it all...

How had he even, for a millisecond, believed that, hello, *he had this?*

He turned off his lights, letting the darkness engulf the car. Then he closed his eyes. *I don't have this, Lord. In fact, all I have is You. If You'll have me.*

The silence behind his words swept through him.

And then, "*You of little faith, why are you so afraid?*"

The voice seemed nearly audible, and he opened his eyes. Leaned up.

Still the storm, the voice of the wind, the pelleting of the snow and ice.

And then, there—across the prairie, the finest wink of a light. It shone out through the pitch and swirl of snow. In fact, if it hadn't been so terribly black out, he might not have seen it at all.

Please stay on.

He reached for his emergency bag and pulled out the sleeping bag and a Maglite. Then he tightened down his hat, pulled up the furry hood of his parka, tightened his boots, took a breath, and pushed out of the truck.

He landed in a foot or more of snow, but the truck had flattened the fencing, so he worked his way over the mangled wire. Then he shook out the sleeping bag, pulled it around himself, and headed for the light.

A blizzard across the prairie of Montana was nothing like the snowstorms in Slovenia.

"It's gorgeous, right?" Retti sat in one of the big rocking chairs, wrapped in a quilt, her feet in lambswool slippers.

Sibba wore the same attire—quilt, slippers. And they both held a mug of hot cocoa, courtesy of their aunt, who'd stepped out for a bit to listen to the howl.

"It sounds like the ocean waves, although sometimes it's simply thunder gathering in the distance," Sibba said.

"I like to think of it as the breath of God."

"And you're not afraid of that?"

Retti looked her, blowing on her cocoa. "Why would I be? If God is for us, who can be against us?"

Her question hung with Sibba even after they finished the cocoa. *Why would I be?*

They talked about Slovenia, and Sibba told her about learning how to disable bombs, and Retti thought it was cool. And then Retti told her about how her entire family had been praying for Grandpa Henry for years.

And for her.

And Sibba had sat there, under the warmth of the great quilt, and wanted, for some reason, to cry.

"I'm headed in. A warm bath is calling my name." Retti stood up.

"I think I'll sit out here, just a little longer."

"You done with your cocoa?"

Sibba handed her the mug. Retti took it, then paused at the door. "Just wait until you wake up in the morning. The day after the storm is even more glorious. The whole world will be white, and it'll look like the ocean swept past, leaving frozen waves and sparkles. And the sky will be a breathtaking blue." She winked at Sibba. She opened the door, and light and heat spilled out.

"Retti," Sibba said. "Can you turn off the light?"

"You want to sit out here in the dark?"

"Yes."

Be one with the storm and still cocooned inside her warm quilt. *Into the middle of our darkness, God reaches out and saves us.*

Yes, maybe He did.

The light went off, and the darkness swirled around her. She'd put the blanket up around her head, so only her face showed. Even so, the cold bit at her nose. She thought of the cows, huddled together, companions against the storm.

But a partner, in love, walks the road with you. Helps to make sense out of the life we live. Gives it meaning.

Yes. And first thing tomorrow, when the storm lifted...she was going to find Jonas. Because maybe she didn't have to know how to love him. Maybe she simply...did. One step, one amazing day at a time.

She should go in. The cold had started to nip around her legs, despite her warm slippers. She got up, adjusted the quilt, and was turning toward the door when something flashed in her periphery.

Turning back, she stood there, listening to the wind moan. Darkness.

Then—there, another flash.

A *light*.

Except, it wasn't coming from the drive but...the cow pasture? She turned and opened the door to the house. "Uncle Marek—I think there's someone in your field."

Her uncle got up and headed to the door. Peered out into the night a long while.

"There, see it?"

"I'll get my coat. You should come in." He turned on the porch light.

But she didn't, and she didn't know why, but something kept her on the porch. Maybe curiosity.

Maybe hope.

Because it was crazy, this thought that—no. Stop.

Still, as Uncle Marek stepped out of the front door, garbed in a thick parka, heavy boots, a scarf, gloves, and carrying a flashlight, she nearly followed him out into the snow.

Oh, don't be absurd. But she couldn't help it. "*Hey. Remember me? Storm chaser? I'm exactly the person you want around when the lights go down and the wind kicks up.*"

Wow, she could even hear his voice. His laughter. Clearly, hope had gotten too strong a grip on her.

Uncle Marek reached the light, having gone past the fence, out into the field. And now they were walking back, together.

So yes, a person, although he—or she, just calm down Sibba—was no more than a blob, no form, as if—

The person came into the faintest glow of light. They were draped in what looked like a blanket. Probably some refugee who got stuck on the road. She didn't know why she thought...aw, see, this was why she should stay firmly rooted in reality, in her nice one-meter space.

She turned toward the door—

"Sibba!"

She stilled, glanced back at her uncle. He was closing the gate, his back to her.

"Sibba!"

The refugee flung off his hood, snow casting into the glow of the porch, sparking against the light.

No. What—

He came up to the porch, tucking the blanket under his arm.

But his blue eyes were fixed on her. Snow clung to his hair, a slight smattering of whiskers, and dusted his parka like he'd, well, like he'd hiked through a blizzard to find her.

"Jonas?" Her voice came out in a whisper.

He hit the top step, his breath forming in the night air. "Hey."

What? She dumped her quilt and launched herself at him, her arms around him, holding on.

"Oh," he said, and then his arms caught her. "Hi."

She leaned back, her eyes in his. "I knew it." She pressed her warm hands to his cold face. "I knew it was you."

"You...what?"

"I saw your light and...and I hoped you'd come, right here. To me."

His smiled curled up slowly. "Huh."

And then he leaned down and kissed her. His lips were cold on hers, and his kiss was sweet, but she held him there, kissing him, tasting him, believing in him.

Believing in their tomorrows.

"Wow. I see how it is," said Uncle Marek as he came up on the porch. He lifted an eyebrow.

Jonas lifted his head, looked at her uncle. "Jonas Marshall."

"I figured." He looked at Sibba. "The weatherman?"

She nodded. Grinned.

"Better come in and get warm," Uncle Marek said and tromped inside. Closed the door.

Leaving them alone on the porch.

Jonas unzipped his jacket.

She picked up her quilt. "I just...how did you find me?"

He laughed, grabbed her hand and pulled her to himself,

cocooning her inside his jacket. He was warm and strong and safe. "I just followed the storm."

Then he bent his head and kissed her again. And as the snow swirled around them and the wind howled, she knew...

Right here, in the eye of love, was where she was staying.

What Happens Next

It was a longshot, Ned knew it, but he couldn't break free of his hold on the idea that Shae had returned home.

Back to Mercy Falls, Montana, where her uncle Ian lived and where, when the dust settled, she knew she was safe.

At last.

And sure, she'd spent years hiding from the murderer who'd killed someone she loved, and even, eventually, tried to kill her too, but those were long ago days.

Four years long ago.

And since then, she'd made Mercy Falls, and her uncle Ian's new ranch, her home base. Probably because here, she also remembered the girl she'd been—Esme Shaw. That girl had loved horses, and life. And while Esme had had her issues, it was the brave, stubborn, feisty girl of her past that Shae had tapped into when she'd faced her killer. When she'd followed Ned to San Diego, then Pensacola, and back. And the person who'd helped her start her online graphic arts business.

So, yes, Shae and Esme were one, and that meant Ned had a good shot that his gut was right on this as he rented a truck and headed north from the Kalispell airport.

He liked Montana. His cousins lived south of here on a ranch in Geraldine, just outside the border of Glacier National Park. He liked their life—raising bulls for the rodeo circuit, and recently, according to Ford, they'd added bison to their grazing herd.

But mostly he loved their land, endless rolling hills, the jagged mountains rising to the north, the scent of wildflowers, and expansive blue sky. Out here, everything felt...big. Big dreams. Big...life.

Not that he didn't like Minnesota—he loved the pockets of lakes, the deep green of the vineyard, the sense of community. But being out here, in Montana, he felt like he could take deeper breaths. Let the world spin out of his hands.

Let it go.

Maybe that's why Shae came here too.

Please.

He turned east, toward Mercy Falls, and drove through the small town with the bridge over the Flathead River, the false-front buildings, a few of them advertising huckleberries. Then he headed south, toward the PEAK Search and Rescue team HQ. He hadn't called Ian, but best guess was that the man was at the base that he'd founded.

The small house that had once sat on Ian's land, before the Shaw ranch had been purchased by country music star Benjamin King and his wife, rescue chopper pilot Kacey, had gotten a makeover since the last time he'd been here for their wedding reception.

The house now boasted a two-story addition, and on the property, a massive garage added. The doors were open, and inside he spotted a new truck as well as an airplane—and behind the property, a long runway.

Maybe the plane belonged to King—his music career had soared in the last few years, his private label adding new talent. Ned had watched King receive the Entertainer of the Year award last year, to add to his collection of other CMA awards.

He pulled up beside a truck with the PEAK team logo on the

side and got out. His hiking boots thumped on the wooden deck, and he took a breath before he pulled open the door.

His entrance stopped a conversation in the main room, one with a couple of flatscreen televisions on a far wall, a massive table in the center of the room inlaid with a detailed map of Glacier National Park, and a few desks around the room, sporting computer monitors.

The great room attached to the kitchen, and the scent of spicy chili seasoned the room. He hadn't realized he was hungry.

A door led off the great room—once upon a time, the office of Chet King, Ben's dad and former Vietnam chopper pilot. He'd teamed with Ian after Shae went missing to form a search and rescue team, which eventually led to PEAK.

Four people, two sitting on stools at the counter, two more leaning against the table, looked at him.

He recognized a couple of the guys. Gage Watson, his long hair pulled back into a ponytail, wearing a PEAK team pullover and a pair of cargo pants. If Ned remembered right, the man had been a champion snowboarder before he joined PEAK.

And Ty Remington—he'd helped Ned in the search for Creed and a bunch of cross-country runners four years ago when a tornado ripped through southern Minnesota. Ty wore a flannel shirt, a pair of jeans, and cowboy boots, and all he needed was a Stetson to fit into an episode of Yellowstone. He looked up at Ned, and a slow smile found his face. "Ned?"

"Hey," Ned said, his hand out.

Ty came to meet him. "What's going on?"

"Not much. I...uh. I was looking for Ian Shaw."

The other two people had gotten off their stools. One, a younger man with a lumberjack build, had black hair and sported black whiskers. He wore a denim shirt with a vest emblazoned with the PEAK symbol. "Harrington Bly."

Oh, the man had an Australian accent. Interesting.

The other was a woman, auburn hair in a braid under a denim ball cap, lean, striking pale blue eyes. "Derby McDonald."

"Ned Marshall."

"Ned's family lives in Minnesota," Ty said. "Wow, it's been years. I heard you were in SEAL training."

"Mm-hmm."

Ty grinned. "Okay, man. Right. So, Ian. Uh, let's see." He ran a hand across his mouth. "Probably at the hospital right now."

Ned stilled.

Gage laughed. "His wife is in labor. Number two." He held up his fingers. "But this time it's a girl. And Ian's lost his mind with joy."

He remembered Shae telling him about her nephew, little Chase Shaw. "I didn't know Sierra was pregnant again."

"Apparently, they're wasting no time."

"Shoot."

Ty raised an eyebrow.

"I just...actually, I was looking for Shae. She isn't in San Diego and..." And now he felt stupid, because, yeah, this was starting to look weird. "Never mind. What hospital?"

"Kalispell. I haven't seen Shae since...earlier this summer, maybe?" Ty said. He looked at Gage, who shrugged.

Yeah, this was a spectacularly stupid idea. "Okay, thanks, guys. Hey, I like the new garage."

"And we've expanded the team. All the way to Australia," Gage said. He put a soft fist into Harrington Bly's shoulder.

Harrington just raised an eyebrow.

"Tell Brette I said hi," Ned said and headed toward the door.

Clouds hung over the far side of the mountains, the storm having cleared western Montana. He'd been detoured to Salt Lake City because of the blizzard, had spent an uncomfortable night in the airport. Had debated renting a car and driving but didn't want to take a chance on the roads. Too easy to skid off into the ditch and freeze to death.

He found a place in the parking lot and headed inside the hospital to the maternity center. Blue carpet, teal walls with painted mountainscapes, quiet music. Stopping at the information desk, he checked in and, sure enough, Sierra Shaw was in labor.

He hadn't thought about the fact that Shae was probably at home, babysitting little Chase, and suddenly that truth clicked in, and the fist inside his chest released.

Yes. She'd been here, probably out of cell phone reach, given the mountains and sometimes spotty cell signal at Ian's place.

Still, he headed toward maternity, waiting at the doors as they buzzed him in, and then spotted Ian at the nurses' station. Tall, dark hair, early forties, Ian Shaw always seemed in command of the room.

Except now. He wore a printed T-shirt, a pair of jeans, a five-o'clock shadow, and his hair deeply tousled.

"Ian?"

He turned. Blinked. "Ned?"

"Hey," he said and came toward him. A nurse handed him a glass of ice chips. "I hear Sierra is in labor?"

He nodded. "Got here about four this morning." He did look tired, his eyes reddened. "She's nearly fully—probably TMI. What—is Shae here?"

The question dropped out Ned's stomach.

Silence. Then, "I...nope. Uh..." And the last thing he wanted to do was stress Ian out even more, but now, shoot, he was stuck. "Actually, Shae and I got into a little disagreement, and I thought she might be..."

"Here? In Montana? What kind of disagreement has her hopping a plane to Montana?" Gone was the stressed out Ian. Welcome to Angry Ian, the former billionaire who knew how to get his way. His mouth tightened.

"Um. It's a long story, but we were in Geneva, and then I got called up, and I've been trying to get ahold of her, but...she won't answer my calls."

Ian stood there, holding the cup of ice. "Won't answer your calls? Did you go to her house?"

"Yes. No—I had a friend stop by. But she's not there and—"

"Mr. Shaw. Your wife is asking for you." A female nurse, petite, wearing pink scrubs, had stuck her head out of a room.

He nodded, turned back to Ned. "Find her. Straighten this out."

"Yes, sir," Ned said.

Ian pointed at him as he walked away. "Find. Her."

"Congratulations on the baby."

Ian held up the cup and disappeared into the room.

Ned headed out to the lobby. Sat on a bench. Pulled out his phone and swiped open Shae's contact. *Where are you, Shae?*

His phone buzzed in his hand, and he answered the incoming video call from Fraser. His brother's face appeared on the screen.

"What's up?"

"Coco found some CCTV footage from Geneva you need to see." He wore a grim look that trickled ice into Ned's gut.

"What?"

"I sent you a link. There's no audio, just the video. Tell me what you think."

Ned minimized the call and opened the text app. Found Fraser's link, then clicked on it.

Then everything inside him seized, his breath gone as he watch Shae storm out of the hotel. Given the sunshine and her attire, it looked like it had been right after their argument.

As he watched, she turned, her eyes widening, as if someone had called her name.

Then that someone walked up to her.

Tall, ponytail, wearing a backpack.

Dana Munson. Maybe. Probably.

And then, as he watched, a car pulled up, and Dana motioned to it. Shae seemed to frown, then look back at the hotel.

Like she might be thinking about returning.

To him.

Then she smiled and shook her head. Mouthed something. He couldn't make it out.

But he clearly made out the shock on her face as Dana took

her arm and then manhandled her into the car, pushing her inside.

Then he got in, shut the door, and it pulled away.

Ned just stared at the screen as the video ended.

"Ned?"

He thumbed open the call to Fraser. He was still wearing that grim look.

"Shae's been kidnapped," Ned said quietly.

Fraser nodded.

"Okay, I'm coming home. And then I'm getting on a plane. Can you ask Coco to run the plate number?"

"Done. And by the way, Ned. You're not going alone. We'll find her. I promise."

Fraser hung up, and Ned closed his eyes, pressed the phone against his head.

Please, Shae, where ever you are, just stay alive.

I'm coming for you.

The epic romance and adventure continues with Ned and Shae's story in NED, book 3 of the Minnesota Marshalls.

Thank you for Reading

Thank you so much for reading *Jonas*. I hope you enjoyed the story.

If you did enjoy *Jonas*, would you be willing to do me a favor? Head over to the **product page** and leave a review. It doesn't have to be long—just a few words to help other readers know what they're getting. (But no spoilers! We don't want to wreck the fun!)

I'd love to hear from you—not only about this story, but about any characters or stories you'd like to read in the future. Write to me at: susan@susanmaywarren.com.

And if you'd like to see what's ahead, stop by www.susanmaywarren.com .

I also have a monthly update that contains sneak peeks, reviews, upcoming releases, and free, fun stuff for my reader friends. Sign up on www.susanmaywarren.com.

Susie May

About Susan May Warren

With nearly 2 million books sold, critically acclaimed novelist Susan May Warren is the Christy, RITA, and Carol award-winning author of over ninety novels with Revell, Tyndale, Barbour, Steeple Hill, and Summerside Press. Known for her compelling plots and unforgettable characters, Susan has written contemporary and historical romances, romantic-suspense, thrillers, rom-com, and Christmas novellas.

With books translated into eight languages, many of her novels have been ECPA and CBA bestsellers, were chosen as Top Picks by *Romantic Times*, and have won the RWA's Inspirational Reader's Choice contest and the American Christian Fiction Writers Book of the Year award. She's a three-time RITA finalist and an eight-time Christy finalist.

Publishers Weekly has written of her books, "Warren lays bare her characters' human frailties, including fear, grief, and resentment, as openly as she details their virtues of love, devotion, and resiliency. She has crafted an engaging tale of romance, rivalry, and the power of forgiveness."

Library Journal adds, "Warren's characters are well-developed and she knows how to create a first rate contemporary romance..."

Susan is also a nationally acclaimed writing coach, teaching at conferences around the nation, and winner of the 2009 American Christian Fiction Writers Mentor of the Year award. She loves to help people launch their writing careers.

Susie is the founder of www.MyBookTherapy.com and www.LearnHowtoWriteaNovel.com, a writing website that helps authors get published and stay published. She is also the author of the popular writing method *The Story Equation*.

Find excerpts, reviews, and a printable list of her novels at www.susanmaywarren.com and connect with her on social media.

facebook.com/susanmaywarrenfiction

instagram.com/susanmaywarren

twitter.com/susanmaywarren

bookbub.com/authors/susan-may-warren

goodreads.com/susanmaywarren

amazon.com/Susan-May-Warren

Also by Susan May Warren

THE MINNESOTA MARSHALLS

Fraser

Jonas

Ned

Iris

Creed

SKY KING RANCH

Sunrise

Sunburst

Sundown

THE EPIC STORY OF RJ AND YORK

Out of the Night

I Will Find You

No Matter the Cost

GLOBAL SEARCH AND RESCUE

The Way of the Brave

The Heart of a Hero

The Price of Valor

THE MONTANA MARSHALLS (family series)

Knox

Tate

Ford

Wyatt

Ruby Jane

MONTANA FIRE

Where There's Smoke (Summer of Fire)

Playing with Fire (Summer of Fire)

Burnin' For You (Summer of Fire)

Oh, The Weather Outside is Frightful (Christmas novella)

I'll be There (Montana Fire/Deep Haven crossover)

Light My Fire (Summer of the Burning Sky)

The Heat is On (Summer of the Burning Sky)

Some Like it Hot (Summer of the Burning Sky)

You Don't Have to Be a Star (Montana Fire spin-off)

MONTANA RESCUE

If Ever I Would Leave You (novella prequel)

Wild Montana Skies

Rescue Me

A Matter of Trust

Crossfire (novella)

Troubled Waters

Storm Front

Wait for Me

MISSIONS OF MERCY SERIES

TEAM HOPE: (Search and Rescue series)

Waiting for Dawn (novella prequel)

Flee the Night

Escape to Morning

Expect the Sunrise

NOBLE LEGACY (Montana Ranch Trilogy)

Reclaiming Nick

Taming Rafe

Finding Stefanie

THE CHRISTIANSEN FAMILY

I Really Do Miss your Smile (novella prequel)

Take a Chance on Me

It Had to Be You

When I Fall in Love

Evergreen (Christmas novella)

Always on My Mind

The Wonder of Your

You're the One that I Want

THE DEEP HAVEN COLLECTION

Happily Ever After

Tying the Knot

The Perfect Match

My Foolish Heart

The Shadow of your Smile

You Don't Know Me

**A complete list of Susan's novels can be found at
susanmaywarren.com.**

Jonas
A Minnesota Marshalls Novel
Copyright © 2023 by Susan May Warren
Paperback ISBN: 978-1-943935-86-4
Ebook ISBN: 978-1-943935-85-7

This book is a work of fiction. Names, characters, places, and incidents are either products of the author's imagination or used fictitiously. Any similarity to actual people, organizations, and/or events is purely coincidental.

Scripture quotations are also taken from the Holy Bible, New International Version®, NIV®. Copyright© 1973, 1978, 1984, 2011 by Biblica, Inc®. Used by permission of Zondervan. All rights reserved worldwide.

For more information about Susan May Warren, please access the author's website at the following address: www.susanmaywarren.com.

Published in the United States of America.

Cover design by Jenny Zemanek, jennyzemanek.com